James Phinney Munroe

The Educational Ideal

An Outline of its Growth in Modern Times

James Phinney Munroe

The Educational Ideal
An Outline of its Growth in Modern Times

ISBN/EAN: 9783337022945

Printed in Europe, USA, Canada, Australia, Japan

Cover: Foto ©Andreas Hilbeck / pixelio.de

More available books at **www.hansebooks.com**

THE EDUCATIONAL IDEAL

AN OUTLINE OF ITS GROWTH IN MODERN TIMES

BY

JAMES PHINNEY MUNROE
FORMERLY OF THE MASSACHUSETTS INSTITUTE OF TECHNOLOGY

———

BOSTON, U.S.A.
D. C. HEATH & CO., PUBLISHERS
1896

Norwood Press:
J. S. Cushing & Co. — Berwick & Smith.
Norwood, Mass., U.S.A.

TO

THE MEMORY OF

A. B. M. AND A. L. M.

PREFACE.

THE following outline of a special phase of development in the history of education is not only incomplete, but also, in a measure, fragmentary. Inadequate as it is, however, the author issues it in the belief that it enters a territory in educational literature not yet fully explored. It seems to him that this territory must be thoroughly known before the present questions in education can be wholly understood, and he hopes that his sketch may lead to an abler study and treatment of this field of human growth.

He begs to acknowledge the valuable assistance and advice given by President Walker of the Massachusetts Institute of Technology, by Dr. Dickinson, late Secretary of the Massachusetts State Board of Education, and especially by Professor Hinsdale of the University of Michigan, who has reviewed and criticised the manuscript and proof of the entire book.

CONTENTS.

vii

CHAPTER VIII.

CHAPTER IX.

CHAPTER X.

THE EDUCATIONAL IDEAL.

CHAPTER I.

INTRODUCTION.

HUMAN LIMITATIONS; A "NATURAL" EDUCATION; GROWTH OF THE EDUCATIONAL IDEAL; ITS OBSCURITY; ITS "HEROES"; ITS ENEMIES: MEDIÆVALISM; CLASSICISM; FEUDALISM; ECCLESIASTICISM; MATERIALISM.

In few things are human limitations more evident than in our judgments of human progress. Our every step is accepted as one in a new direction; our every idea is advanced as one of a new growth. With us, we incline to think, all real reform has begun. Especially is this true, to-day, of educational questions, to whose solving we believe ourselves peculiarly anointed. We feel that to us, for the first time in history, true pedagogic inspiration has come, and that from our hands, after centuries of neglect and misunderstanding, the child is, at last, to receive right education.

It is to remind ourselves of the falseness and narrowness of this attitude that I have ventured to sketch the growth of the educational ideal, and to trace the steps through which it expanded from the narrow pedantry of the Schoolmen into an ever broader understanding of the true function

tion, as of all social forces, is not to be grasped by any one man or group of men. It has been a balancing of hidden tendencies rather than a chronicle of observed attainments. The educational standard is at once a motive and a measure of social change. While the evolution of matter is marked by milestones of transitional types, in the evolution of mind there are no fixed records of progress. A fossil bone may unfold the life-history of a large body of mammalia, but not all the memoirs and letters of the eighteenth century, not all its state papers and secret archives, can show us when and how its bad standards of civilization began to grow into the still imperfect, but better, standards of to-day. While it is true that mankind, not men, make history, it is no less true that the only beacons in the onward sweep of the human flood are men. Without the "hero," as Carlyle calls him, to mark history, we should be swirled on in the torrent of events, ignorant of the vaguest outlines of a channel, powerless even to conjecture whence we came or whither we are going.

But "heroes" are more than historical landmarks. They are important agents in the universal plan.[1] As con-

---

[1] "In all epochs of the world's history, we shall find the Great Man to have been the indispensable saviour of his epoch ; — the lightning, without which the fuel never would have burnt. The History of the World, I said already, was the Biography of Great Men." — CARLYLE, *Heroes and Hero-Worship* (Chicago, 1891), Lect. I. 21.

"Historians are very right in attending solely to great men ; they should only be careful not to represent them as anything that they are not ; they should represent them, not as the masters, but as the representatives of those who do not appear. . . . Under this reservation it is certain, that as every people resolves itself into its great men of all kinds, the history of a people ought to consist, as it does consist, in the history of its great men." — VICTOR COUSIN, *Introduction to the History of Philosophy* (Linberg's translation ; Boston, 1832), Lect. X. 302.

ceived by our limited faculties, all sciences — or history in its broadest sense — are but fragments of a universal science to which man may or may not ultimately attain. Research and speculation, the farther they go, tend to strengthen more fully the belief that man's feeble mind, able now to examine life only in detail, disconnectedly, may gain, in future ages, the power of looking at the world as a whole, of taking such a bird's-eye view, so to speak, of creation, that its plan shall be comprehensible. Only then can there be devised a perfect method of education, in conformity with nature. To bring forward this condition, to assemble the results of the patient toil of specialists, master minds are sent into the world. Without them to generalize and to show us to what point man has come, progress in knowledge would be well-nigh impossible. Each scholar, having explored his little patch, having mapped its topography, would then rest content, oblivious to its relations to other patches explored by other men. The master mind, however, is gifted with the power to extract the essentials of other men's labor, and, grouping them together, to show, in one broad, luminous plan, so large an area, so perfect a section, that the rotundity of the sphere of knowledge is at once made plain. Then it is that men begin to dream of a sight of the eternal cosmos, and, with new light and strength, to work for its attainment.

Treating, then, for the sake of concreteness, the progress of "natural" education as a series of revolutions led by men, rather than as a noiseless expansion of mankind, we may say that the first revolt of education, in modern days, was against mediævalism. This, in its broader aspect, was that social change which we call the Renaissance. From the many great leaders crowding this period, Rabelais stands out as the champion of the new education, not because he laid greater stress upon education than did many others, not because his educational ideas were more formal or more orig-. inal; but because his vision was broader, his weapons were keener, his warfare was more effective. Not content with attacking local abuses and temporary wrongs, he levelled his satire at the sins which had begotten them. He battled, not with the imps of darkness and the brood of hell, but with darkness and hell themselves. In his warfare against mediævalism, the time-spirit was with him; but in his visions of reconstruction, he looked far beyond his age.

Upon the ruins that he and his had made, there was built up a new educational temple, a classic one; but it was dedicated to gods as false as those of the Middle Ages, though infinitely less cruel than they. The classicism of the Renaissance, upon which the schooling of that period rested, was as foreign to the real science and art of education as was scholasticism.

In turn, the monopoly over education which, through the Renaissance, the classicists secured, was shattered, — in England by Bacon, in France by Descartes. As the elder — and as the better — leader in this second revolt, I have chosen Bacon.[1]

---

[1] Descartes was, without doubt, the greater thinker, and from him, more than from Bacon, came that impulse towards pure and ordered thought which was to be so beneficial to civilization. But Bacon, it seems to me, exerted a wider influence upon social progress, for the very reason that he was not altogether ahead of his time. He was tinged with current superstition, his experimentation was desultory and often puerile, his genius was diffusive and, therefore, not always effective. Nevertheless, as, similarly, in the case of Franklin, — whose scientific attainments were far inferior to those of many of his contemporaries, and whose philosophy was certainly not of a high order, — the union in him of homeliness and genius made just that bridge which was needed between the rank superstition of the Elizabethan age and the truly scientific spirit, misdirected as it often was, of the materialistic generations which followed.

The obvious objection to Descartes which might be made in this

. Mediævalism and classicism weakened, there remained feudalism to be cleared away before the light could reach mankind. This work, begun by Luther, was taken up, on the educational side, by Comenius, the founder of real public education. His theories, adorned and refined by Montaigne, co-ordinated and made scientific by Locke, spread slowly, through these men, from Germany and Scandinavia, where Comenius had planted them, into France and England.

Beaten in the open, mediæyalism and classicism took refuge in the Church, and, in a bad alliance, were re-enthroned by the Jesuits. From this new power, Jansenism deposed them, never again to reign.

These successive shocks to the old order of things had practically destroyed the educational city, leaving its inhabitants, the children, naked upon a desert of materialism. To this point, the process had been chiefly one of destruction. From this point, it was to be one mainly of construction. The first architect of the new city which is rising upon the dust of the old, was Rousseau. He laid the foun-

connection, that he was a founder of idealism, not of realism, would not be a valid one. Whatever the ultimate effect of his teachings, their immediate influence was not greatly different from that of Bacon's. Both these leaders of thought freed men from tradition by making them self-active ; in so doing they accomplished all that, at this stage of progress, was necessary.   •

It is interesting to observe that most, if not all, of the French biographers of Descartes are special pleaders. Premising the undoubted superiority of Descartes as an investigator and organizer of scientific thought, they try to prove his superiority to Bacon in everything. His latest biographer, M. Alfred Fouillée, would even persuade us that Descartes anticipated the distinctive researches, among lesser men, of Newton, of Kant, and of Darwin.

See, in this connection, the very vivid, though somewhat forced, characterization of Bacon, Descartes, and Leibnitz in De Gérando's *Histoire comparée des systêmes de philosophie* (Paris, 1804), T. I. 284.

dations and shaped the plan upon which later builders wrought. His errors were rectified by Pestalozzi, by Froebel, by the philosophers and psychologists, by the legion of schoolmasters, and, not least, by the myriad women who, after Rousseau, took their part in educational work, — a part essential to sound and rapid progress.[1]

Dealing, therefore, with these successive educational "heroes," I shall consider, as types and leaders in educational progress, Rabelais, Francis Bacon, Comenius, Montaigne, Locke, the Jansenists, Fénelon, Rousseau, Pestalozzi, Froebel, and, collectively, women.

[1] Of these forces I must, to my regret, wholly neglect one. The influence upon education of the philosophers and psychologists of our century is too wide and too abstruse a problem to be considered here.

CHAPTER II.

RABELAIS.

The Revolt against Mediævalism.

THE MIDDLE AGES; THEIR EDUCATIONAL STANDARDS; THE RENAIS-
SANCE; RABELAIS; HIS CHARACTER; HIS CAREER; HIS WRITINGS;
HIS AIMS; GARGANTUA; OLD AND NEW EDUCATION CONTRASTED;
RABELAIS'S IDEAL EDUCATION; ITS DETAILS; ITS VALUE; PAN-
TAGRUEL; GARGANTUA'S LETTER; MILTON'S "TRACTATE"; RAB-
ELAIS'S FUNDAMENTAL TEACHINGS; THELÊME; PANURGE; VOYAGE
IN QUEST OF THE ORACLE; ITS REAL MEANING; WHAT RABELAIS
ACCOMPLISHED; HIS STYLE.

To understand fully the growth from ancient to modern
ideals, one ought to be able to elucidate the Middle Ages;
for in them, as well as in the elder civilizations, lie the roots
of modern knowledge. Were these, the so-called Dark Ages,
a necessary stage in human progress, a sort of *interregnum*
pending the birth of new forces? Was it essential to progress
that humanity should, on the intellectual side, lie fallow for
centuries in order to produce, in the after years, a richer
harvest? Or were the Middle Ages a mere grouping of
circumstances, a logical result of themselves, a successive
rebirth from their own spawning? However these questions may be answered, it is plain that there existed a long
period of outward intellectual darkness following the time
of the Fathers of the Church, that it continued till the
period of Charlemagne,[1] when there was a faint, spasmodic

---

[1] Much is made of the so-called "Palace School" and "Academy"
of Charlemagne's court, and the monk Alcuin is not seldom dubbed

resurrection of learning, that it dragged on till Abèlard[1] and the scholastics proclaimed a false dawning, and that it extended well into the fifteenth century, when, at last, the sun of the new day rose.

During this long period, such Christian education as existed was mainly of the Church. To prepare men for the religious life, not in the purer spirit of the Fathers, but in the bigotry of doctrine, was the main object of teaching. Learning and priesthood were almost synonymous, but the priest was cramped by instruction, not freed by study. The dry formalism and dead conning of words which the standard of the Church entailed, led, inevitably, to the dreary hootings of scholasticism. This owlish learning, growing more outrageous as its metaphysics became more absurdly deep, soon lost all point of contact with humanity. Its husks of syllogism drove all appetite for real learning from the mind of the student, and he contented himself, ignorant of better intellectual food, with a smattering of Latin, a jargon of philosophy. In his sloven lips the Latin grew to be as false as the philosophy. Whatever the remote cause of the degradation preceding the Renaissance, its immediate source was, plainly, the low standard of education; for, when the sun of real learning dawned upon this intellectual

his Minister of Public Instruction. While Charles, undoubtedly, made honest and serious endeavor to improve the condition of his household and his loosely federated subjects, it is easy to exaggerate both the extent and the success of his efforts. Where the mists of ignorance are as heavy as they were in the ninth century, even so small a rush-light as that burned at Aix-la-Chapelle casts gigantic reflections and is easily mistaken for an educational lighthouse.

[1] For Abèlard and the University of Paris, of which, virtually, he was the founder, consult Compayré, *Abèlard;* and Laurie, *Rise and Early Const. of Univ.*

[NOTE. — *Whenever the titles of books are not given in full, they will be found, extended, in the Bibliography on p. 233.*]

morass, what seemed dead and corrupt was quickened, the means of growth — the printing-press, the compass, and a thousand other material aids — arose, and, in an instant, historically speaking, Europe was transformed, reformation came, naturalism gained place, and modern civilization began.

To resolve the myriad forces of the Renaissance, tracing each to its source and measuring its results, would be impossible. Every nation of Europe did its part in the work of promoting true learning, but from France, modern "Mother of arts and eloquence," came the first great prophet, the leader of revolt, the seer of real education, François Rabelais. He was the first modern pleader for the copartnership of Nature in the bringing up of youth. No veil of tradition could blind him to the path which education should take. His words, true then, are no less true to-day. His plans, Utopian then, are far from their fulfilment now.

Some one[1] compares Rabelais's writings to a Gothic cathedral of the florid type. Viewed point by point, the building is cumbered with petty and curious detail; fancy, in its adornment, runs mad and grows obscene; incongruity is everywhere. But contemplate this mass from a distance, merge details in the outline of the whole, and there appears the perfection of architecture, the flower of the art. One must look at Rabelais in this way, seeing the beauty, the majesty, of his thought, forgetting the flippancy, the grotesqueness, the indecency, of its detailed form.

The man was, in a measure, an outgrowth of his time. His character, individual as it was, received its mould from the forces of the hour. Moreover, he was a native of

---

[1] Lenient, *La satire en France au XVI⁰ siècle.* " Rabelais n'est point encore un disciple de l'architecture mathématique inaugurée par la Renaissance : il a tous les caprices, l'exubérante confusion et la riche prolixité de l'architecture gothique."

Touraine, that fantastic garden of France, where extraordinary physical vitality is linked with wonderful imagination, astonishing fertility of resource, an inexhaustible fund of Gallic *bonhommie*. In these traits are all the elements of such a character as that of Rabelais: courage that could withstand the force of long-accepted doctrines, imagination that could set up and make real a world other than that known of tradition, laughing sunniness of temper that could carry reforms impossible to gravity and dulness. We fancy discerning in Rabelais some of the tavern-keeping spirit of his father, of the raillery and joviality, that, real or assumed, have always an eye to the business of the inn.

Rabelais's existence was no better — it was certainly no worse — than that of his contemporaries. He was a hanger-on of the Papal court while protesting against its abuses. He was, in youth, a scandal to a monastery itself scandalous. He enjoyed benefices won by cringing and kept by favor. He was unchaste in an age when chastity was unmanly. He was drunken in a time when sobriety was a reproach. He was slavish and sycophantic in an era and kingdom where these qualities were the surest means of success. His life was a continual denial of his teachings, or, better, his teachings were a stinging protest against the life that he and his fellows led. In the tumult of the breaking up of the old and the rearing of the new, he stands, a ribald prophet, preaching the new faith in the old tongue.

That he knew himself a genius superior to his age, is undoubted. Such satire as his sprang from a mind that must have gauged its power and despised its surroundings. Such blows as his came from a hand that felt itself gigantic. The spurious death scene, in which he exclaims, "Drop the curtain; the farce is played," expresses his attitude. He had lived a farce. Knowing such great things, he had done such mean ones. To such vision as his, the sixteenth century was a vulgar masque, a carnival of beastly appetites and low aims, played by men of god-like possibilities.

Born the son of an inn-keeper [1] in Chinon, that obscure cradle of the Plantagenets,[2] he dies the friend of popes and kings, the idol of all save those whom he had scourged. Vowed in early life to St. Francis, he becomes, in middle age, a Benedictine with large benefices. Arrayed with the Reformers, he escapes their usual fate, and expires in the full material enjoyment, if not in the full odor, of sanctity. Attacking the Church as few others in France had dared to do, he remains to the last a *protégé* of Rome. His patron, Du Bellay,[3] falls at the accession of Henry II., but Rabelais

[1] Rabelais's early history is very vague. It is generally believed that his father was an inn-keeper, although some authorities maintain that Rabelais was the son of an apothecary, while it is not impossible that the two vocations were united. Nothing is known of his mother, and even the date of his birth is in dispute. If in 1483, then many years of his life cannot be accounted for, and his books must have been finished in extreme old age. If, on the other hand, the date 1495 is accepted, there is difficulty in reconciling it with trustworthy tradition.

[2] Geoffrey, son of Fulk the Black, was the first of the Counts of Anjou to receive the nickname "Plantagenet." He it was who married Matilda, the widowed empress, and became, by her, the father of the future Henry II. of England.

For an interesting account of Chinon and of the Counts of Anjou, see *Old Touraine*, by Theodore A. Cook. (New York, 1893, 2 vols.)

[3] "Le troisième des frères du Bellay, Jean. . . . Ce bon et pieux personnage, le parrain de Gargantua, fut plus tard ministre du roi pour ses petites affaires secrètes du côté des Turcs, le bon ami de Barberousse et le correspondant de Soliman. Evêque de Paris, cardinal, il ne fut pas loin, dit-on, d'être pape. La chose eût été piquante. Rabelais était son Évangile. Il a travaillé plus que personne à créer le Collége de France." — MICHELET, *Hist. de France*, T. 8 ("Réforme"), 383.

gains rather than loses by Francis's death.[1] Hated alike by good Catholic and rigid Calvinist, he withstands their clashing wrath. The storm that he aroused seemed powerless to reach him, falling on lesser figures, not on his. He was too worldly to sacrifice himself, too keen to commit himself, too powerful to be suppressed. He passed through the tempest of the Reformation, one of its foremost figures, one of its hardest fighters, with no hurt to himself. He was bold as Luther, but he possessed nothing of Luther's martyr-spirit. He exposed the Church with his right hand while clutching her favors with his left. He was first a man of the world, only incidentally a reformer. Both he and Luther were strong because they reached the people, but their channels of influence ran in opposite ways.

His medical career, wherein, in middle life, he studied at Montpellier[2] and practised at Lyons, was characteristic, not only proving the marvellous facility of his mind, but showing how adroitly he could shift the frock for the gown and the gown for the frock, as better served his immediate ends. To the close of his life he practised medicine, while remaining a priest, and, passing his declining years in the cure of Meudon, he was still *Doctor* Rabelais. To this chameleon grasp of opportunity his safety in those ticklish times was due. His work as a physician, moreover, turned his mind to writing. His vast erudition, enriched by medi-

---

[1] Largely through the favor of Diane de Poitiers. See *Notice historique sur la vie et les ouvrages de F. Rabelais*, par L. Jacob, bibliophile (pseudonym of P. Lacroix), Paris, 1868. (Prefaced to *Œuvres de F. Rabelais.*)

[2] "The records of the Faculty of Montpellier bear the name of Rabelais, as candidate, under the date of Sept. 17, 1530, and, as bachelor, under that of Nov. 1 of the same year." — FLEURY, *Rab. et ses œuv.*, Ch. XIII. He was not made Doctor of Medicine, however, until May 22, 1537, after a sojourn at Rome.

cal research, the freedom of study and analysis permitted in the schools of healing, his work in editing old texts, combined to lead him to authorship. Well after the middle point of life, he composed, in the intervals of a busy existence, "while eating and drinking," as he expresses it, the five books which have made him immortal.

The Pantagrueline books are of the type of the second part of Faust. There is a like, though lesser, intellectual sweep, a similar lack of continuity, a like evidence of growth out of a different and smaller scheme. There is, in both, a strange mingling of the human and superhuman, adding to the strength while taking from the unity of the design. As in Goethe's masterpiece, one's interest is not so much in the theme or in the characters as in the summing-up of humanity, the propounding of the hardest questions of existence. Each is a growth, not a creation. Each is a philosophy rather than a romance.

The manner of their composition is interesting, and is plainly to be traced. First appeared,[1] in satire of the extravagant romances of the day, the *Chronique Gargantuine.* A year or two later,[2] was published the first book of *Pantagruel,* still extravagant, still monstrous, but dealing with eternal problems. Both meeting with extraordinary success, the *Chronique* was rewritten to serve as an introduction to *Pantagruel,* which became, thereafter, the second book. This enlarged *Gargantua,*[3] Rabelais's greatest production from the standpoint of education, is, therefore, a thing of patches. A bit of profound truth, a rare prophecy, alternate with chapters of grossest foolery, relics of the old extravagance.

The way now being plain, the mental drift determined,

---

[1] In 1531 or 1532.   [2] 1533.

[3] Published in 1535.

there appeared, in 1546, under shelter of royal sanction,[1] the second book of *Pantagruel,* the third of the series. This, intellectually, is his masterpiece; it is satire at the highest.   The fourth and fifth books, devoted to the voyage of Pantagruel in search of the Oracle, while more homogeneous than the earlier ones, are, for our present purpose, far inferior, and possess no vital interest.   To a study of Rabelais as a whole, however, they are the key.

Here it seems proper to identify and defend my position as to the ever-mooted question of Rabelais's purpose in these books.[2]   Either he was a gross panderer to vulgar,

[1] Privilege of Francis 1st, dated Sept. 19, 1545.

[2] Two quotations will serve to exemplify the antipodal position of the critics of Rabelais.   Michelet says of him (*Hist. de France,* VIII. 428) : "What was he?   Ask, rather, what he was not.   A man versed in every study, every art, every tongue, the true *Pan-ourgos,* universal agent in things scientific and political, who was everything and was fitted for everything, who contained the genius of the century and lavished it without stint. . . .   A bold navigator upon the deep sea that had engulfed the old gods, he sets out to seek the great Perhaps ; . . . already America and the new isles, already the chemical substances extracted from plants, already the motion of the blood, the circulation of life, the interdependence of the bodily functions, press forward in the Pantagruel in sublime pages which, under a light and ironical form, are, none the less, the religious hymns of the Renaissance."   Contrast with this outburst, the judgment of Sir James Stephen (*Lectures on the History of France,* London, 1857) : "A genuine epicurean gifted with gigantic powers, but of cold affections and debased appetites ; ever worshipping and obeying his one idol, Pleasure, though at one time she bids him soar to the empyrean and at another commands him to wallow in the sty. . . .   Deep and fatal are the traces of his example and of his fame in the literary history of his native land.   With him commences the lineage of those eminent spirits who have waged war in France against the moral and religious convictions and even against the social decencies of the Christian world ; a war productive of some of the sorest troubles, or rather, let us say, of some of the heaviest chastisements, which have rebuked the offences of the nations of modern Europe."

corrupted tastes,—in which case we must believe his insight to have been blind accident,—or he was a reformer
wise as the serpent, covering his wisdom so skilfully
that the dulness of the multitude did not reject it nor
the craft of the Church ferret it out. The adventures
of Gargantua and Pantagruel must be classed, either as
scandalous romances without form or purpose except to
debauch, or as one of the great reforming agencies of the
Renaissance. There can be, it seems to me, no middle
belief. If we cannot be satisfied that we have here but one
more of the Middle Age chronicles, then we must see in
Rabelais's work a conscious plan, a moral medicine, dis-
guised in such shape as the manner of the time suggested.[1]

The chronicle begins with a description of an orgy in
which is uttered the famous apostrophe to drinking, one of
the best examples of the fecundity and floridity of Rabelais's
vocabulary. It defies adequate translation, for it is a very
riot of words, real and imagined, thrown one upon another
in a whirlwind of rhetoric. It is followed by the birth of
Gargantua, who is son to Grandgousier and Gargamelle,
giants as is he. After a chapter or two devoted to the

[1] We must keep in mind, too, the entire inconsistency of these
chronicles. In the sixteenth century, literature had not been brought
within bounds. The critical sense was so little developed that form
was almost neglected. More than this, the romances which were the
fashion of the day had fitted the common mind to a comprehension
and appreciation of the exaggerated and grotesque only. When, then,
Rabelais treats his characters, first as giants of prodigious size, then
as mortals of common stature, and when, as is often the case, one of
heroic mould shares the adventures of an ordinary man, it is a matter
of no moment to the progress of the satire. It is as idle to criticise
this incongruity as to find fault with the perspective of a vigorous
Japanese drawing; yet this inconsistency forms a staple argument
with those who would prove that Rabelais is nothing more than a
literary buffoon.

prodigious doings of Gargantua, to his rearing and the cut of his clothes, to the manner of his eating, and to other details, all grotesque, come those great chapters which embrace the beginning and the end of right education, — chapters whose diligent study and faithful application would revolutionize pedagogics. The fine irony and delicious satire of the first, describing false training, are excelled only by the dignity and serene wisdom of the second, expounding true education.

I will pass over the description of Gargantua's gluttony, his gross playing and swinish sleeping, his uncleanliness and stupidity, his eternal mumbling of prayers, and will quote only from the description of his intellectual training: —

"In the first place he was taught by a wonderful master of sophism, Holofernes, who instructed to such purpose that he could say his ABC by heart, backwards. And for this were needed five years and three months; " — absolute figures are characteristic — "then were read to him *Donat*,[1] *le Facet*,[2] *Theodelet*,[3] and *Alanus*[4] *in parabolis*, for the space of thirteen years, six months, and two weeks ; . . . then were taught to him the *De Modis Significandi*[5] and the commentaries of . . .,"[6] but I will omit the list, which, as usual, Rabelais gives at length — "This for the space of eighteen years and eleven months, and he knew it so well that, at his examina-

---

[1] "*Ælii Donati de octo partibus orationis libellus.*" This Latin grammar was in such universal use in the mediæval schools that *Donat* became synonymous with *Grammar*.

[2] "*Liber faceti morosi docens mores hominum.*"

[3] "*Ecloga Theoduli.*" Allegory, in dialogue, against paganism.

[4] Alain de Lisle, a Cistercian monk of the twelfth century, known as *Doctor universalis*.

[5] By Jean de Garlande.

[6] *Gargantua*, Liv. I., Ch. **XIV.**

tion, he said it by heart, backwards. And he proved upon his fingers, to his mother, that *de modis significandi non erat scientia.* Then he was taught the *Compost* [1] for the space of sixteen years and two months, when his perceptor " — not without cause, we must think — "died. . . . Then was placed over him an old cougher," — fossil would be our modern slang, — who taught him a host of treatises, "in the reading of which he became so wise that we have never since seen his equal."

Now this slow haste of fifty years — time, too, is on a gigantic scale — is not pleasing to the old Grandgousier, especially when he finds his son, after all this cramming of scholastic lore, to be inferior, both in manners and in understanding, "to one of the young men of the present time," — that is, of the time of which Rabelais dreams, — "who may have studied not more than two years, for such an one has better judgment, better address, better manners, better conversation and behavior towards the world than he." [2] To prove this, such a young man is brought in, and marvellous is the contrast. [3] This object lesson suffices. Grandgousier loses no time in putting his son under the tutor of this model youth, and, after more nonsense, including the purging of the young giant's memory of all the dreary rubbish which had choked it, the new task is begun. Having ridiculed out of existence the old way of teaching, Rabelais shows us, as he foresees it, a picture of the new. [4]

Here is an outline of the day's work, divested of the Rabelaisian word-juggling with which, in the original, it is overlaid. Gargantua arose about four o'clock in the morning. While he bathed, passages from the Scriptures were

[1] A treatise on the calculation of the calendar.
[2] *Gargantua*, Liv. I., Ch. XV.
[3] *Ibid;* Besant, *Read. in Rab.*, 13.
[4] Ch. XXIII. and XXIV.

read to him, distinctly and clearly, with proper emphasis. Subsequently, his tutor went over the extracts, explaining difficult and obscure points to him. They then observed the sky, noting if it were of the same aspect as on the night preceding. This done, he was dressed, during which time his lessons of the day before were reviewed. Sometimes, in so doing, hard points arose, the discussion of which occupied several hours, but, ordinarily, this review ended with the dressing. This over, they went out of doors, — always engaged upon the subject of the lessons, — and played tennis and other games, properly exercising the body as they had, heretofore, the mind. Being now in a good sweat, they were wiped and rubbed down and their shirts were changed.

While waiting for dinner, extracts from the lessons are recited, clearly and carefully. "Now comes Master Appetite, and they sit down at table. At the beginning of the repast, some pleasant tale of ancient valor is read to them; then, if they please, the reading is continued, or they converse cheerfully together, talking of the virtues, properties, efficacy, and nature of everything on the table. So doing, they soon learn what the ancient authors have taught us in these matters. Then, finishing the repast with confections, they wash their faces and hands in cold water, and give thanks to God for his bounty." This done, cards are brought, not for play, but for the learning of a thousand little tricks and inventions, all founded upon arithmetic; by which means Gargantua comes to love the science of numbers, and, by dint of playing with cards and dice every day, grows so learned in it, "that Tunstal confessed freely that he himself knew only the rudiments."[1]

[1] This must be a polite sarcasm. The Bishop of Durham, while a scholar, intimate with Erasmus, was not conspicuous as a mathematician. He had been recently at Paris, in the train of Wolsey.

"And not only this, but other mathematical sciences, geometry, astronomy, music," were learned in kindred ways.

An hour thus employed, digestion accomplished, he bent himself to the main studying of the day for the space of three hours, reviewing former lessons, taking up new ones, writing, drawing, and lettering. This over, he sallied forth, and was taught, by a young gentleman of Touraine, the art of horsemanship. To this were added the accomplishments of sword-play, lance-play, and hunting. Then followed swimming lessons. Issuing, all glowing, from the water, he ran, climbed trees, wrestled, and indulged in every sort of athletic exercise. To train his lungs, he shouted "with such a voice as Stentor never had." Exercise over, he was rubbed, dried, and freshly clad, and went out into the fields, studying plants, trees, and flowers. Returning to the house, they partook of supper, and, "mark you, while their dinner in the middle of the day was light and frugal, their supper was copious and generous. Wherein is the true principle of diet." Grace said, they betook themselves to singing and the playing of instruments, and to the pastimes with cards, sometimes varying their occupations by visiting men of letters and travellers from foreign lands. In the evening, before going to bed, they searched the heavens, noting the figuration and aspect of the stars. Then, with his tutor, Gargantua reviewed, briefly, after the manner of the Pythagoreans, all that he had read, seen, learned, done, and heard, in the course of the day. "Finally, adoring and glorifying God, he went to rest." And weary must he have been.

On rainy days, Gargantua, instead of the outdoor exercises, studied the arts and sciences, and their applications, visiting the workshops of artisans; instead of botanizing, he visited the shops of druggists and apothecaries, studying the art of healing. On such days the supper was more frugal, "in order that the intemperate dampness of the air, communicated to the body by necessary proximity, might, by this means, be corrected."[1] By the methods thus stated, study "became rather like a pastime of kings than the labor of a scholar." However, to rest the mind from the tedium of continued application, he took, once a month, a complete holiday in the open air, playing, leaping, singing, and reciting Virgil.

Here we have the germ — more than the germ, the perfect flower — of a well-rounded education. Here we have the dependence, close as possible, of instruction upon daily life and common things; here we have the review by which the fact is fixed and its relationship to other facts made clear; here we have the perfection of physical exercise; the splendid picture of the youth, glowing from his bath, racing, climbing, rubbed and clad afresh; here we find practical technology, and the rational search of nature; and, finally, we have, throughout, the fine spirit of reverence, which is as simple as it is profound. A wonderful dream and foresight of the best aims of to-day! The whole science and art of education, a text for a thousand treatises![2]

I might extract from Rabelais's writings many additions to this general scheme of a true education. I content myself, however, with giving, almost in its entirety, the letter which Gargantua, grown old, sends to his son Pantagruel, after the young man has gone to Paris to complete his studies.[3] To those who declare Rabelais to be an atheist, a railer, a corrupter of morals, a scoffer at decency, this letter is a sufficient answer.

[1] This was the age, it will be remembered, of belief in "humours" and in the direct agency of external influences upon them.

[2] Cf. Eugène Lévêque, *Les mythes et les légendes de l'Inde et la Perse*, p. 548 (Paris, 1880) for a source of Gargantua's education in that of Bharata, given in the *Râmâyana*.

[3] *Pantagruel*, Liv. II., Ch. VIII.

" . . . Now therefore, with just and right cause, I give thanks to God, my preserver, in that He has permitted me to see my withered age reflourish in thy youth. For when, at the pleasure of Him who rules and ordains all things, my soul shall leave its mortal house, I shall account myself not wholly to die, but simply to pass from one place to another, while in thee and through thee I continue in my very image, visible to the world, living, seeing, and conversing among my friends as I used. The which my conversation has been, not without sin, I confess (for we are all sinners, continually beseeching God to forgive our trespasses), but, by Divine aid and grace, without reproach. Wherefore, in so far as dwells in thee the image of my body, so equally should be enkindled in thee the qualities of the soul, by which alone shalt thou be judged as the guardian and keeper of the immortality of our name; and my pleasure in seeing this would be small if that the least part of me, which is the body, should remain, and the best, which is the soul, and through which alone our name may be a blessing to men, should be degenerate and bastard. The which I say through no distrust of thy virtue, which has been already proven to me, but the rather to encourage thee to strive on from good to better. And what I herein write is not so much that thou shouldst live in this thy virtuous course, but that thou shouldst rejoice in so living and in so having lived, refreshing thyself thereby with courage for the future. To perfect and consummate which end, I may remind thee how I have spared nothing; but so have propped thee up as if I had no other treasure in the world save in the seeing of thee, during my life, whole and perfect, equally in virtue, honesty, and valor, as in all liberal and right knowledge; and so to leave thee after my death, as a mirror reflecting me thy father, and if not to bring thee to such a point of excellence as I might wish, still to inspire the thirst for its attainment.

"But, while my late father of blessed memory, Grand-gousier, bent all his study to what might profit me to all perfection and human knowledge, and while my labor and study corresponded to, yea, exceeded his desire, still, as thou canst well understand, the times were not so full and fit in learning as now, and such abundance of teachers as thou hast had was not. The times were still dark, savoring of the terror and calamity of the Goths, by whom good literature had been utterly destroyed. But, by the favor of God, its light and dignity have been, even within my day, restored, and I see in it such growth that, now, I should fail of entrance into an upper class of little boys,[1] I who, in my time, was esteemed (not without reason) the most learned of the age.

. . . .

"Wherefore, my son, I admonish thee that thou employ thy youth to good profit in study and in virtue. Thou art in Paris, thou hast for thy tutor Epistemon, whereby, the one through noble examples, the other, through quickening instruction, may forward thee. I expect and desire that thou shouldst learn perfectly the languages. First Greek, as Quintilian advises; secondly, Latin; and then, Hebrew, because of the Holy Scriptures. Likewise, Chaldee and Arabic; and form thy style, as to Greek, after Plato; as to Latin, after Cicero. Let there be no history which is not firm in thy memory, to which end cosmography will help thee. Of the liberal arts, I gave thee a taste of geometry, arithmetic, and music when thou wast still little, no older than five or six; pursue the rest and search out all the laws of astronomy. As to astrology and the Lullian art,[2] leave

---

[1] " Petitz grimaulx."

[2] Lully's aim seems to have been as high as that of Francis Bacon, which was to find a key to universal knowledge. The result in the

them; they are abuses and vanities. Know by heart the texts of civil law and compare them with the teachings of philosophy.

"Now, as to the facts of nature, addict thyself studiously to the learning of them, so that there be no sea, river, or lake of which thou knowest not the fish; so that all the birds of the air, all the plants and fruits of the forest, all the flowers of the soil, all the metals hid in the bowels of the earth, all the gems of the East and South, none shall be foreign to thee.

"Most carefully peruse the writings of physicians, Greek, Arab, Latin, despising not even the Talmudists and Cabalists; and by frequent searching gain perfect knowledge of the microcosm, man.[1] And at certain hours of the day, turn to the Holy Scriptures. First to the New Testament and Epistles, in Greek, then to the Old Testament, in Hebrew. In short, let me behold in thee an abyss of learning; for, as thou becomest a man and great, thou must come out from this tranquillity and calm of study, learning chivalry and arms, wherewith to defend my house and to succor our dear friends from hurt of evil-doers. I would that thou shouldst shortly learn how much thou hast profited, the which thou canst no more easily do than by maintaining theses, publicly against all comers, frequenting, too, the company of the learned.

"But, because, as saith the wise Solomon, wisdom enters not the wicked heart, and knowledge without conscience is but the ruin of the soul, it behooves thee to serve, love, and

case of the former, however, was little more than an alphabetical and geometrical word-juggling. See the interesting account of him in H. C. Lea's *Hist. of the Inquisition of the Middle Ages* (New York, 1888), III. 578.

[1] Perhaps a too free rendering of " *et par frequentes anatomies acquiers toy parfaicte congnoissance de l'aultre monde, qui est l'homme.*"

fear God, putting in Him all thy hope, all thy thought; and, by a faith founded on love, cleave thou to Him so that thou shalt never be torn from Him by sin. Have a care of the follies of the world. Fix not thy heart on vanities; for this life is transitory: but the world of God endureth forever. Serve thy neighbors and love them as thyself. Revere thy teachers, shun companions whom thou wouldst not resemble, and receive not in vain the graces with which God has endowed thee. And when thou shalt perceive thyself to have acquired all this knowledge which I have pointed out to thee, return to me, that I may behold thee and give thee my blessing before I die.

"My son, the peace and grace of our Lord be with thee. Amen.

"From Utopia,[1] this 17 day of the month of March.

"Thy father,.

"*Gargantua.*"

In these inadequate quotations is embraced the message of Rabelais.[2] All else he wrote is but the setting to this pearl.

[1] A reprint of the first edition of More's *Utopia* was published at Paris in 1518.

[2] There is a singular parallelism between the principles laid down by Rabelais and those contained in the famous tractate, *On Education*, of Milton. This marked resemblance is due in part, of course, to the fact that both courses of study were, as Milton says of his own, "Likest to those ancient and famous schools of Pythagoras, Plato, Isocrates, Aristotle, and such others, out of which were bred such a number of renowned philosophers, orators, historians, poets, and princes all over Greece, Italy, and Asia, besides the flourishing studies of Cyrene and Alexandria"; but, as the following necessarily disconnected extracts will show, the likeness is so close as to suggest, at least, a great admiration upon the part of the Puritan Englishman for the Frenchman, puritan in far different fashion, who preceded him by about a century. Milton says, concerning the education of young men: ". . . First, they should begin with the chief and necessary

The contempt of sham, the ridicule of pretence, the hatred
of tyranny, which appear again and again in the medley of

rules of some good grammar, . . . and while this is doing, their speech
is to be fashioned to a distinct and clear pronunciation. . . . Next,
to make them expert in the usefullest points of grammar, and withal
to season them and win them early. to the love of virtue and true
labour, . . . some easy and delightful book of education would be
read to them, whereof the Greeks have store.

"But here the main skill and groundwork will be, to temper them
such lectures and explanations, upon every opportunity, as may lead
and draw them in willing obedience, inflamed with the study of learning and the admiration of virtue ; stirred up with high hopes of living
to be brave men and worthy patriots, dear to God and famous to all
ages. That they may despise and scorn all their childish and ill-
taught qualities, to delight in manly and liberal exercises. . . . At
the same time, some other hour of the day, might be taught them the
rules of arithmetic ; and soon after the elements of geometry, even
playing, as the old manner was. After evening repast, till bedtime,
their thoughts would be best taken up in the easy grounds of religion
and the story of scripture.

"The next step would be to the authors of agriculture. . . . It will
be then seasonable for them to learn in any modern author the use of
the globes, and all the maps, first, with the old names, and then with
the new ; or they might be then capable to read any compendious
method of natural philosophy.   ·

". . . Having thus passed the principles of arithmetic, geometry,
astronomy, and geography, with a general compact of physics, they
may descend in mathematics to the instrumental science of trigonom-
etry, and from thence to fortification, architecture, enginery, or navi-
gation. And in natural philosophy they may proceed leisurely from
the history of meteors, minerals, plants, and living creatures, as far as
anatomy.

"Then also in course might be read to them, out of some not tedious
writer, the institution of physic, that they may know the tempers, the
humours, the seasons, and how to manage a crudity. . . . To set
forward all these proceedings in nature and mathematics, what hin-
ders but they may procure, as oft as shall be needful, the helpful
experience of hunters, fowlers, fishermen, shepherds, gardeners,

his five books, are but reiterations of his plea for the manliness, the liberty, the piety, that are the foundations of

apothecaries; and in the other sciences, architects, engineers, mari-
ners, anatomists; who doubtless would be ready, some for reward,
and some to favour such a hopeful seminary. And this will give them
such a real tincture of natural knowledge, as they shall never forget,
but daily augment with delight."

Here follow recommendations to study ethics, politics, and civil law.

"Sundays also and every evening may be now understandingly
spent in the highest matters of theology and church history, ancient
and modern; and ere this time the Hebrew tongue at a set hour
might have been gained, that the scriptures may be now read in their
own original; whereto it would be no impossibility to add the Chaldee
and the Syrian dialect.

"And now, lastly, will be the time to read with them those organic
arts, which enable men to discourse and write perspicuously, elegantly,
and according to the fittest style, of lofty, mean, or lowly. Logic,
therefore, so much as is useful, is to be referred to this due place. . . .
To which poetry would be made subsequent, or indeed rather prece-
dent.

". . . This institution of breeding which I here delineate shall be
equally good both for peace and war. Therefore about an hour and a
half ere they eat at noon should be allowed them for exercise, and
due rest afterwards; but the time for this may be enlarged at pleasure, according as their rising in the morning shall be early.

"The exercise which I commend first, is the exact use of their
weapon; . . . this will keep them healthy, nimble, strong and well in
breath. . . . They must be also practised in all the locks and gripes of
wrestling, wherein Englishmen were wont to excel. . . . The interim
of unsweating themselves regularly, and convenient rest before meat
may, both with profit and delight, be taken up in recreating and com-
posing their travailed spirits with the solemn and divine harmonies of
music, heard or learned.

". . . They are, by a sudden alarum or watchword, to be called
out to their military motions, under sky or covert, according to the
season . . . first on foot, then, as their age permits, on horseback, to
all the art of cavalry; that, having in sport, but with much exactness
and daily muster, served out the rudiments of their soldiership, . . .

this scheme of education. He would not destroy the Church, for, relentlessly pointing out her corruptions, he carefully maintains her spiritual supremacy; but he would tear down the abuses of religion, which had made a mockery of priesthood and a travesty of learning. He did not cavil at the law, but upheld her majesty by scourging the "Catch-poles," [1] the "furred cats," [2] the "Bridlegeese," [3] who had converted the halls of justice into auction rooms. So reverent was he of his profession, medicine, that he could find no words too stinging for quacks and charlatans. He would strip life of all the mummery and falsehood which monks and pedants had wrapped about it, and would bring man face to face with nature. He would make of religion a spontaneous act, the normal result of a study of God's works, not the unmeaning formalism of a corrupted Church. He would found philosophy upon legitimate search and reasoning, not upon forced syllogisms. He hated asceticism and scholasticism with the scorn of an honest mind that had tested the hollowness of both. He knew that only in the sound body and the reverent mind can real learning flourish.

they may . . . come forth renowned and perfect commanders in the service of their country.

". . . . Besides these constant exercises at home, there is another opportunity of gaining experience to be won from pleasure itself abroad . . . learning and observing all places of strength, all commodities of building and of soil, for towns and tillage, harbours and ports for trade.

" Now lastly, for their diet there cannot be much to say, save only that it would be best in the same house ; for much time else would be lost abroad, and many ill habits got; and that it should be plain, healthful, and moderate, I suppose is out of controversy." — *Prose Works of John Milton*, III. 462. (London, H. G. Bohn, 1848.)

[1] Besant, *Read. in Rab.* 239.

[2] *Ibid.* 326.

[3] *Ibid.* 193 (" *Bridoye* ").

He saw that to conquer nature, to make her the ally of man, she must not be thwarted, as by the monks and scholars, but must be made a friend, yielding to him who humbly seeks, her deepest secrets. He discerned the glorious average of man, that even balancing of body, mind, and soul, which, in maintaining spiritual equilibrium, makes us one with God. Everywhere he saw men slaves to each other and to themselves. To be released, he knew, they must free themselves from their lower natures. But he saw, as none other did, that self-emancipation does not come through asceticism or through transcendentalism, but from bodily vigor, honest work, hard study, healthy thinking, and reverent communion with nature.

This spiritual liberty is taught in his first book, the *Gargantua*, in the chapters on education, contrasting, as we have seen, the old training, as it existed, with the new, as he conceived it. The lesser forms of freedom, that from kings and that from priests, are exemplified, in the same book, by two incidents, the first showing to what follies lust of power led King Picrochole; the latter, picturing, in the Abbey of Thelême, the perfect religious life.[1] It is not

---

[1] One extract will suffice to show the wholesomeness of Rabelais's conception of religious liberty: "Their entire life was governed, not by statutes, laws, or rules, but by their own free will and choice. They arose when they pleased, drank, ate, worked, slept, as the humor moved them. No one awakened them, none forced them to drink, eat, or do aught else. For so Gargantua had established it. Their rules were included within this one sentence, Do What Thou Wilt. Because free persons, well-born, well-bred, of good conversation, have a natural instinct and spur urging them to virtuous living and restraining them from vice — namely, honor. The same persons, brought down and held under vile subjection and restraint, turn aside from a noble affection toward virtue, the better to throw off the yoke that enthralls them. For we are prone to enter into forbidden things and to long for what is denied us. But, being free, all strove in

necessary to dwell upon the war of Picrochole and Grand-gousier, for its treatment is not original, except in the surprising humor of the satire against predatory warfare and foolish ambition.[1] Neither is it possible for us to follow Rabelais in his characteristically florid description of the Abbey of Thelême — a description so exact in its details that modern architects have drawn its plan.[2]

I have said that interest does not attach so much to the figures as to the philosophy of Rabelais's creations. I should have made exception of the third book, — the second *Pantag-ruel*, — for in this the study of character is masterly. In it are contrasted three marked types, in the persons of Pantagruel, the result of two generations of rational training; of Friar John, the man of noble instincts made beastly by monkish training; of Panurge, the man of the world, the fruit of all the evil influences of the day. Through these three men, the education of the monastery and that of the dying chivalry are brought into sharp contrast with the new

pleasant rivalry to do the will of each. . . . So nobly did they apply themselves to learning that not one among them but could read, write, sing, play upon instruments, speak five or six languages, and compose therein both in prose and in verse. Never were knights so brave, so gallant, so skilled on foot and on horseback, so adroit in arms, as they. Never were ladies so perfect, so dainty, less froward, more ready with the hand and needle in all womanly occupations, than those.

"For which reason, when the time came that any, either at his parents' wish or for other cause, would go from the Abbey, with him he would take one of the ladies, her to whom he had sworn fealty, and they would marry. And if they had lived in devotion and friendship in *Thelême*, still more did they in marriage, preserving their fond affection to the end of their days."

[1] See Fleury, *Rab. et ses œuv.*, Ch. V.; and Besant, *Read. in Rab.* 32.

[2] See Fleury, Ch. VI.; and Besant, 58. For the plan, consult A. Heulhard, *Rabelais, ses voyages en Italie; son exil à Metz*, 8. (Paris, 1891.)

education taught by Rabelais. Perhaps we are justified in taking Friar John as the type of pure animalism, in which corruption is only superficial; Panurge as the type of pure intellect, whose debasement sinks him lower than the beasts; and Pantagruel as the perfect type, the balance of body, brain, and soul, made possible by proper education.

From a dramatic standpoint, Panurge is Rabelais's greatest creation. He ranks with the typical characters of Shakespeare.[1] From the moment when, entering the romance, he greets Pantagruel in twelve different languages, to the end of the fifth book, Panurge serves, not only as the chief mouthpiece of Rabelais's satire, but as a necessary foil to the high and manly — the truly ideal — character of Pantagruel. His self-conceit, his swaggering, his crafty improvidence, his low cunning, his abject cowardice in face of actual danger, above all, the utter misuse and waste of his keen intellect and brilliant wit through the moral deformity of the man — are admirably depicted. But a study of him, interesting as he is, goes beyond our limits. It is around him that the last three books are grouped. The exertions of Pantagruel and his followers, their questioning of fate by divers methods, their journeyings to foreign lands, and their final and arduous quest of the Oracle of the Bottle, are all in search of an answer to the question of Panurge, — which is, no less, the question of to-day, — "Shall I marry?" The philosophy, the satire, as well as the narrative of these books, hangs, often by slenderest threads, to the main proposition, which is, superficially, Is marriage the means to greatest happi-

---

[1] In this connection see Wilhelm König, *Ueber die Entlehnungen Shakespeare's inbesondere aus Rabelais und einigen italienischen Dramatikern;* in *Jahrbuch der Deutschen Shakespeare-Gesellschaft* (9ter Jahrgang, Weimar, 1874), 195.

ness? but which is, deeply, Can knowledge be attained outside the sphere of the senses?

The answer comes at last. Every test of the occult
known to Rabelais — and his erudition, which he delights
in showing, is immense [1] — has been tried with negative
results. There remains the Oracle of the Bottle, the way
to which is long and difficult. Through adventures extraordinary the shrine is reached. The necessary hocus-pocus is
made, the bottle answers, uttering but one word, "Drink."

Omar Khayyám, the Persian, gives us the same answer: [2] —

> "Then to the Lip of this poor earthen Urn
> I lean'd, the Secret of my life to learn :
> And Lip to Lip, it murmur'd — ' While you live,
> Drink ! for, once dead, you never shall return.' "

Is this the whole of life? Are we, as Panurge exclaims
when he hears the Oracle, "as wise as we were last year?"
Or is there a deeper meaning, the command that we shall
not question the unknowable, but shall drink deep at the
spring of nature, making the most of life, taking the good
and the bad as they come, safe in the faith that God is?

In this confused and ribald allegory, Rabelais led the way
out of ancient superstition into modern science. More than
this, he taught in it that the study of nature, observation of
her laws, imitation of her methods, must be at the root of

---

[1] "His" (Rabelais's) "genius is like the sea, yielding both pearls
and slime ; like nature, producing indifferently the nettle and the rose
and pronouncing them both good. His science and his memory are as
gigantic as his fancy ; medicine, law, theology, metaphysics, ethics,
history, criticism, poetry, eloquence, he has read them all and has
retained them all." — PAUL STAPFER, *Laurence Stern ; sa personne
et ses ouvrages.* (Paris, 1870.)

[2] *Rubáiyát*, Fitzgerald's rendering. Quatrain XXXV. (Tenth
American ed. ; Boston, 1885.)

every true system of education. He showed that the nature-spirit is the true spirit of good teaching. Ever since his day civilized mankind has been trying to learn this lesson of his and to apply it in the schools. For three centuries the leaders in education, under his indirect inspiration, have been slowly and painfully transforming the false pedagogy of the cloister into the true pedagogy of out-of-doors. Writers and teachers, schools and universities, have been engaged in a halting and irregular struggle to transfer education from a metaphysical to a physical basis, to lead it away from a habit of deductive speculation into one of inductive research. This transfer Rabelais made boldly and at once. He did not, of course, elaborate the educational ideal of to-day, but he plainly marked out the lines upon which that ideal is framed. He taught truth and simplicity, he ridiculed hypocrisy and formalism, he denounced the worship of words, he demanded the study of things, he showed the beauty of intellectual health, of moral discipline, of real piety. Best of all, he enunciated the supreme principle of nature, which is *ordered freedom*.

The freedom which he advocated is not that of the individual, but that of the citizen. He taught, not license, but social freedom, in which the liberty of all is conditioned upon the restraint of each, and the liberty of each is secured only by the mutual restraint of all. The watchword of his Abbey of Thelême is not simply, in its interpretation, "Do what thou wilt"; it is, "Do what thou wilt, unselfishly." Upon free action modified by interdependence, the scheme of nature rests. From the solar system down to the tiniest molecule there is no departure from this principle.

Rabelais was a leader in thought, therefore, because he recognized the supreme law to which is due the harmony of nature. He was a leader in education because he showed that it, too, must rest upon this law. He reconciled uni-

versal liberty with universal restraint. He showed that
the only true system of education must recognize fully the
freedom of the individual while teaching the immutability
of eternal law, and while seeking, ceaselessly, the workings
of that law. He pointed out the only way along which
humanity could progress. He outlined, in short, the career
of civilization.

Hence it is that no one whom we are to consider later
deals so broadly with education as did Rabelais. His was
a master mind that planned for all time and all men. His
scheme is vague, it is impracticable; but it is the essence
of which other systems are the inadequate fulfilment.
Other men have taught as he did, but few have sketched so
broadly, and fewer still have written so aptly and in a
manner so suited to their time. It is a manner which,
happily, is now not only obsolete, but impossible.[1] Strong
as are his writings, their direct sway was ended long ago.
The work is still going on; its end is centuries ahead;
Rabelais's own words, however, can influence it no longer.
The books which, in too many instances, conceal his
thoughts, are, to most decent persons, forever sealed.[2]

---

[1] Mr. Besant, than whom Rabelais has no more earnest champion,
says, in summing up his genius: "Cheerful, light-hearted, full of good
sense, of faith, hope, and charity, an advocate of all good things, an
enemy of all hypocrisies ; and yet he has written so that those who
read him have to show a reason why they read him, so that those who
praise him have to explain why they praise him ; so that no woman
can ever read him, and so that priests have just cause to condemn
him, independently of his derision and mockery of their pretensions.
The pity of it!" — *Rabelais*, 194.

[2] Those who are interested in Rabelais, but who are repelled by the
indecency and obscurity of his writings, cannot do better than read
the excellent volumes of M. Jean Fleury (*Rabelais et ses œuv.*), who
has succeeded in making, not only an intelligible and straightforward,
but also a decent narrative out of the Rabelaisian books. He gives,

For general use, they are dead; but the impulse which they gave is still a living and a growing force.

furthermore, a satisfactory sketch of Rabelais's life, and, to his own judgments and explanations, adds those of many able commentators. The most readable English rendering of Rabelais is that of Mr. Walter Besant (*Readings in Rabelais*).

CHAPTER III.

FRANCIS BACON.

THE REVOLT AGAINST CLASSICISM.

RABELAIS A TYPE ; HIS DIRECT INFLUENCE ; OVERTHROW OF MEDIÆ-
VALISM ; CLASSICISM ; BACON ; HIS CAREER ; HIS FALL ; HIS CHAR-
ACTER ; HIS ASPIRATIONS ; THE "GREAT INSTAURATION" ; HIS
OTHER WRITINGS ; THE INDUCTIVE METHOD ; HIS CONTRIBUTIONS
TO SCIENCE ; TO THOUGHT AND METHOD ; HIS RELATIONS TO CON-
TEMPORARY REFORMERS ; HIS INDICTMENT OF CLASSICISM ; HIS
METHODOLOGY ; THE "IDOLS" ; SENSE-TRAINING ; EMANCIPATION
FROM SELF ; FROM WORDS ; FROM DOGMAS ; BACON'S PRINCIPLES ;
THEY UNDERLIE MODERN EDUCATION ; HIS PEDAGOGY ; HIS PLANS
FOR HIGHER LEARNING; A LEADER IN EDUCATIONAL THOUGHT;
HIS TEACHINGS ; HIS INTELLECT ; HIS INFLUENCE ; HIS STYLE.

IN placing Rabelais first among the leaders in the progress
towards the ideal education, it should be understood that he
is taken as a type — I believe, the best type — of that host
of reformers who saw in education the chief hope of
advance.   Few of the leaders of the Renaissance failed to
give weight to this factor of growth, but in none, it seems
to me, is seen that grasp and prophecy of the power of right
training which is found in Rabelais.   His ideas, put forth
from no pedagogic standpoint, anticipate all later writers
upon education.   His system, dimmed by obscenity and
flippancy, is itself pure as crystal.   It expands to embrace
novel conditions; it may be analyzed to meet specific
problems.

To perceive — or to read into it — these varied qualities, however, required the light that came with later human growth. The immediate result of Rabelais's work was little more than a partial destruction of old errors and abuses. With the surest scalpel, satire, he laid bare the gangrene of mediæval education; in the universal language, humor, he called mankind to see and heal the sore. Here his direct influence ceased. The child whom he had freed from the scholastics fell at once into the hands of the classicists. They imprisoned him in the narrow range of the Greek and Latin civilizations, and human progress, paradoxically, tended towards a retrogression of two thousand years. Deep within it were nurtured, however, the finer, enduring ideas of Rabelais, there to survive for two hundred years and to impel education, finally, into the light of the nineteenth century.

Mediævalism, by Rabelais and his contemporaries, had been overthrown; in its place arose classicism. Against this lesser foe the battle was yet to be fought. The first effective champion of education in this new phase of its advancement was Francis Bacon.

To write of Bacon is to become a partisan, for in few men has the dual nature, the good and the evil, been more strongly marked.[1] To dismiss his sins by attributing them to a subtle furtherance of his labors is as impossible as to condemn his patient work by founding it on vanity. To-day we say of him, "Admirable!" to-morrow, "Despicable!" His "meanness,"[2] more than weakness, was a monstrous blemish; his greatness, more than talent, was sublimest

---

[1] Cf. Lord Campbell's antithetical and rather unjust summary of Bacon's career. *Lives of the Lord Chancellors*, opening of Ch. LI.

[2] Cf. Pope's too brilliant epigram : —

> "If parts allure thee, think how Bacon shin'd,
> The wisest, brightest, meanest of mankind!"
> — *Essay on Man*, Ep. IV.

genius. He sounded the gamut of human experience fully, but with discord. The false note of his personality constantly offends.

He was born to eminence.[1] Son to Elizabeth's Lord Keeper of the Seal, he was, as in his boyhood he felicitously expressed it, "Two years younger than her Majesty's happy reign."[2] Through his mother's sister, he was nephew to Lord Burghley. With such a start, a youth of ordinary parts could scarcely fail of making a place for himself in an age so kind to its favorites. To Bacon's genius everything was possible. As a child, if anecdote be true, he is found already in the eye of favor. As little more than a boy, he takes high place in the Commons. In his eighteenth year, serving on a mission to France, he earns warm praise.[3] But at the opening of his career his father dies, his expected income shrinks to a pittance, the Cecils, upon whose aid he had counted, forsake him, and he begins that sorry quest which is never wholly to be given up, the seeking of royal favor and preferment. With law as his profession, with science and letters as his well-marked avocation, he plies, instead, the unwholesome trade of a courtier.

He attaches himself to Essex, then in high favor, furthers him with Elizabeth, — losing no chance to advance his own fortunes, — is privy, we fear, in some degree, to the rash and stupid plans of that hot-headed nobleman; and, when the crash comes, having privately and honestly, we must believe, tried to avert it, he accepts the certainty of Essex's doom,

---

[1] Francis, youngest son of Sir Nicholas Bacon, by his second wife, Ann Cooke, was born at York House, London, Jan. 22, 1561.

[2] See this and other anecdotes in Dr. Rawley's *Life of Bacon*, which Spedding has prefixed to his edition of the *Works*.

[3] Sir Amias Paulet, in whose train Bacon went, commended him to the Queen as "of great hope, endued with many good and singular parts." — FOWLER, *Bacon*, 3.

deliberately arrays himself against his bosom friend, and, at the Queen's command, calmly sets in motion the machinery that forces him to the scaffold.[1] This business of Essex is the sorriest fact in Bacon's career.[2] His later political fall and the acts which led to it are minor to this first moral degradation. And it avails him little. Elizabeth must have scorned the instrument of her wrath no less than she regretted its effect. The last fretful years of the friendless Queen are not ones in which to show favor to him who, by his legal skill, has deprived her of her latest favorite.

Under James, however, Bacon anticipates better days, and he hastens to study, as he had conned those of Elizabeth, the foibles of the new monarch. Though these are legion, the easiest honorable avenue to favor leads through the pretentious pedantry of the King. Bacon hurries, therefore, to put forth the *Advancement of Learning,* in which, by a skilful presentation of its dignity, of its possibilities for progress under so wise a king, he judiciously calls attention to his plans, under favoring circumstances, for its advancement.

This and other subserviencies have their effect. Slowly his political fortunes, for which through twenty-three years Bacon has striven and manœuvred, are advanced. At the King's accession he is knighted, " gregarious," [3] with three

---

[1] See Abbott's *Bacon and Essex.* It is well to read Mr. Abbott's estimate of Bacon as given in this and in his *Account of his Life and Works,* before accepting the more favorable judgments of Mr. Spedding and Professor Fowler.

[2] Bacon himself characterizes like conduct in his essay *Of Wisdom for a Man's Self :* " It is the wisdom of rats that will be sure to leave a house somewhat before it fall ; it is the wisdom of the fox that thrusts out the badger who digged and made room for him."

[3] See his letter of July 16, 1603, to Cecil : " For my knighthood, I wish the manner might be such as might grace me, since the matter will not ; I mean, that I might not be merely gregarious in a troop."

hundred others; the next year he is made King's counsel; in 1607 he becomes solicitor-general; in the following year the clerkship of the Star Chamber, whose reversion he had long awaited, falls to him; in 1613 he reaches the attorney-generalship; and, finally, in 1618, at the age of fifty-eight, he is made lord chancellor. The three years following, during which he is created Baron Verulam and Viscount St. Albans, are the most prosperous of his life. Politically, he is one of the great figures of Europe; his *Novum Organum*, just published, gives him high rank among philosophers; his essays make him one of the lights of a brilliant literary age.

But, in 1621, the retribution of his petty arts, his frantic striving, his time-serving, comes in full measure. The moral justice of his downfall is as magnificent as it is unusual. The charges of his indictment are, in the times of the Stuarts, insufficient to condemn him. They are but shadows of his real offence. His crime is having made himself the "King's man." [1] He has carried the King's prerogative to its highest pitch. He has dealt in royal rather than in human justice. To please James, he has served Buckingham, and such service entails corruption. [2] The spirit and temper which, later, will behead Charles, are abroad; they demand a victim, and Bacon is sacrificed. The weak King deserts him as Bacon had deserted Essex. He is tried on twenty-eight charges, throws himself on the mercy of the Lords in a letter half-proud, half-grovelling, [3] but is sentenced heavily. Sick in body, harassed in mind, banished and disgraced, he must see, at last, the pitifulness of the

---

[1] "I have been," he says, appealing to James, "ever your man and counted myself but an usufructuary of myself, the property being yours."

[2] See, for example, Mr. Heath's report of his investigation of the Steward case. Spedding, *Life*, Appendix to Vol. VII. 579.

[3] Spedding, *Life*, VII. 242.

splendor that he has, with such pains, gained, and lost.   He
must see, too, the rank which might have been his, and
stainlessly.   But no.   Driven temporarily from the sunshine of the court, he retires to Gorhambury, and, while
devoting himself to his rightful, but neglected work, has
still a morbid thirst for royal favor.   He bends himself, in
the hope of appeasing James, to a long-planned History
of England, finishing so much of it as to cover the reign of
Henry VII.   By this, and by servility to Villiers, he returns
to partial favor, but never to office.   After five years, after
vainly suing for the provostship of Eton, he dies, in 1626, a
broken and disappointed man.   Having caught a cold in
experimenting with snow, he expires, a martyr to science, but
a sacrifice in reality to inordinate and misdirected ambition.

It seems to me that, both in his political life and on the
side of the affections, Bacon exhibited the worst defect of
the scientific habit.   The analytical spirit, which to the
highest degree he possessed, spares nothing in its vivi-
sections.   Life, love, the dearest virtues, are to it but
manifestations, normal or morbid, of natural phenomena.
Therefore, they may be tabulated, experimented upon, dissected, maimed, and perverted without moral responsibility.
Especially was this tendency strong in Bacon, for he believed
in the ultimate simplicity of things, and sought, ever hope-
fully, that "New Instrument" which should make of the
investigation of nature a mechanical process.   As with
compasses the rudest hand can draw a perfect circle, so by
his "Instrument" the commonest mind was to be empowered
to search and know the infinite.   To this end, to the devising of this rule or plan, — whatever it was, — by which
"Forms," or first causes,[1] should be made clear, his whole

---

[1] For a discussion of 'Bacon's use of the word "Form," see
Ellis's *Gen. Preface to the Philosophical Works*, § 8; Spedding,
Works, I.

life, if we may credit his repeated assertions, was bent. He was no mere physicist, although he advanced not far beyond the limits of visible things. Had time and power been his, he would have so perfected his "Instrument," he believed, that the soul should be not less accessible than the body.[1] To his bold mind, therefore, king, courtiers, friends, and enemies, were all food for experiment.

The exceptionally great intellect, the genius which can, in a measure, comprehend eternity, must fall into an extreme attitude. Either it must conceive an abnormal respect towards moral principles, abhorring their infraction in the least degree as tending to an unbalance of the universe, or it must run to the opposite habit of regarding the niceties of ethics as vain and petty in the face of the immensity of time and the oblivion of eternity. Bacon, unconsciously, may have viewed his weaknesses from this latter standpoint. Furthermore, he never divested himself of the elevated spirit which impelled him to publish his first youthful production as the "Greatest Birth of Time."[2] To his mind, so far above the common, common laws of morality, he may have reasoned, were not to be applied; the cause of science was bound up in him and would be checked by his delay; therefore his progress must not be stayed by petty obstacles of right and wrong, of duty and sincerity. Humanity could well bear, he may have thought, some slight out-

---

[1] "It may also be asked (in the way of doubt rather than objection) whether I speak of natural philosophy only, or whether I mean that the other sciences, logic, ethics, and politics, should be carried on by this method. Now I certainly mean what I have said to be understood of them all ; and as the common logic, which governs by the syllogism, extends not only to natural but to all sciences ; so does mine, also, which proceeds by induction, embrace everything." — *Nov. Org.* (Spedding, § cxxvii.).

[2] See his letter to Father Fulgentio ; Spedding, *Life*, VII. 531.

rage at the hands of him who was to be its greatest benefactor.[1]

But it is with his intellectual personality rather than with his moral shortcomings that we are chiefly concerned. And, while this side of his nature is far brighter than the other, it is still to be taxed with the unfulfilment of wide plans, with the inadequate realization of high ideals.

From his earliest years Bacon seemed aware of the defectiveness of the contemporary standards of knowledge.[2] He was conscious of the fact that the Humanists, no less than the Scholastics, had not only failed to comprehend true learning, but had set up in place of it a false learning which was barren and mischievous. He saw that, by furnishing their minds and those of their successors with these spurious attainments, they were refusing entrance to the solid teachings of the natural world. He perceived that they were making themselves deaf, blind, and benumbed, in order to keep intact that Greek and Latin heritage, precious as far as it went, but wholly inadequate, which they had so recently reclaimed. His life-aim seems to have been to turn the learned world squarely about, to make it look forward instead of backward, outward into the face of nature, rather than inward into its dark and narrow self. Nature, not man, he perceived, must be the starting-point of inquiry; her laws, not man's vagaries, must be the object of study; her sure methods, not human guesswork, must be the model of research.

[1] See Fischer's analysis of Bacon's character on the thesis of its moral flexibility.

[2] " Whilst he was commorant in the university, about sixteen years of age, (as his lordship hath been pleased to impart unto myself), he first fell into the dislike of the philosophy of Aristotle; not for the worthlessness of the author, to whom he would ever ascribe all high attributes, but for the unfruitfulness of the way." — RAWLEY, *Life* (Spedding, *Works*, I.).

With a courage born of genius, he set himself, therefore, to the task of finding the elements of nature, or, rather, of devising an instrument for their discovery. Stupendous, unending, is the work which he designed. We find it set forth in the introduction to the *Great Instauration*, we see a hope of realizing it in everything which Bacon wrote. He proposed:[1] —

First, to show the present state of human knowledge, not only in those assured and settled fields of invention and discovery which his generation possessed, but in those "waste regions," or barren territories, which, though ready and fit to do so, the human mind had not yet taken the trouble to occupy.

Secondly, to demonstrate how human reason should be trained to the further investigation of phenomena, and in what manner the principles of nature should be sought out; in other words, to show "the true relation between the nature of things and the nature of the mind."

Thirdly, to collect, sort out, and arrange the beliefs, experiences, and attainments of mankind, forming thereby a treasury or storehouse to "supply a suckling philosophy with its first food."

Fourthly, to set up a sort of model of philosophical inquiry, selecting from the second and third parts such typical forms and methods as should strikingly present the whole image of learning; to articulate, in short, the skeleton of natural philosophy.

Fifthly, to set forth the empirical results which he had already attained by the old methods of inquiry. This part would become superfluous and would disappear, however, when,

Sixthly, he should have attained and demonstrated the

---

[1] Cf. Spedding, *Works*, IV. 22.

true Philosophy of Nature, the aim and crown of all that had gone before.

"The completion of this last part," he says,[1] "is a thing both above my strength and beyond my hopes."

Of this great scheme he did, indeed, complete but a fragment. The first portion, that describing the present state of knowledge, is partly covered by the Latin translation and enlargement of the *Advancement of Learning*.[2] The portion devoted to the use of the understanding is begun in his finest work, the unfinished *Novum Organum*.[3] To the third part belong the *Sylva Sylvarum*, the *Historia vitæ et mortis*, the *Historia densi et rari*, the *Historia ventorum*, etc.[4] To cover the fifth portion, we have but isolated treatises, incomplete observations, unfinished tabulations, tentative experiments, guess-work, rumor, and old-wives' tales. While, until the others should be completed, the fourth and sixth portions were, of course, impossible.[5]

[1] Spedding, *Works*, IV. 32.

[2] Retranslated into English in Spedding, *Works*, IV. and V.

[3] Spedding, *Works*, IV.

[4] Spedding, *Works*, II. and V.

[5] It is a nice question whether or not Bacon's pitiful place-hunting, much as it hurt his character, really curtailed his achievements. Were his efforts fragmentary and incomplete because other cares and interests pressed upon him, or were they so because his canvas was too large for human hand to fill? Is it not probable that in the magnificent sketch of the *Great Instauration*, the picture of human learning past, present, and to come, we have all that Bacon could have produced, all that he needed to produce, to take the place that is his in the world's history? Would the complete elaboration and filling in of his gigantic outline have been any more successful than are those portions which he did bring to his idea of perfection? The lesser treatises on physics, the enlargement of the *Advancement of Learning*, while rich and suggestive, while often flashing forward into the achievement of to-day, are distinctly inferior to his more general writings. His intellect was of that colossal build which cannot cope with details.

Fragmentary and chaotic as his work was, however, far as it fell below the most modest of his plans, he did enough to achieve enduring fame and to revolutionize the methods of philosophy and research.   What more could ambition, even as insatiate as his, expect to realize? [1]

The goal which Bacon set for himself, the manner in which he proposed to reach it, necessitated his emphasis of the richness of the inductive, his exposure of the poverty of the deductive, processes, as a means to intellectual growth.   He showed that the vice of the philosophies founded upon Aristotle lies in their insufficiency.   "It cannot be," he affirms,[2] "that axioms established by argumentation should avail for the discovery of new works; since the subtlety of nature is

His was one of the master minds which gather up the spirit of the past, glean from it the elements of progress, and set them forth, as on tables of stone, for future generations.   Their schemes and hopes are too large for mortal achievement, but not too high for mortal aspiration.   Just as in Rabelais we saw the utter impracticability of his system, so, with Bacon, the "Great Instrument," which he promises but never reveals, is too sacred for human use, but its quest is a true goal for the effort of mankind.   Longfellow, imbued with the spirit of Richter, says, in *Hyperion* (Ch. VIII.): "It has become a common saying, that men of genius are always in advance of their age ; which is true.   There is something equally true, yet not so common ; namely, that, of these men of genius, the best and bravest are in advance not only of their own age, but of every age.   As the German prose-poet says, every possible future is behind them."

[1] "Is it nothing to have conceived, at the fit moment, the thought which would open a new era for science ?   Is it nothing to have predicted and well-nigh to have pre-delineated an immense revolution, at its dawning ?   It seems to me that none before Bacon truly felt the grandeur of nature, and that it is this feeling which he disseminated along with an enthusiasm for science.   Since he wrote, the genius of observation, its head raised, advances as an equal of the genius of thought." — DE RÉMUSAT, *Bacon*, 397.

[2] *Nov. Org.*, §§ xxiv. and xxv.

greater many times over than the subtlety of argument. But axioms duly and orderly formed from particulars easily discover the way to new particulars and thus render sciences active.

"The axioms now in use, having been suggested by a scanty and manipular experience and a few particulars of most general occurrence, are made for the most part just large enough to fit and take these in: and, therefore, it is no wonder if they do not lead to new particulars. And if some opposite instance, not observed or not known before, chance to come in the way, the axiom is rescued and preserved by some frivolous distinction; whereas the truer course would be to correct the axiom itself."

On the other hand, Bacon had fullest respect for deduction, properly used. "For our road," he says,[1] speaking of the investigation of phenomena, "does not lie on a level, but ascends and descends; first ascending to axioms, then descending to works."

This scientific "road," this path of research which must go up from particulars as well as down from generals, was, in Bacon's day, an unfamiliar route, and it led into wholly unexpected fields of thought, whose fertility was astonishing. The votaries of philosophy had become so accustomed to invoking their goddess from above, of looking for her descent from clouds of wordy speculations and hazy generalizations, that it amazed and confused them to find that she must rise instead of descend, and that she can rise only out of an accumulation of mean and trivial facts. Through Bacon's teachings, however, they came to understand this truth, and, once comprehending it, they made rapid progress, revolutionizing the material and intellectual world.

Bacon's own use of the inductive principle was not, how-

---

[1] *Nov. Org.*, § ciii.

ever, very fruitful. He seldom applied it either wisely or searchingly. He made, therefore, few valuable contributions. to exact science. He is not for a moment to be compared, in this respect, with contemporaries like Galileo, or Kepler, or even Gilbert. He was impatient of searching, he was bewildered, perhaps, by the mass of materials, valuable and trumpery, which he had diligently heaped together, by the elaborateness of the methods through which he proposed to sort them, by the very magnitude of the scientific scheme which he had himself created. The inductive principle yielded little in his hands; but in the hands of those whom he — and he alone — inspired it produced the bountiful harvest of modern civilization.

A gift to humanity greater, however, than the emphasis of the inductive method, greater than would have been the Instauration itself — that supreme Philosophy of Nature and that Instrument for its discovery — was the pointing out, by Bacon, of the immensity of the field of nature, his survey of its boundaries, his demonstration that within its area lie the beginning and the end of human knowledge, and his proof that mental strength and spiritual insight can come only as a result of its interpretation. "For," he writes,[1] "man is but the servant and interpreter of nature: what he does and what he knows is only what he has observed of nature's order in fact or in thought; beyond this he knows nothing and can do nothing. For the chain of causes cannot by any force be loosed or broken, nor can nature be commanded except by being obeyed. And so those twin objects, human Knowledge and human Power, do really meet in one; and it is from ignorance of causes that operation fails."

How Herculean is the labor of this search for causes, how

[1] Spedding, *Works*, IV. 32.

endless is the toil which the study of nature demands, we know only too well. With all our progress, all our advance in scientific knowledge, we see plainly enough that the enterprise is hardly under way. We are slightly in advance of Bacon, but final knowledge is immeasurably in advance of us. This sixteenth century philosopher had a dim hope of accomplishing a work which, since his time, ten generations of laborers have only just begun.

But in the very magnitude of the task which Bacon presented, and in the magniloquence of its presentation, lay its value. Had it been less ambitious, it would have loomed up less massively through the contemporary fog of scientific ignorance, and would not have given, as it has, to learning a new goal, to education a new beacon. He who would make head against custom and the drift of his time, must make a noise and a promise of wonders. Else will he be wholly overborne. Because of Bacon's large view of things, he saw, beyond petty applications and specific details, the final goal towards which learning must strive. Because of his large manner of presenting his views, the world, both learned and vulgar, saw too this goal, and changed its course accordingly.

Bacon was almost alone in understanding the real intellectual needs of the time.[1] Luther and like leaders of reform unmasked the Schoolmen and exhibited the poverty

[1] ". . . the history of human knowledge points out nobody of whom it can be said, that, placed in the situation of Bacon, he would have done what Bacon did; — no man whose prophetic genius would have enabled him to delineate a system of science which had not yet begun to exist! — who could have derived the knowledge of what *ought to be* from what *was not*, and who could have become so rich in wisdom, though he received from his predecessors no inheritance but their errors." — JOHN PLAYFAIR, *The Progress of Mathematical and Physical Science, since the Revival of Letters in Europe*, Part I., § ii.

and meanness of mediæval learning; but, with the exception
of Rabelais, they turned back to the ancients for light and
inspiration.   Luther, advocating in his vigorous fashion,
as no one had yet maintained, the necessity for popular
education,[1] upheld, nevertheless, the supremacy of the dead
languages, and would train peasants by teaching them
Latin, Greek, and Hebrew.   Melanchthon, the educational
leader of Protestantism, busied himself chiefly with the
niceties of scholarship.[2]   Montaigne, gently and placidly,
as was his nature, chid pedantry, deprecated scholasticism,
advocated no education rather than one corrupting to the
moral nature, and, in his rambling way, was a sort of
Renaissance Rousseau;[3] but he was far too mild to figure
as a leader.   Sturm of Strasburg and his docile pupil
Ascham were frankly and narrowly grammarians.[4]   Then

---

[1] Writing, " I blush for us Christians when I hear it said, ' Instruction is good for priests, but unnecessary for the laity.' Such speeches
justify too well what other nations say of us Germans. . . . I tell
you we must everywhere have schools for our boys and girls, to the
end that the man shall be fit for his duties and the woman for direct-
ing her household and rearing, in a Christian way, her children."
Quoted from *Libellus de instituendis pueris; magistratibus et senatori-
bus civitatum Germaniæ Martinus Luther*, by Compayré, *Hist. crit.
des doct. de l'éduc. en France*, I. 152.

[2] " He was, above all else," says Compayré (*Hist. of Ped.*, 113), "a
professor of *Belles-Lettres*."

[3] Cf. *Montaigne and Locke*, p. 119.

[4] Not but what both these men had many excellent and progressive
ideas on the subject of education. Sturm's school was one of the
most famous of his time ; Ascham's influence upon his royal pupils
and, through them, upon the standards and methods of English teaching, was excellent. But Ascham expresses, undoubtedly, the highest
ideals of both when he says (*Scholemaster*, Book II.), "If a good
student would bend himselfe to read diligently ouer *Tullie*, and with
him also at the same tyme, as diligently *Plato*, and *Xenophon*, with
his bookes of Philosophie, *Isocrates*, and *Demosthenes* with his ora-

unsurpassed as such, but with little aim beyond a perfect accidence. As for Erasmus, what has been said of his literary, might well be applied to his mental atmosphere; he "thought in Latin, got angry in Latin, loved and hated in Latin. Never did a literary idea come to him in Dutch or German. His nurse's speech gave him current idiom for converse with his servant: but, beyond that sort of uses, his mind could take shape only through Latin signs." [1]

The list might be indefinitely extended of these good and zealous men, these men of wide mental horizon, who were yet not far enough in advance of their age to understand, to again quote the ever-felicitous Bacon, that "when men have once made over their judgments to others' keeping, and (like those senators whom they called *Pedarii*) have agreed to support some one person's opinion, from that time they make no enlargement of the sciences themselves, but fall to the servile office of embellishing certain individual authors and increasing their retinue." [2]

To these blind followers of antiquity, Aristotle was the god of education, and Cicero, his prophet. Having unearthed the fragments of Greek and Latin learning, having rid them

tions, and *Aristotle* with his Rhetorickes: . . . and not onelie write out the places diligentlie, and lay them together orderlie, but also to conferre them with skilfull iudgment by those few rules which I haue expressed now twice before: if that diligence were taken, if that order were vsed, what perfite knowledge of both the tonges, what readie and pithie vtterance in all matters, what right and deepe iudgement in all kinde of learnyng would follow, is scarce credible to be beleued.

"These bookes, be not many, nor long, nor rude in speach, nor meane in matter, but, next the Maiestie of Gods holie word, most worthie for a man, the louer of learning and honestie, to spend his life in."

[1] Nisard, *Erasme (Renaissance et réforme)*, Ch. XII. 198.

[2] Preface to the *Great Instauration* (Spedding, *Works*, IV. 14).

of the barbarities of the Schoolmen, having devised means of
bringing these precious inheritances before the learned and
the vulgar, they rested content. But Bacon did not. He
saw clearly the limitations of the classical wisdom. "Antiquity," he declares,[1] "deserveth that reverence, that men
should stand thereupon and discover what is the best way;
but when the discovery is well taken, then to make progression. And to speak truly," he continues, "*Antiquitas
sæculi juventus mundi*. These times are the ancient times,
when the world is ancient, and not those which we account
ancient, *ordine retrogrado*, by a computation backward from
ourselves."

He leaned upon the old learning, using it as a sort of
fulcrum for the new. He realized that the moving of the
world was yet to be done, and in his "New Instrument" he
believed to see the lever.[2] The warring sects of the older
philosophies ignored, to a great degree, facts and things,
and reasoned in circles, from themselves back to themselves.
They anticipated the methods of those political economists
who deduce untenable propositions from the fallacious premise of a perfect, solitary man. Learning for learning's
sake was the scholastic principle; the elaboration of useless
learning was their dismal practice.

But Bacon scorned so narrow a position. Enumerating the
"peccant humours" which "discredit learning," he says:[3]

---

[1] *Adv. of Learn.*, Book I., § V. 1 (Wright). See also, *Nov, Org.*,
§ lxxxiv.

[2] It should be remembered that the real "New Instrument," that
by which the world is being moved in such a breathless way with us,
is not the one which Bacon, vainly indeed, but ever persistently, tries
to elucidate. It is the, to him, secondary instrument by which his, the
elusive, was to have been discovered. The real "New Instrument"
is, of course, the patient mind persistent in its study of nature.

[3] *Adv. of Learn.*, Book I. (Spedding, *Works*, III. 294).

"But the greatest error of all is the mistaking or misplacing of the last or furthest end of knowledge. For men have entered into a desire of learning and knowledge, sometimes upon a natural curiosity and inquisitive appetite; sometimes to entertain their minds with variety and delight; sometimes for ornament and reputation; and sometimes to enable them to victory of wit and contradiction; and most times for lucre and profession; and seldom sincerely to give a true account of their gift of reason, to the benefit and use of men. . . . But as both heaven and earth do conspire and contribute to the use and benefit of man; so the end " (of knowledge) "ought to be . . . to separate and reject vain speculations, and whatsoever is empty and void, and to preserve and augment whatsoever is solid and fruitful: that knowledge may not be as a courtesan, for pleasure and vanity only; or as a bond woman, to acquire and gain to her master's use; but as a spouse, for generation, fruit, and comfort."

To Bacon knowledge is always in process, never complete. The discovery of new truths makes necessary new methods; as man grows he finds ever more to learn, and nothing, with him, is final; no advance serves except as a resting place and spying point from which to press on to new discoveries. The ancients and scholastics, however, accepted their hasty generalizations as immutable truths, considered them, arbitrarily, as the beginning and end of elemental knowledge, and, like spiders, as Bacon calls them,[1] evolved nature out of themselves. As they had no means, even had they wished, to test either their premises or their conclusions, each philosopher could not fail to bring forth an individual philosophy, alien to all others. "Hence," observes Bacon,[2]

---

[1] *Nov. Org.*, § xcv.
[2] Preface to the *Great Instauration* (Spedding, *Works*, IV. 15).

"the wisdom which we have derived principally from the Greeks is but like the boyhood of knowledge, and has the characteristic property of boys: it can talk, but it cannot generate; for it is fruitful of controversies, but barren of works."

Like these Greeks, he believed in the ultimate simplicity of nature. He was convinced that the infinitely complex of the universe[1] is founded upon the absolutely simple, and deduces therefrom his doctrine of "Forms," or first causes. But he consistently maintained, as the Greeks did not, that these elements cannot be assumed. They must be delved for, and the digging is a task of centuries. "I have made a beginning," he declares in the plan of his *Great Instaura-tion*,[2] "a beginning, as I hope, not unimportant: — the fortune of the human race will give the issue; — such an issue, it may be, as in the present condition of things and men's minds cannot easily be conceived or imagined. For the matter in hand is no mere felicity of speculation, but the real business and fortunes of the human race."

Having turned his face to the West, by denying the supremacy and adequacy of antiquity, he begins, a philosophic Columbus,[3] to chart the unfamiliar seas that lie before him. As clearly as he sees the errors of the past,

[1] Or, as he regarded it, of the terrestrial system. He never accepted the Copernican theory. He says, *e.g.*, in the *Descriptio Globi Intellectualis* (Spedding, *Works*, V. 517), ". . . in the system of Copernicus there are found many and great inconveniences; for both the loading of the earth with a triple motion is very incommodious, and the separation of the sun from the company of the planets with which it has so many passions in common, is likewise a difficulty . . . and some other assumptions of his, are the speculations of one who cares not what fictions he introduces into nature, provided his calculations answer."

[2] Spedding, *Works*, IV. 32.

[3] Cf. *Nov. Org.*, § cxiv.

he anticipates the snares of the future. He knows that the pursuit of nature is a task far heavier than that of the barren word-philosophies. "The subtlety of nature is greater many times over than the subtlety of the senses and understanding," he declares.[1] And again,[2] "It is idle to expect any great advancement in science from the super-inducing and engrafting of new things upon old. We must begin anew from the very foundations, unless we would revolve forever in a circle with mean and contemptible progress." But the only tool with which man can explore this subtle nature and lay this foundation, is his own mind. It is essential, therefore, to examine the mind and determine its competence.

In this analysis Bacon evolves his famous figure of the four Idols which perplex the human mind. This quaint classification is the key to his philosophy.

"There are four classes of Idols," he writes,[3] "which beset men's minds. To these, for distinction's sake, I have assigned names, — calling the first class Idols[4] of the Tribe; the second, Idols of the Den; the third, Idols of the Market-place; the fourth, Idols of the Theatre."

"The Idols of the Tribe have their foundation in human nature itself, and in the tribe or race of men. For it is a

[1] *Nov. Org.*, § x.

[2] *Ibid.*, § xxxi.

[3] *Ibid.*, § xxxix. *et seq.*

[4] By *idola*, usually translated idols, Bacon does not mean false gods, but distortions of the true image of nature. "The human Mind," he says (*Nov. Org.*, Pickering's ed., London, 1850, p. 17), "resembles those uneven mirrors which impart their own properties to different objects, from which rays are emitted, and distort and disfigure them." In the preceding aphorism (xl.) he says, "The doctrine of *Idols* bears the same relation to the *Interpretation of Nature* as that of the con-futation of sophisms does to common logic." See, in this connection, Hallam, *Lit. of Europe*, Part III., Ch. III., § 60.

false assertion that the sense of man is the measure of things. On the contrary, all perceptions as well of the sense as of the mind, are according to the measure of the individual and not according to the measure of the universe. And the human understanding is like a false mirror, which, receiving rays irregularly, distorts and discolors the nature of things by mingling its own nature with it."

"The Idols of the Den are the idols of the individual man. For every one (besides the errors common to human nature in general) has a cave or den of his own, which refracts and discolors the light of nature; owing either to his own proper and peculiar nature; or to his education and conversation with others; or to the reading of books, and the authority of those whom he esteems and admires; or to the differences of impressions, according as they take place in a mind preoccupied and predisposed or in a mind indifferent and settled; or the like."

"There are also idols formed by the intercourse and association of men with each other, which I call Idols of the Market-place. . . . For it is by discourse that men associate; and words are imposed according to the apprehension of the vulgar. And therefore the ill and unfit choice of words wonderfully obstructs the understanding. Nor do the definitions or explanations wherewith in some things learned men are wont to guard and defend themselves, by any means set the matter right. But words plainly force and overrule the understanding, and throw all into confusion, and lead men away into numberless empty controversies and idle fancies."

"Lastly, there are idols which have immigrated into men's minds from the various dogmas of philosophies, and also from wrong laws of demonstration. These I call Idols of the Theatre; because in my judgment, all the received systems are but so many stage-plays, representing worlds of their own creation after an unreal and scenic fashion."

Under these four heads may be gathered Bacon's wonderful contributions to the advancement of real learning, and, therefore, to the progress of right education. In his *Novum Organum*, in his *Advancement of Learning*, in its enlarged Latin version, the *De Augmentis Scientiarum*, in his lesser works prefiguring and amplifying these, we never lose sight of the fundamental principles upon which the warfare against these idols must be carried on.

The Idols of the Tribe, the inherent imperfection of humanity, will yield only to infinite patience of effort, to infinite diligence of investigation. I say infinite, because human weakness is such that there must always remain much in nature that is above man's comprehension, beyond his power of investigation. His senses are naturally gross and imperfect; presumably there is a limit to their cultivation and refinement. Beyond this limit knowledge cannot go. For, however high our imaginations and aspirations may take us, however exalted may be our beliefs, our knowledge must stop at the confines of our senses; and however far beyond these our speculations go, they must, to have any human value, spring from and be anchored to those exact cognitions which can be attained only through sight, hearing, touch, taste, and smell.

It is because of this that modern education lays, properly, such stress upon the training of the senses. Since, directly or indirectly, all that we know, all that we think, all that we believe, must rest finally upon the sensual powers, it is of the first importance that those powers should be properly trained and directed. To expect the highest intellectual and moral attainments in a man whose senses have been left entirely without education, is to ask an impossibility. It is to demand the most exquisite workmanship without

providing proper tools or permitting adequate apprentice-
ship.

The Idols of the Den, man's personal bias, can be escaped
only by self-effacement. Everything that man sees, everything that he thinks, must be submitted, sooner or later, to
an exact scrutiny. The researches and speculations of each
must be tried by the investigations and beliefs of all, similar studies must be compared, diverse results must be
reconciled, in order that the personal element in research
shall be wholly eliminated and the inter-relationships of
phenomena established, so to speak, externally, in order
that these phenomena may be recognized, finally, as facts,
not as reflections of the individual who studies them.

Similarly, in teaching, the chief aim must be to take the
child, by slow and gradual steps, out of the self by which
his infant consciousness is bounded, into that world of
nature by contact with which he is to be developed; and,
thence, back again into that subjective territory wherein
must be cultivated his ethical and spiritual tendencies. The
child's early education must be mainly extensive in order
that his later training may be more strongly intensive; for
only by a wide objective experience is he fitted to undertake
that subjective self-discipline which moral education entails.

The Idols of the Market-place, man's poverty of outward
expression, may be overcome by an appeal to things, by a
breaking loose from words; action, not disputation.

Under this head Bacon emphasized most strongly the
defects in the prevailing spirit of education. An empty
worship of words had produced the barren quibbles of
scholasticism. For this the classicists had substituted a
philology scarcely more fruitful. Names without meaning,
ideas without connection, distinctions in which the things
distinguished had no substance, speculations whose bases
were unknown,— these made up the Barmecide feast offered

to the children of Bacon's day. In place of it he opened to them the boundless field of nature, and the endless opportunity for real education which its exploration gives.

The Idols of the Theatre, man's slavery to passing doctrines, will fall with the dislodging of all sects and dogmas. He who interprets nature must be absolutely free. It is this principle of intellectual and moral freedom, so easy to apply, — now that we have been taught how, — to the higher education, which is so difficult of right application in the primary teaching. It is upon this point, perhaps more than upon any other, that pedagogical thought and experiment are, at this moment, focussed.

These truths, in their many aspects, these fundamentals of a sound, progressive learning, Bacon showed forth as none before had displayed them. About them, as main propositions, his philosophical writings may be grouped. Upon these truths, moreover, modern teaching founds its endeavor. Patient study of the child, active investigation by the child, self-emancipation on the part of both teacher and pupil, self-conducted and unbiassed experiment upon things and logical inference from facts, entire liberty of thought and opinion, — these are the corner stones of the New Education. Kindergartens, object-lessons, laboratory work, nature-study, the mechanic arts, — all are concrete expressions of these fundamental principles.

Upon these Bacon stands, a leader of modern thought. Natural education, which is but the searching and following of nature, derives from this man, as from no one before him, the impulse of its growth. In outlining the methods and aims of scientific research, he laid down, at the same time, the laws of education.

But he gave little heed to the specific problems of pedagogics. His gaze was too wide to busy itself with details. He says, it is true, in the sixth book of the Latin transla-

tion of the *Advancement of Learning*,[1] "As for the pedagogical part" (of the transmission of knowledge) "the
shortest way would be, consult the schools of the Jesuits;
for nothing better has been put in practice." But to perceive how little he knows of these schools, we need but to
read further among the "hints" that he "gives as usual."
He says: "For the order and manner of teaching, I would
say, first of all, — avoid abridgment and a certain precocity
of learning, which makes the mind over-bold, and causes
great proficiency rather in show than in fact. Also let some
encouragement be given to the free exercise of the pupils'
minds and tastes; I mean if any of them, besides perform-
ing the prescribed exercises, shall steal time withal for
other purposes to which he is more inclined, let him not be
checked. Observe, moreover (what perhaps has not hitherto
been remarked), that there are two ways of training and
exercising and preparing the mind, which proceed in opposite
directions. The one begins with the easier tasks, and so
leads on gradually to the more difficult; the other begins by
enforcing and pressing the more difficult, that when they are
mastered, the easier ones may be performed with pleasure.
For it is one method to begin swimming with bladders,
which keep you up, and another to begin dancing with heavy
shoes which weigh you down. Nor is it easy to tell how
much a judicious intermixture of these methods helps to
advance the faculties of the mind and body."

Now this is exactly contrary to the methods of the
Jesuits.[2] The pupils of the Society of Jesus were never,
intellectually, free, however easy and complaisant may have
been the rule of their masters. The Jesuit teachers permitted range of study; their admirable method was not so

[1] Ch. IV. (Spedding, *Works*, IV. 494).
[2] For an exceedingly just and temperate analysis of the Jesuit teaching, see Compayré, *Hist. of Ped.*, 139.

rigid that it forbade excursions outside its limits, but this authorized ranging was frivolous and barren.   The brighter pupils were encouraged to an enlarged exercise of their minds, but, unfortunately, this exercise was a mere beating of the air with the weapons of syllogism, a fencing with shadowy words.

Abridgment, too, which Bacon so strongly condemns,[1] was a corner stone of the Jesuit teaching. The elegant superficiality at which it aimed was built upon extracts from and summaries of the vast range of human thought. This surface-teaching gave that "precocity of learning" which inflated their pupils with a tenuous vapor of false knowledge.

The Jesuits were, purposely, behind their age; they were degenerate heirs of scholasticism, not even loving learning except as it gave them spiritual gain.   They hated the spirit of progress which filled the world about them, they wanted civilization and thought to stay their courses at the point where the Society of Jesus could control them.   They helped in the resurrection of the ancient authors, they systematized them most wonderfully, but they deliberately crushed and stifled all that was intellectually best in their pupils, and did all they could to render the minds under their tuition unfit for that very work of investigation which Bacon saw was vital to the progress of the world.

As, unfortunately, in so many things, Bacon looked only at the outside of Loyola's system. He knew it was better than the chaos which preceded it; he saw its splendor, its exactness, its immediateness of result, and he accepted it, sublimely ignorant that it was hostile to him at every point.

In questions of higher education, however, he has much

---

[1] *E.g.*, in the *Advancement of Learning*, Book II., § ii. 4.   ". . . the corruptions and moths of history, which are epitomes."

to suggest. In Salomon's House[1] he depicts an academy of arts and sciences, in the *Advancement of Learning,* he outlines,[2] clearly, the conditions upon which, alone, true intellectual greatness for a country can be achieved.

Salomon's House, the heart of the splendid government of the "New Atlantis," is, as Bacon describes it, not only a place for discovery and invention of every imaginable sort, but also a museum of all known products, processes, and "engines," a vast experiment station for inquiries concerning physics, hygiene, agriculture, zoölogy, pharmacy, metallurgy, and the other myriad processes of applied science. So far as his knowledge went, he seems to have forgotten nothing in the planning of it, and, in a crude way, he foretells many modern discoveries and inventions.[3] In the thirty-six "fellows" whose duties he describes, he plainly fore-imagines such an association for scientific research as was realized, eighteen years later, in the germ of the Royal Society.[4] The travellers, or Merchants of Light, the Depredators who glean from books, the Mystery Men who collect the experiments of others, the Pioneers who experiment for themselves, the Compilers who tabulate experiments and researches, and, finally, the Benefactors, Lamps, Inoculators, and Interpreters, who, out of the mass of materials collected by the others, devise and discover, in their several capacities, new benefits and knowledge for humanity, — all these fanciful officers are to find their prosaic successors in

[1] In *The New Atlantis* (Spedding, *Works,* III. 156).

[2] See Spedding, *Works,* III. pp. 322–328, and IV. pp. 284–290.

[3] There is little to amaze us in this, since in Bacon's time, no less than in our own, the longing imagination could foretell many things that the brain and hand seemed, at the time, powerless to realize.

[4] The Royal Society was not definitely established until 1660, and did not receive its charter until 1682, but its foundations were laid in 1645.

the members of the many learned bodies founded upon the model of the Royal Society.

In the introduction to the second book of the *Advancement of Learning*, Bacon discourses upon the three agents for the preservation and furthering of knowledge; namely, universities, libraries, and the "persons of the learned." ·He advocates the founding of a real university, one not alone dedicated to the professions, but "left free to the arts and sciences at large"; adequate salaries and proper rewards to teachers and investigators; an enlargement of the scope of experimentation through the establishment of laboratories in almost every branch of learning; the continual revision of the methods and aims of teaching in order to conform them to the needs of the times; the substitution, for the mutual jealousy and distrust of the seats of learning, of "more intelligence mutual between the universities of Europe"; and, finally, a systematic inquiry into the state of knowledge, a "census of the sciences," such as Bacon himself purposed carrying out in the *Great Instauration*. These large and solid plans are only beginning to be realized to-day, nearly three centuries after.

Without making, therefore, any immediate contribution to pedagogics beyond these wide prophecies for the higher education,[1] without contributing many things of value to exact learning, without making, either to physics, to law, or to history,— his chosen fields for particular inquiry,— any direct additions of great moment in the progress of civilization, Bacon yet did that which makes his career one of inestimable worth to the world. At a time when men were in a ferment of growth and mental productiveness, when the

[1] Unless we except the fragmentary *Letter and Discourse to Sir Henry Savill, touching Helps for the Intellectual Powers* (Spedding, *Works*, VII. 97), and certain of the *Essays*, particularly that immortal one, *Of Study*.

conditions were right for the rapid breeding of new ideas, new discoveries, new principles, he marked out, clearly and justly, the direction in which those ideas, discoveries, and principles should be sought, the way in which they could be made available. He crystallized, so to speak, the energetic but amorphous mass of thought, speculation, and inquiry which the Renaissance had produced. By doing this he made progress not only surer but more easy;[1] for when it is shown what we ought to do and in what manner it should be done, more than half the task of any investigation is accomplished. While Bacon pointed out, lucidly, the right aim of human endeavor, he indicated, no less clearly, the path by which it could be reached. He showed, among other truths, —

That civilization must look forward, not backward; that it must be a growth out of the conditions of to-day, not a fixed state modelled on the past.

That it must depend upon living nature, not upon dead antiquity, for light and guidance.

That it must rest upon investigation, not upon speculation.

That investigation must be upwards from observed facts, not downwards from arbitrary premises.

That man, in his researches, must be ever on the watch against himself; that he must learn to distinguish universal truth from human error, general principles from personal prejudice, facts from names, the eternal harmony of God from the partial and warped theories of men.

Bacon and his writings mark, plainly, the beginning of

---

[1] On the effect of Bacon's ideas, see an interesting paper by Macvey Napier (Trans. of the Royal Society of Edinburgh, VIII. 373). *Remarks Illustrative of the Scope and Influence of the Philosophical Writings of Lord Bacon.*

a new era in human thought and methods of study.[1] They inaugurate, therefore, a marked advance in pedagogics; for, however strongly they may cling to old forms and symbols, educational ideas follow, closely and accurately, the progress of civilization. He who leads an advance in modes of thought must be, perforce, a prophet of educational growth. In breaking away from classicism, in codifying, if I may use the term, the inductive processes, in propounding the true aim of learning, Bacon did such service to the cause of right education as few, if any, before or since, have been able to accomplish. All the advance that has been made in education has been upon the lines which he laid down.

His was not the strongest intellect of his age, but it was the most human. Others thought more learnedly than he; many others more accurately. In various directions he was singularly ignorant and blind. But, besides that marvellous mental grasp of his, which made it possible for him to plan the *Great Instauration*, and to finish so much of it as was

---

[1] "Two men stand out, 'the masters of those who know,' without equals up to their time, among men — the Greek Aristotle and the Englishman Bacon. They agree in the universality and comprehensiveness of their conception of human knowledge; and they were absolutely alone in their serious practical ambition to work out this conception. . . . We shall never again see an Aristotle or a Bacon, because the conditions of knowledge have altered. Bacon, like Aristotle, belonged to an age of adventure, which went to sea little knowing whither it went, and ill furnished with knowledge and instruments. . . . This new world of knowledge has turned out in many ways very different from what Aristotle and Bacon supposed, and has been conquered by implements and weapons very different in precision and power from what they purposed to rely on. But the combination of patient and careful industry, with the courage and divination of genius, in doing what none had done before, makes it equally stupid and idle to impeach their greatness." — CHURCH, *Bacon*, pp. 190 and 193.

necessary to make its scope comprehensible, he had the rare faculty of making learning popular without making it cheap.[1] This·is a quality essential to enduring influence. However high the great intellect and soul may soar, their flight is barren unless they keep contact with earth, and bring down their ecstasies to the level of common men. Intellectually as well as socially, the recluse is an anomaly in the civilized world. However abundant and valuable may be the dis- coveries of the individual, they can be quickened only by contact with humanity at large. From this point of view, Bacon's unhappy love of authority was, perhaps, not unfor- tunate. It gave him added sway, it kept him before men, made them curious about him, and assured that attention to his writings which he did not fail to solicit.

Having gained attention, he easily kept it; for, quite apart from the matter of his writings, his manner was captivating even to Englishmen of the earlier Jacobean days, when the language was fresh and when the few men

---

[1] With all the faults of Macaulay's estimate of Bacon, no one has found better words in which to describe his influence than these: " Great and various as the powers of Bacon were, he owes his wide and durable fame chiefly to this, that all those powers received their direc- tion from common sense. His love of the vulgar useful, his strong sympathy with the popular notions of good and evil, and the openness with which he avowed that sympathy, are the secret of his influence. There was in his system no cant, no illusion. . . . In his opinions on all . . . subjects he was not a Stoic, nor an Epicurean, nor an Academic, but what would have been called by Stoics, Epicureans, and Academics, . . . a mere common man. And it was precisely because he was so that his name makes so great an era in the history of the world. It was because he dug deep that he was able to pile high. It was because, in order to lay his foundations, he went down into those parts of human nature which lie low, but which are not liable to change, that the fabric which he reared has risen to so stately an elevation, and stands with such immovable strength." *Lord Bacon*, 466. See, also, Fowler, *Bacon*, 197.

who wrote well, wrote marvellously well. Bacon's style is wonderfully flexible; in the very cumbersomeness of many of his passages there is a ponderous dignity which gives weight to what he says. It is bald or sonorous, pithy or elaborate, as the theme demands. Especially is it homely. He refuses no illustration because of its meanness, but transfigures it by the genius of his diction. Through this homeliness his message to mankind was made immediately available. His high and remote ideas were, by this means, transmuted into the coin of common speech and brought into the currency of popular thought. No author, except Shakespeare, is so quotable. Fanciful, and even grotesque, as many of his similes and metaphors are, they have the power of wakening the train of thought which he wished to stimulate. Truly, as he fulsomely said of James,[1] his "manner of speech is prince-like, flowing as from a fountain, and yet streaming and branching itself into nature's order, full of facility and felicity, imitating none, and inimitable by any."

And we may well apply to him, also, what he said further[2] of his king, that he "standeth invested of that triplicity, which in great veneration was ascribed to the ancient Hermes; the power and fortune of a king, the knowledge and illumination of a priest, and the learning and universality of a philosopher."

From this pedestal of rank, of authority, of wisdom, and of genius, Bacon pointed out the modern road which, each generation less haltingly, — because the education of every succeeding generation has advanced a little towards Bacon's ideal, — mankind has been, since his time, slowly following.

---

[1] *Adv. of Learn.*, Book I. ¶ 2.   [2] *Ibid.*

CHAPTER IV.

COMENIUS.

THE REVOLT AGAINST FEUDALISM.

FOUR PATHS OF EDUCATION; BACON'S ALONE EXPANSIVE; COMENIUS;
A FOLLOWER OF BACON; VIVES AND RATICH; COMENIUS'S CAREER;
HIS WRITINGS; HIS WEAKNESSES; THE "GREAT DIDACTIC"; ITS
GENERAL PRINCIPLES; ITS PROPHECY OF THE PUBLIC SCHOOL; ITS
ENCYCLOPEDISM; ITS FOUR SCHOOL-PERIODS; THE PRINCIPLE OF
METHOD; OTHER PRINCIPLES; OTHER TEXT-BOOKS; THE "JANUA";
THE "ORBIS PICTUS"; ORIGIN OF HIS PRINCIPLES AND METHODS;
HIS EXPANSION OF EARLIER IDEAS; HIS CONTRIBUTIONS TO THE
EDUCATIONAL IDEAL.

DATING from the Revival of Letters, education may be
said to have taken four paths: through Luther towards
a common school that should fit for a knowledge and interpretation of the Bible; through Melanchthon, Sturm, and
Ascham, to a classicism which found in the Greek and
Latin authors all knowledge other than that inspired;
through the Jesuits to an ordered discipline of the intellect;
through Bacon towards a study of nature as the source of
knowledge and the manifestation of the Divine. The tendency of each of these paths was good. In their beginning,
the systems following them were, as far as they went, excellent. We cannot overestimate the effect of Luther's clamor
for popular education, narrow as that education proved itself
to be. In rescuing and purifying the classic texts, the
Humanists contributed, in no small degree, to human prog-

ress, however the application of their ideas may have retarded immediate growth. In their perfect organization and in their gentle methods, the Jesuits set an example of the highest value, notwithstanding the fatal defects of their system. As for Bacon, his spirit was, as I have tried to show, one of the main sources of modern education; but, without dilution and adaptation to the needs of society, his teachings would have been almost barren of pedagogic results.

As time went on, however, the direct influence of the leaders of these movements, of Luther, of Sturm, of Loyola, of Bacon, waned, and the inevitable perversion of their systems supervened. Luther's plans, committed to his wrangling successors, partook of their controversies, and the village schools became battle-grounds of dogma. The system of Sturm that, in his hands, tended to unlock the moral as well as the rhetorical treasures of the ancients, fell, after his death, into the dry routine of textual criticism;— a routine that was, and still is, a curse to the English schools.[1] The method of the Jesuits, externally so fair, developed into a soulless machine, crushing youth into a mould of intolerance, unmanliness, and deceit. Bacon's philosophy alone seems to have contained the elements of growth, and in treating of Comenius I hope to show how these elements were fostered and developed. Later we shall study the revolt against the Jesuits; we shall gain

[1] As recently as 1878, Professor Alexander Bain wrote, in his *Education as a Science* (N.Y. 1892, 380): "The classical system has been the practical exclusion of all other studies from the secondary or grammar schools" (in England). . . . "The pressure of opinion has compelled the introduction of new branches — as English, Modern Languages, and Physical Sciences; but either these are little more than a formality, or the pupils are subjected to a crushing burden of conflicting studies. . . . In the evening preparation it is found that the classical lessons absorb the greater part of the attention."

also, I trust, some idea of the decline of classicism. Let me here try to show how from a union of Bacon's philosophy and Luther's democracy there resulted the public school. The problem that Luther was too busy, Bacon too lofty, to undertake, was solved by the son of a Moravian miller, a wanderer on the face of the earth. The most influential teacher of the seventeenth century, one of the greatest figures in the history of education, is this Moravian, whose Latin name is Johannes Amos Comenius.

Throughout his stormy career two influences dominate him; that of Bacon's philosophy, and that of the spirit of the Reformation. To the first is due his comprehensive scheme; to the second, his labors in behalf of common schools. To Bacon and to Luther he owes his main ideas, but to two other men he acknowledges himself, in lesser degree a debtor. These are Vives and Ratich. The first, a Spaniard, tutor to the Princess Mary until, because of his opposition to the King's divorce, he was driven from court,[1] waged vigorous war against the Aristotelian supremacy.[2]

[1] Professor Brewer (*The Reign of Henry VIII. Reviewed and Illustrated from Original Documents.* London, 1884, 2 vols.) puts Vives in a rather different light. After stating, on contemporary authority, that Vives was one of the few Spaniards whom, during the negotiations relative to divorce, Katharine was permitted to retain, he says (II. 318): "It appears that he was compelled by the King, who was now grown wholly unscrupulous, to reveal the subjects of his conversations with the Queen ; and he justly complains of this outrage to which he, who was one of her council and a subject of the Emperor" (of Spain) "had thus been exposed ; 'not,' he says, 'that it could injure any one to relate it, even if it were published at the church doors.' He had intended to return to Spain in May, but, at the King's request, remained until Michaelmas, and during the winter, at Katharine's desire, gave the Princess Mary lessons in Latin."

[2] "Vives must be regarded as the most important philosophical reformer of this period" (the early Renaissance), "and as a forerunner

The second, a pedagogic adventurer of no mean influence, went about from court to court, offering to disclose, for a substantial reward, a new and short method of learning languages. The pedantic court of Weimar took him up, and he made much stir in the European world; but his influence was not permanent. He enunciated, however, certain principles of value, the chief of which are these: —

"Everything according to the order and course of nature."

"Everything in the mother-tongue first."

"Everything without violence."

"Matter before form."

"Everything through experience and the investigation of particulars."[1]

From the teachings of many besides these four, Comenius sought, with greater or less result, the aid that it was his nature to crave. Like Bacon, he lit his torch at every man's candle,[2] but, unlike Bacon, he had no wish to extinguish the spark that had enkindled him. Never was there a great man more modest than he. Duty, the flame of zeal, not love of authority, impelled him to publicity. Could he have found in his reading — and he searched with extraordinary pains — a method which even partially fulfilled his ideal, he would have accepted it without hesitation and would have effaced himself in the preaching of it. He studies all authors available to him ; he writes, to all

of Descartes and of Bacon. His whole life was an uninterrupted struggle against Scholasticism. . . . Vives was one of the clearest heads of his century." — LANGE, *Hist. of Materialism* (Thomas's trans.), I. 228.

[1] Cf. Browning, *Educ. Theories*, Ch. IV. ; Quick, *Educ. Reformers*, Ch. IX.

[2] A phrase used by Rawley (Spedding, *Works,* I.). "And for himself, he contemned no man's observations, but would light his torch at every man's candle."

parts of Europe, letters of inquiry, begging for suggestions. Only as a last resort does he himself formulate
a system, and in it he has no wilful pride or overcon-
fidence. The vacillation and fluctuation of his writings
show that he was always receptive, always ready to throw
aside his own ideas in order to accept those of another.
Simple, single of purpose, patient, untiring, steadfast
under continued adversity, the old Bishop is a pathetic
figure, made heroic by life-long sorrow. The little church
of the United Brethren finds its best exponent in this
leader of hers whose birth occurred more than three hundred years ago.

Born [1] in a village of Bohemia, he came of a Slavic family
named Komenski, attached to the sect of the United
Brethren. His parents dying while he was still in infancy,
he became a charge upon the community, and was given
such a schooling as the primitive village afforded. Slight
as this was, the precious attributes of piety, earnestness,
simplicity, and belief in Christian brotherhood were secured
to him by the Moravian atmosphere. At sixteen years of
age, though ignorant of Latin, the sole vehicle of learning,
he gave sufficient promise to obtain for him a ministerial
training. He was sent by the Brethren to Herborn, in
Nassau. There and at Heidelberg he completed his education. Too young, on his return to Bohemia to take a
pastorate, he was given the rectorship of a school. Here
he worked diligently, attempting a reform of the Latin
teaching, until, four years later, he was made pastor of the
parish at Fulneck, the most flourishing of the Moravian
churches. There he married, and there he spent the last
years in which he was to see happiness. In 1621, the hor-
rors of the Thirty Years' War having begun, Fulneck was

---

[1] March 28, 1592.

sacked by the Spaniards. Comenius lost everything, including his books and manuscripts.[1]

The next six years were years of wandering and hiding, until, by the final edict of dispersion, he was driven out of his fatherland into Poland. He established himself at Lissa,[2] near the frontier, was rector of the Moravian school there, and, inspired by the difficulties of teaching, became filled with a holy and unflagging zeal for the improvement of education. In the fresh enthusiasm of this time, he wrote the *Great Didactic*,[3] in which are given his ideas in their first purity, before they became, as in later years, confused and somewhat mystical. Here he began, too, the text-books which were to occupy so much of his life.

At the death of his father-in-law, bishop of the persecuted brethren, Comenius was chosen to succeed him, and, for the remainder of his life, in addition to his labors for education, he busily writes to the scattered brothers, cheers them with hope of relief from exile and persecution, and fills them with visions of a union of Christian sects.[4] The good man seems, indeed, to have been an indefatigable letter-writer. He sought intellectual help from all quarters, entering into correspondence, among others, with Hartlib[5] — Milton's Hartlib — the friend and promoter of works of education. This philanthropist became immensely interested in Comenius's larger projects. The union of Chris-

---

[1] Some authorities say that his wife and child also perished, but it is more probable that they died in the following year, perhaps as a result of hardships.

[2] Called also, Lesna and Leszno.

[3] *Didactica Magna; universale omnes omnia docendi artificium exhibens:* etc., etc. See Laurie, *Comenius*, p. 70.

[4] See Note 1, p. 92.

[5] For an account of this interesting man, see Masson, *Milton*, III. 193.

tendom and, as a means to it, the marshalling of all learning into a universal philosophy, were dreams that met with an immediate response in his enthusiastic mind. He could not be satisfied until he had persuaded Comenius to visit England. Accordingly, in 1641, the Moravian appeared, prepared to lay his plan of a *pansophia*, or school of all knowledge, before the Long Parliament. But that body was more concerned with the immediate problems of democracy than with costly experiments upon Bacon's theories.[1]

Mortified and bitterly disappointed, Comenius was preparing to return to Poland, when he received, through his friend, Louis de Geer, an urgent call to Sweden. His partisans in London begged him to remain until a lull in political affairs should permit of the pushing forward of his *pansophia*, already, so far as it was heeded at all, most favorably looked upon. England was stormy and uncertain, however, while the northern kingdom, guided by its great Chancellor, seemed on the road to power and peace. Hopes were held out to him, too, that a removal to Sweden might not delay his plans, but that the Scandinavians, equally with the English, might be hospitable to his pansophic scheme. But these hopes were dashed even at his first interview with Oxenstierna. That keen and busy statesman was far too impatient of delay to be satisfied with so shadowy a proposal.

In a famous discussion of two days,[2] this "Eagle of the North,"[3] as Comenius calls him, shows himself as practical as he is broad. He attacks the Schoolmen, derides Ratich,

[1] Strafford had just been executed, and, while Comenius awaited the pleasure of Parliament, the "Remonstrance" was published and the "Privilege of the House" was invaded by the King.

[2] Reported by Comenius in the preface to the second volume of his collected works. See Laurie, *Comenius*, 41.

[3] *Aquilonaris aquila.*

to whom he had already appealed in vain for practical suggestions, shows the folly of the *pansophia*, and makes it
plain to Comenius that Sweden wants school-books, not
pedagogic dreams. The friends in England learning of
this, clamor for his return, accusing him of apostasy from
the great purpose of his life. But the readiness of the
Swedish government to give immediate help, the offer of
De Geer to maintain him for a number of years, contrasted
with the turbulence of England, win the contest. He retires to Elbing, in Prussia, there to devote six years, in
the unquiet security of dependence upon the somewhat
arbitrary De Geer, to preparing text-books for the little
Swedes. Bitterly, in his old age, does he repent this sacrifice of his strength. "How badly have I imitated," he
cries,[1] "that merchant seeking for good pearls, who, when
he had found a pearl of great price, went away and sold all
he had and bought it! O, wretched sons of light, who
know not how to imitate the wisdom of the children of the
world! Would that I, having once struck the pansophic
vein, had followed it up, neglecting all else! But so it
happens when we lend an ear to the solicitations clam-
oring outside us, rather than to the light shining within
us."

His obligations to Sweden fulfilled, Comenius returns to
Lissa, but soon, listening to other "outside solicitations,"[2]
goes to Patâk, in the Tokay district of Hungary, under the
patronage of the Transylvanian princes. Although, in so
doing, he surrenders his *pansophia*, this period is one of
comparative happiness to him. His patrons are liberal,
they give him latitude in the application of his theories,

---

[1] Laurie, *Comenius*, 54.
[2] Bayle would have us believe that Comenius's life was always led
in the direction of the largest creature comforts.

he sees a beginning that may develop into *pansophia*.[1] But his episcopal duties recall him to Lissa, war follows him, the Swedes capture the city, he unwisely writes, it is said, a panegyric on Gustavus, the Poles rise, recapture the city, and he narrowly escapes. Everything he owns is destroyed, including precious manuscripts, on which he had labored for forty years. Again he is a fugitive, wandering hither and yon, at last finding asylum in Amsterdam with Laurence de Geer, the son of his old patron, dead not many years.[2] Here in this Dutch city, an exile even from the Poland that had sheltered him, his spiritual flock scattered to every corner of Europe, his *pansophia* wholly unrealized, he passes peacefully, except for the assaults of the Schoolmen, the remainder of his melancholy life. During these last years he revises his many writings, by the liberality of De Geer and other Dutch merchants, publishes them in four huge volumes, cheers, as best he can by correspondence, the hunted Moravians, and, becoming more and more a mystic, letting his fancy stray into ever wilder pastures, dies in his eightieth year.

Wide as were the wanderings of this pious old man, they narrowly missed extension even to America. For we read in Mather's *Magnalia:*[3] —

"That brave old man, *Johannes Amos Commenius,* the *fame* of whose worth has been *trumpetted* as far as more

---

[1] For an account of his school at Patâk, see Theodor Lion, *Comenius,* p. 97 *et seq.*

[2] "Il se sauva en Silesie, et puis au païs de Brandebourg, ensuite à Hambourg, et enfin à Amsterdam, où il trouva des personnes extrêmement charitables. La pluie d'or, qui tomba sur lui dans cette ville, l'obligea de s'y arrêter pour le reste de ses jours." — BAYLE, *Dict. hist. et crit.,* I. 912.

[3] Cotton Mather, *Magnalia Christi Americana* (Hartford, 1820, 2 vols.), II. 10.

than *three* languages (whereof everyone is endebted unto his *Janua*), could carry it was indeed agreed withall, by our Mr. *Winthrop* in his travels through the *low Countries*, to come over into *New England,* and illuminate their *Colledge* and *country,* in the quality of a *President:* But the solicitations of the *Swedish* Ambassador, diverting him another way, that incomparable *Moravian* became not an *American.*"

What a fertile source of speculation is this paragraph! If Comenius had yielded to "our Mr. Winthrop," and if thereby Dunster had been succeeded by this vigorous reformer instead of by the testy yet pliable Chauncy,[1] what might not have been the difference of result. How unlike its real history might have been the growth, not alone of Harvard College, but of the whole country! Throwing off the shackles of English tradition two hundred years earlier than it in fact did, what might not this university have accomplished! The chief leader of New England thought, its early emancipation from the humanities would have altered the whole course of American history. The great Oxenstierna ought, perhaps, to be added to the list, already too long, of conservative forces governing New England.

During his long and troubled life, Comenius produced a vast pile of writings, many of them vain repetitions, and not a few of them, I imagine, dreary as any of the stuff brought forth by the scholastics. His chief works are the *Great Didactic,* produced in his early days at Lissa ; the *Janua Linguæ Latinæ reserata,* or " Gate of the Latin Language unlocked," written at the same period, and to which his world-wide fame was due; the additions to the *Janua,* namely, the *Vestibulum,* or "Threshold," the *Atrium,* or

---

[1] See Quincy, *History of Harvard University* (Cambridge, Mass., 1840), I. 24 ; also *Magnalia,* I. 418.

"Entrance Hall," the *Palatium*, or "Treasure-house"; and finally, most famous of all, the *Orbis sensualium Pictus*, or "World of Visible things Portrayed." [1]

Comenius was always hampered by the voluminousness of his ideas, and, paradoxical as it may seem, by the catholicity of his reading. Filled with zeal, he had the zealot's fault of hobby-riding. Diffident of his own powers, he grasped at any notion of other men that seemed to point in his direction. A strain of mysticism in his character, a vein of fancifulness in his intellect, often led him astray. Several times he was the abject dupe of charlatans, a fact of which the malicious Bayle takes minute account. In one of his lesser works, he throws away all his fundamental principles, merely that he may logically follow a fanciful conceit. He is always, indeed, in a state of vacillation. The main points of his system which he evolves in the *Great Didactic* are repudiated in the later editions of the *Janua*. In the *Vestibulum* and the *Orbis Pictus*, he returns to these principles, only to leave in the *Atrium* and *Palatium* his position undefined. It would be a waste of time to follow him in these vexatious turnings and doublings. What he saw clearly and taught well has endured. What was confused and contradictory has been sent to deserved oblivion. [2]

---

[1] First published at Nuremberg, in 1657.

[2] I ought, in fairness, to confess that I have shirked the duty of following him in the original Latin, possessing neither the ability nor the patience to traverse the twenty-three hundred pages of his ponderous treatises. I have placed dependence upon modern interpreters of him, especially upon Professor Laurie, of Edinburgh, who did undertake the weary task, who gives a careful analysis, with full extracts, of the writings, and who declares his aim to have been the omission of nothing "characteristic, useful, or historically important." But, even with work so materially lessened, it is not easy to avoid confusion of

It is best, perhaps, to consider here the chief points of the *Great Didactic,* since in this, his earliest work, he is most consistent. In it, moreover, his really original notions are, in the main, developed. Having done this, we shall be ready to examine his enlargements of this treatise, to study the sources from which he drew inspiration, and, finally, to discover in his amplification of these radical ideas, the value of his contributions to the growth of rational education.

He starts out with the propositions, the first two founded on Bacon, that —

"Man should know all things."

"He should have power over all things and over himself."

"He should refer himself and all things to God, the source of all." [1]

Knowledge, virtue, piety, — on these he builds his structure of education. "The seeds of these three," he says, [2] "are in us by nature; that is, our first, original, and fundamental nature, to which we are to be recalled by God in Christ." "Nature gives the seeds of knowledge, morality, and religion," he says in another place, [3] "but it does not give knowledge, virtue, and religion themselves. These have to be striven for. [4] . . . Man then has to be edu-

mind and, therefore, of statement, in dealing with Comenius's principles.

For the text of the *Didactica Magna,* I have followed, mainly, the German translation of Dr. LÏon, availing myself, moreover, of his marginal indication of the section numbering used by Comenius.

[1] *Didactica Magna,* 24. See Laurie, *Comenius,* 72; and LÏon, K. 4, § 6.

[2] Laurie, *Comenius,* 72.   [3] *Ibid.,* 74.

[4] "Diese werden durch Reden, Lernen, Handeln erworben. Daher hat nicht über jemand den Menschen definÏrt, er sei ein *Schulbares Geschöpf;* er kann nur Mensch werden, wenn er unterrichtet wird." —BEEGER U. ZOUBEK, *Grosse Unterrichtslehrer,* 43.

cated to become a man; . . . in order that the human
being may be educated to full humanity, God has given him
certain years of childhood during which he is not fit for
active life; and that only is firm and stable which has been
imbibed during the earliest years."

Then follows a remark of profound significance in these
days. "The care of children belongs properly to their parents, but they need the help" — help, not usurpation — "of
those specially set apart for education, . . . and there is,
consequently, a need for schools and colleges." "Schools
should be instituted in every part of the empire, and the
whole of the youth of both sexes should be sent to these.
Schools have been truly called . . . workshops or manufac-
tories of humanity where man may be trained to be — 1. A
rational creature; 2. A creature lord of other creatures and
of himself; 3. A creature which shall be the joy of his
Creator. That only I call a school which is truly *officina
hominum*, where minds are instructed in wisdom to penetrate all things, where souls and their affections are guided
to the universal harmony of the virtues, and hearts are
allured to divine love."

In these few pregnant sentences, Comenius announces
four doctrines new in his day,— parental responsibility for
education, universal education, coeducation, and a complete, rounded education.[1] As an early preacher, if not the

---

[1] "All children, rich and poor, well-born and lowly, boys and girls,
should be taught in schools ; in all should God's image be implanted ;
each should be fitted for his future career. Each should learn everything ; every man is a microcosm. Not that each can attain to all
knowledge, but all who, in this world, would be doers and not mere
lookers-on, must be so taught that they may learn to analyze the principles, conditions, and purposes of all vital things, present or to come."
— *Didact.*, 45. Quoted by Von Raumer, *Gesch. d. Päd.*, II. 58. See
Lion, 217.

first important preacher of these principles, Comenius may truly be regarded as the father of the public school. First, the school system of Germany, secondly, our American system — absurd as it seems to give a nationality to methods — followed and follow on these lines. Having enunciated these principles, wild and revolutionary to most of his contemporaries, he proceeds to the details of organization.

"A certain fixed time," he says,[1] "ought to be set apart for the complete education of youth, at the end of which they may go forth from school to the business of life truly instructed, truly moral, truly religious."

"The time that is required for this is the whole period of youth; that is to say, from birth to manhood, which is fully attained in twenty-four years. Dividing the twenty-four years into periods of six years each, we ought to have a school suited to each period, viz.: the school of—

1. Infancy: the mother's lap up to six years of age.
2. Boyhood: the vernacular public school.
3. Adolescence: the Latin school or gymnasium.
4. Youth: the university and travel."

"The Infant School" — again note the lesson for to-day — "should be found in every house, the Vernacular School in every village and community, the Gymnasium" (the word being used in the German, not in our restricted sense) "in every province, and the University in every kingdom or large province."

In his scheme of the mother-school he adopts the idea of Bacon, that a little of everything should from the first be taught. He develops this tentative notion, however, into absolute encyclopedism. As this outline of the mother-

---

[1] *Didact.*, 164, 165, 166 (Lïon, K. XXVII., p. 446). Quoted by Laurie, p. 131.

school is an epitome of his main pansophic idea, I will give it, quoting Professor Laurie somewhat at length.[1]

"In the infant school (which is the family)," Comenius says, "the elements have to be taught of everything necessary to the building up of the life of man, and we shall show that this is possible by running over the different departments of knowledge." He demonstrates then that the child acquires rudimentally a knowledge of —

"1. *Metaphysics,* by ordinary observation of *is, is-not, where, when,* etc.

"2. *Physics,*[2] by knowing the elements (water, earth, air, fire, rain, etc.) and the parts of his own body.

"3. *Optics,* when he learns light, darkness, etc.

"4. *Astronomy,* when he learns to name sun, moon, etc.

"5. The beginnings of *Geography,* when the child understands what a mountain is, a plain, a valley, a river, a village, a city, a state.

"6. *Chronology,* in learning what an hour is, a day, a week, a month, a year, yesterday, to-day, and to-morrow, etc.

"7. *History,* in learning what has recently happened,[3] and the way in which it happened, and how this or that man conducted himself.

"8. *Arithmetic,* by finding out the much and the little, by counting up to 10, and by the simplest forms of addition and subtraction.

"9. The rudiments of *Geometry,* in discovering great

---

[1] *Comenius,* 133 *et seq.*

[2] Used in the broad sense (*Naturwissenschaften*). See Beeger u. Zoubek (note), 264.

[3] "Every week Comenius appointed an hour for the reading aloud of newspapers (*prælegantur ordinariæ mercatorum novellæ*), in order to learn contemporary history and geography." — VON RAUMER, *Gesch. d. Päd.,* II. 85.

and small, long and short, broad and narrow, thick and thin, a line, a circle, etc.

"10. *Statics*, in observing the light and heavy, and by balancing things.

"11. *Mechanics*, by causing the children to carry things from one place to another, to arrange things, to build and take to pieces, to tie, and untie.

"12. The beginnings even of *Dialectic* are taught by question and answer, and by requiring direct and adequate answers to interrogations.

"13. *Grammar* is acquired by the child in its elements through the right articulating of his mother-tongue, letters, syllables, words.

"14. *Rhetoric*, by hearing the use of metaphors in ordinary conversation, and of the rising and falling inflection in speech.

"15. The foundation of a taste for *Poetry*, by learning little verses.

"16. The daily exercises of household piety, including the singing of easy psalms and hymns, will give the elements of *Music*.

"17. The rudiments of *Economics*,[1] by noting the relations of father, mother, domestic servant, and the parts of a house and its furnishings.

"18. Of *Polity* less can be learned, but even in this sphere some knowledge of the civil government and the names of governors and magistrates may be acquired.

"19. But above all, the foundations of *Morality* have to be firmly laid — by training to temperance in all things, cleanliness of habits, due reverence to superiors, prompt obedience, truthfulness, justice, charity, continual occupation, patience, serviceableness to others, civility.

---

[1] *Hauswirtschaftslehre* (Lion, and Beeger u. Zoubek).

"20. In *Religion* and *Piety* the beginnings are to be laid. The elements of the Christian religion should be committed to memory, and the child should be trained to recognize the perpetual presence of God, his dependence on Him, and to see in Him a punisher of evil and a rewarder of good. Simple prayers should be taught, and the child led to bend the knee and fold the hands in prayer.[1]

In the vernacular school, covering the years from six to twelve, the same encyclopedic plan is followed; but, wonderful in those days, instruction is to be given wholly in the mother-tongue.[2] He plans that this shall be pre-eminently a useful school, that all children shall be taught, in these years, all things which may be of direct value in the actual business of life. He realized, as too few of those concerned since in education have done, that this matter of the practical is a great question, which must be faced in the planning of all public schools. His course prescribes reading, writing, arithmetic, mensuration, geography, general history, "so much of economy and polity as is necessary for the understanding of what goes on around him," singing, ethics, and religion. He adds,[3] "A general knowledge of the mechanical arts should be given, that boys may better understand the affairs of ordinary life, and that opportunities be thus given to boys to find out their special aptitudes."[4] Here is the origin of manual training, as, in Rabelais, appeared the first suggestion of technology. From the insufficiency of his scheme for this period, it seems plain that the problem of this formative epoch in education was no less difficult than it is now.

In the third, or gymnastic period, he is more at home.

---

[1] *Didact.*, 168–171. See Lïon, K. XXVIII. 452.
[2] See his reasons (Lïon, K. XXIX. 461 *et seq.*).
[3] *Didact.*, 174 ; Laurie, 139.
[4] Cf. *Didact.*, 182 ; Lïon, 482.

Not only is the problem easier, but in the fortunate years at Paták, he had opportunity to experiment with a school of this general character. He yields so far to custom as to base his gymnastic course upon the time-honored *Trivium* (grammar, dialectic, and rhetoric), and *Quadrivium* (arithmetic, geometry, music, and astronomy), these being the seven liberal arts of the Humanists. But to these arts he adds physics, — experimental and applied, — geography, chronology, history, ethics, and theology. These subjects he purposes teaching so well and so thoroughly that "there is nothing in Heaven or Earth, or in the Waters, nothing in the Abyss under the earth, nothing in the Human Body, nothing in the Soul, nothing in Holy Writ, nothing in the Arts, nothing in Economy, nothing in Polity, nothing in the Church, of which the little candidates of Wisdom shall be wholly ignorant." [1]

The claim is preposterous, but the aim is good, and the means to attain pansophic knowledge is summed up by Comenius with truth and brevity. [2] "To secure a good education to a child, three things are necessary, — good teachers, good books, good methods." To enable one teacher to superintend the work of many pupils, he proposes a monitorial system, suggestive of that which Bell and Lancaster put to such pernicious use in England more than a century after. Good teachers must themselves be raised up, text-books on his pansophic plan must be written, and, these obtained, there will remain only the need of a good method.

Comenius advises a mild, but firm, discipline, and distinguishes between the two kinds of offences, reserving chastisement for those against morals. In his *Dissertatio de sermonis Latini studio*, he gives most valuable hints to teachers for the carrying out of his pedagogic principles.

---

[1] Quoted by Laurie, 191.   [2] Laurie, 192.

These hints are of that class of truism which is seldom kept firmly in mind, and reference to which gives one always a pleasant sensation of novelty.   Here are a few of them: [1]—

"Let the teacher not teach as much as he is able to teach, but only as much as the learner is able to learn."

"Let nothing ever seem so easy as to relieve the teacher of the duty of striving, in various ways, to make it more perspicuous."   •

"Never let the pupils be overburdened with a mass of things to be learned."

"Three things always are to be formed in the pupil, viz.: mind, hand, and tongue."

"Never dismiss any topic which has been begun until it is thoroughly finished."

"Whatever is taught let it be taught accurately."

The university, he proposes, shall be not only a place for the teaching of all arts and sciences, for the acquiring of all knowledge, but also the home and centre of research, discovery, and invention.   Here we find forestalled that very modern tendency, the broadening of the field of college work.   To this final division of the schools, only the flower of youth is to be admitted.   All ordinary boys must be sent from the public schools at the end of the gymnastic period or, perhaps, at the close of the vernacular school; they must take their places as farmers, mechanics, and shopkeepers. [2]

Comparing the richness of his programme with the poverty

[1] Laurie, 127.   See, also, quotations from *Methodus Novissima* given in *Amer. Journ. Ed.*, V. 290 *et seq.*

[2] "Die Arbeit der Academie selbst wird leichter und erfolgreicher von Statten gehen, wenn erstens nur die auserwählteren Geister, die Blüthe der Menschen, dorthin geschickt werden ; die übrigen aber zum Pfluge, zum Handwerk, oder Handel — je nachdem sie dazu geboren sind — sich hinwenden." — Lïon, 482 (*Didact.*, 181).

of the school courses of his day, Comenius saw that he must devise some means whereby the immensity of the task which he sets may be covered in the same space of time as that given, heretofore, to a beggarly smattering of the humanities. He solves the problem by an appeal to "Method." "Order is the soul of the world; order sustains nature in all its parts; order, too, is the eye of the school; from nature must be taken this order of the school."[1] This question of method he returns to again and again. Professor Laurie,[2] reviewing his principles, says:—

"The school-time must be so ordered that every year, month, week, day, hour, may have its own task. The tasks should be so arranged that they are within the powers of the average mind: in this way the more ordinary natures will be stimulated, while the more precocious and brilliant will be retarded to their advantage. Pupils should be admitted only at the beginning of the school year. On no day should boys do more than six hours' work, and those all in public and in school. The rest should be given to relaxation and domestic duties. The school is the proper place for *school* work; moreover, home-work is apt to be badly done, and badly done work is more hurtful than no work at all. The hours should not be consecutive; the morning should be devoted to studies that call into requisition the intellect, the judgment, and the memory; the afternoon to the discipline of hand, voice, style, demeanor."

"The occupations of the pansophic school are not all of equal importance. They may be classed as primary, secondary, and tertiary. The primary are those which contain the essence or substance of Wisdom, Virtue, Piety, and Eloquence, such as Languages, Philosophy, and Theology; the secondary are auxiliary to these, such as History; the

---

[1] Laurie, 77. Cf. *Didact.*, 61–63 (Lïon, 245 *et seq.*).   [2] p. 193.

tertiary only indirectly contribute to the primary occupations, *e.g.* all that pertain to vigor of health and mental alacrity, such as recreation and sports. But all the occupations and studies have a place *at each successive stage* of progress, and are to be presented *according to the same method.*"

"At the same time, the order of the instruction is subject to certain general laws: for in the younger classes we have to appeal chiefly to the senses, and to cultivate observation; and, as the pupils advance, we draw more on the activity of the memory, the intellect proper, and the power of expressing what is known."

This principle of method is his primal doctrine. For his strenuous advocacy of it the world owes its chief debt to Comenius. The Jesuits, also, taught order; upon method the system of Loyola and Aquaviva rests. But theirs is not, like Comenius's, the order of nature; it is the arbitrary and rigid rule of the cloister. Comenius may have borrowed inspiration from them, but he gave life to a principle which, in their hands, was wholly fruitless, if not, indeed, pernicious.

In addition to this fundamental aid of "Method," by which alone many years heretofore wasted will be saved to the child, Comenius finds other ways of instruction so "that arts may be shortened with a view to rapid learning." These are, in the main, the underlying principles of all good systems of teaching; namely, a dependence upon induction, a strict adhesion to step-by-step methods, the making of learning pleasant so that desire for study shall be aroused, the careful gauging of instruction to the capacity of the pupil, a constant appeal, where possible, to the senses, and, finally, encyclopedism, that is, the presentation to the pupil of all varieties of knowledge at all periods of his advancement, suiting the complexity of the view to the age and capacity of the child. This final principle is accepted to-day, in general, only so far as to secure at every stage of the pupil's development, an equal and steady advance of all his faculties.[1]

Upon these principles Comenius intended to build up his text-books, but the deficiencies to which reference has been made, — that is, his inability to properly digest his ideas and materials, and a certain whimsical temperament, — combined with the magnitude of the task of overthrowing suddenly the deep-laid systems of his day, warped his well-conceived plans in their execution. Thus the *Janua,* which brought him high and immediate fame, departs widely, in its later editions,— those which have the seal of his approval,— from his principles ; it departs so widely, indeed, as to advise the absurd method of teaching Latin by presenting the lexicon and the grammar to the pupil before allowing him to read and speak the tongue.

In the first form of the *Janua,* however, and in the *Vestibulum,* which is an introduction or "Threshold" to it, his plan is rational and in accord with his truer understanding. His method there is to begin with the origin of the universe, to take up then the "elements," — as in those days fire, air, water, and earth, were named,— to follow with a study of plants, of animals, and of man, to develop next the arts and sciences, and to conclude with the attributes and providence of God.

Although modified in the many editions which appeared, his underlying idea is so to present this encyclopedic knowledge that it shall be both easy and interesting to the child, and in such a form that one or many languages may be, at the same time, learned. To this end, he arranges

---

[1] Cf. Herbart, *Science of Education,* Bk. II. (Felkin's Trans., Boston, 1893), 122.

words and sentences in parallel columns, those in Latin or in the other languages to be learned being given in literal translation from the vernacular. Those in the mother-tongue are studied first; the things and actions which they represent are made perfectly plain and familiar to the pupil before the foreign equivalents are taken up. These are then made as clear and common to the child as those in the native speech. By this process, he believed, not only would a perfect and complete knowledge of all things, spiritual and temporal, be gained, but in its acquisition the grammar and vocabulary of any language could be attained without sensible effort.

In the *Orbis Pictus*, which for a hundred years or more was the primer of the German peoples, he carried this idea still further, remedying a defect which had greatly diminished the value of the *Janua* and *Vestibulum*. He associated with every topic studied a woodcut, suitably numbered and annotated, so that when the actual object, whose use whenever possible he makes imperative, could not be obtained, its image should be before the pupil's eyes. With infinite trouble he found an engraver compe-tent to prepare these woodcuts, and edition after edition of this novel picture-book appeared in Europe, to make less hard the thorny path of learning. To Comenius, therefore, we owe not only the vital principle of object-teaching, but also the first school picture-book, the forerunner of the legions of to-day.

This book, of which Hoole's English-Latin version has recently been reprinted,[1] is delightfully naïve. It is pref-aced by an alphabet founded upon the cries of animals, — a novel, though scarcely accurate, method. That the "Bear

[1] By C. W. Bardeen, Syracuse, N.Y. The plates and Latin text are taken from the first edition of 1657, but the English text is from the English edition of 1727.

grumbleth mm " and the "Dog grinneth rr " might, however, vivify the twenty-six crooked symbols to the unhappy
abecedarian. To illustrate the system of the *Orbis Pictus,*
let me quote from two of the lessons. The first is on
"Flying Vermin," as Hoole quaintly translates *Insecta Vo-
lantia.* The "vermin" are pictured in a hilly landscape,
and are duly numbered for reference.

"The *Bee,* 1. maketh honey which the *Drone,* 2. devour-
eth. The *Wasp,* 3. and the *Hornet,* 4. molest with a sting ;
and the *Gad-bee* (or Breese), 5. especially *Cattel;* but the
Fly, 6. and the *Gnat,* 7. us. The *Cricket,* 8. singeth. The
Butterfly, 9. is a winged *Caterpillar.* The *Beetle,* 10. cov-
ereth her wings with *Cases.* The *Glow-worm,* 11. shineth
by night." [1] The second lesson which I quote is, fortunately, a somewhat advanced one. It is upon the "Tor-
menting of Malefactors " (*Supplicia Malefactorum*). So
many are the tortures that the illustrations, happily, are
small and indistinct.

"*Malefactors* are brought from the *Prison* (where they are
wont to be tortured) by *Serjeants,* or *dragg'd* with a *Horse,*
to place of *Execution. Thieves* are hanged by the *Hang-
man* on a *Gallows, Murtherers* and *Robbers* are either laid
upon a *Wheel,* having their *Legs broken,* or fastened upon a
Stake. Witches are burnt in a *great Fire.* Some before
they are executed have their *Tongues cut out,* or have their
Hand cut off upon a *Block* or are burnt with *Pincers.* They
that have their life given them are set on the *Pillory,* or
strapado'd, are set upon a *wooden Horse,* have their *Ears
cut off,* are *whipped with Rods,* are branded, are banished,
are condemned to the *Gallies,* or to perpetual Imprisonment.
Traytors are pull'd in pieces with four *Horses.* " [2]

Comenius carried the idea of object-teaching still far-

---

[1] Bardeen, 31.   [2] Bardeen, 159.

ther. In the *Schola Ludus,* borrowing the idea of dramatic
representation, perhaps, from the Jesuits, he elaborated a
series of schoolroom plays, in which the pupils, representing objects and qualities, harangued one another upon the
topic in hand until it and they were exhausted. That these
insufferably dreary dialogues were, in his time, immensely
popular, is a vivid comment upon the barrenness of school
life two hundred and fifty years ago.[1]

A sufficient analysis of Comenius's methods has now, I
think, been given to prove that Bacon's scheme of universal knowledge is at the foundation of the Moravian's plans
for educational reform. Starting with the *Great Instauration,* he develops it into encyclopedism. Borrowing the
philosophy of Bacon, he enlarges it and makes it available.
His use of the inductive method, his appreciation of the
patience and careful searching that are necessary to a real
education, his attacking of all problems by the way of
the senses, his striking, though often absurd use of anal-

[1] It may be a matter for surprise that Comenius, with such clear
notions of the true end of education, with such impatience as he enter-
tained of the time wasted in the schools of the humanists, should
have based all his teaching, as, except in the *schola vernacular,* he
did, on the study of Latin, making this the pedestal from which to
survey the universe. He explains it himself by declaring that this
tongue is the sole vehicle of learning and that its construction makes
it a peculiarly valuable instrument of teaching. But, in calling Latin
the "Universal" language, he discloses, it seems to me, the secret of
his partiality. Never did he forget his dream of bringing all Christen-
dom together. An exile, he had visions of a universal country with
Christ as its spiritual head. He traced to the dispersion at Babel the
beginning of the bloody dissensions in the midst of which he lived.
From his thirtieth to his sixtieth year, Europe was torn by the Thirty
Years' War, and his people were hunted, by other Christians, because
of a difference in creed. By making the knowledge and use of Latin
universal, he fondly believed war would cease, and world-wide peace,
destroyed by difference of language, would reign again.

ogy, — these he owes to Bacon. But if his debt to the
Englishman is large, Bacon's obligation to him is no less
for making these principles, remote and indefinite as they
originally were, useful to the world. The duty that, in
carelessly recommending the Jesuit schools, Bacon imagined
he fulfilled, Comenius really discharged in putting forth
his *Didactic* and his text-books. "I was troubled," the
good Bishop exclaims, "because the noble Verulam while
giving the true key of Nature did not unlock her secrets,
but only showed by a few examples, how they should be
unlocked, and left the rest to future observations to be extended through centuries."[1] This leisurely unravelling, a
work for profound scholars, Comenius brought down from
its lofty vagueness and put into the hands of children, that
each, every day, might do his share of the task. It is
largely because he did this that the skein of the world has
been in the last two centuries so swiftly untangled.

The principle of method Comenius borrowed from the
Jesuits, but, as we have seen, he quickened it by resting
upon nature instead of upon art. His method, from the
point of exactness and sureness of result, is far inferior to
that of the Society of Jesus, but his, imperfect as it is,
makes men, while theirs, finished as clockwork, produces
automatons.

His plea for popular education is an echo of Luther's,
but Luther's aim was simply to make Protestants, learned
only in the Bible and the faith, while Comenius's end was
such a perfect training in wisdom, virtue, and piety, that all
men and all women should be fitted to take part in a reformation of the world, and in the founding of a Church
Universal.

From Ratich, as we have seen,[2] he obtained many of his

[1] Laurie, 34.   [2] p. 70.

ideas; through him, too, as well as through Vives, he learned to distrust Aristotle. Moreover, he shared with Ratich the profound influence of Bacon; but, unlike that strange semi-charlatan,[1] he scorned to hold his labors in patent for the highest bidder; rather he hurried, almost too eagerly, to give them to the world. As he devoutly expresses it: "What the Lord has given me, I send forth for the common good."

From the humanists he gained little except a distrust of classicism. His Latinity had a different basis, an alien aim. He accepted the ancient writings as a part — though a small part — of knowledge; they received them as the whole of wisdom. He employed Latin partly as a convenience, partly in furtherance of his pan-Christian scheme, but he had no fondness for perfection of form. He used the tongue carelessly, he introduced barbarisms and coined words with a freedom that disgusted the purists whose sole aim was the criticism of texts and readings.

No single thought did he borrow, however, which by his genius he did not make of greater worth. The talents which he received from his masters increased in his hands a hundredfold. To a world that has well-nigh forgotten him, he left a splendid legacy, the conception and example of a public school; a people's school in which all boys and all girls shall be taught, according to their capacities and needs, all things; in which order and method shall intelligently reign; in which discipline shall be mild and emulation healthy; in which the eye and the hand, the ear and the touch, shall have equal training with the mind; in which the moral and spiritual nature shall be given full chance to expand. A rational school, in short, truly educating the child in Wisdom, Virtue, and Piety.

[1] See Von Raumer's account of Ratich (properly Ratke or Ratichius), translated in *Am. Journ. Ed.*, V. 229.

CHAPTER V.

MONTAIGNE AND LOCKE.

The Child has Senses to be Trained.

REACTION AGAINST ECCLESIASTICISM ; MATERIALISM ; MONTAIGNE AND
LOCKE ; THEIR PHILOSOPHY ; SENSATIONALISTS AND SUPERNALISTS ;
INFLUENCE OF MATERIALISM ; MONTAIGNE'S CHARACTER ; THE
"ESSAIS" ; MONTAIGNE AND LOCKE CONTRASTED ; LOCKE'S LIFE ;
HIS CHARACTER ; HIS WRITINGS ; THE "ESSAY CONCERNING HUMAN
UNDERSTANDING" ; ITS PRINCIPLES ; ITS FALLACIES ; ITS INFLU-
ENCE ; THE "CONDUCT OF THE UNDERSTANDING" ; THE "THOUGHTS" ;
THE "DE L'INSTITUTION DES ENFANS" ; THE TWO ESSAYS COM-
PARED ; THEIR MAIN TEACHINGS ; FREEDOM AND SELF-RELIANCE.

THE Age of Faith, sunk into an age of fatuity, was
rudely brought to a close by Luther. It was succeeded,
gradually but irresistibly, by an era of materialism. So
intense was the revolt against old idols that, in their destruction, the truths which they represented shared, for a
time, their fate. This inevitable reaction against blind
belief took effect most quickly in France, whose mercurial
people register the faintest change in mental atmosphere.[1]
The slower Anglo-Saxon temperament adapts itself less
readily to new conditions, and not until well into the
eighteenth century was it prepared to produce a Hume and
a Bentham. Hence it is that Montaigne and Locke, men

---

[1] Notwithstanding this sensitiveness of the Celt to new ideas, it is
generally the Anglo-Saxon, as Buckle shows (*Civil. in Eng.*, I. 436),
who institutes the reforms which grow out of those ideas.

of essentially the same trend of thought, men who represent similar tendencies, flourished more than a hundred
years apart. The English philosopher was born in 1632,
ninety-nine years later than his Gascon prototype.[1] Since,
from our English point of view, the influence of the gos-
siping Frenchman was far less than that of the learned
Locke, it seemed best to postpone acknowledgment of the
undoubted, though indirect, influence of the former until
it could be brought into juxtaposition with that of the
latter.

These two honest gentlemen represent the most genial
and wholesome side of materialism. The first is a skeptic,
the second an agnostic,[2] in manly fashion, with no affecta-

---

[1] Michael Eyquem de Montaigne was born in Périgord, in 1533;
John Locke in Somersetshire, in 1632.

[2] Locke was not an agnostic in the narrow sense of the word. His
agnosticism embraced both the attitudes so well defined by Prof. F.
Max Müller in a recent article. (*Nineteenth Century*, No. 214, p. 895):
"In one sense I hope I am . . . an agnostic . . . in relying on nothing
but historical facts and in following reason as far as it will take us in
matters of the intellect, and in never pretending that conclusions are
certain which are not demonstrated or demonstrable; . . . but if
Agnosticism excludes a recognition of an eternal reason pervading the
natural and the moral world, if to postulate a rational cause for a
rational universe is called Gnosticism, then I am a Gnostic, and a
humble follower of the greatest thinkers of our race from Plato and the
author of the Fourth Gospel to Kant and Hegel." Throughout his
life Locke remained a stanch Puritan, a believer in revelation. His
last years were given to a demonstration of the *Reasonableness of
Christianity* (*q.v.*). But, heartily and honestly as he accepted the
theology of the English Church, he did so, it seems to me, purely on the
grounds of its "reasonableness." Convinced that human nature and
the conditions of life demand, for their explanation, the existence of a
Supreme Mind, he accepted the idea of God as revealed in the Scriptures and as interpreted by the Protestant Church. For, as evidence
of such a Supreme Mind cannot be obtained through the channels by

tion of despair. Their natures are so far from being morbid, they find man — frail and ignorant as he is — on the whole so good and pleasant a creature, that they see no reason to lament his limitations. Montaigne would háve recoiled with disgust, Locke with horror, from the later cynicism of the *philosophes*. They can have had no vision of the moral dyspepsia which their intellectual banquet was destined to induce. The skepticism of Montaigne is so full of faith, albeit in man rather than in God, that it is free from offence. The materialism upon which Locke builds his high tower of argument vanishes when that elaborate structure confronts the Deity.

Nevertheless, it must be kept firmly in mind that, in placing education upon a physical instead of upon a metaphysical basis, their aim was widely different from that of Comenius, of Rabelais, and, indeed, of Bacon.[1] In the

which, alone, all other knowledge comes, it must be obtained through revelation ; and revelation, equally with phenomena, must have an interpreter. "God, I own, cannot be denied to be able to enlighten the understanding by a ray darted into the mind immediately from the Fountain of Light," he says (*Essay*, Bk. IV., Ch. XIX., § 5). Revelation was to him, therefore, an added bulwark of reason. "Whatsoever is divine *revelation* ought to overrule all our opinions, prejudices, and interests, and hath a right to be received with full assent. Such a submission as this, of our *reason* to *faith*, takes not away the landmarks of knowledge ; this shakes not the foundations of reason, but leaves us that use of our faculties for which they were given us." (Bk. IV., Ch. XVIII., § 10.) Cf. Courtney, *Stud. at Leisure*, 124 ; and *infra*, 109.

[1] "He" (Bacon) "did good service when he declared, with all the weight of his authority and of his eloquence, that the true end of knowledge is the glory of the Creator and the relief of man's estate. . . . To those who wish to discourage philosophy in order that ignorance of second causes may lead men to refer all things to the immediate agency of the first, Bacon puts Job's question, 'An oportet mentiri pro Deo,' — will you offer to the God of truth the unclean sacrifice of a lie ? " — ELLIS, *Gen. Pref. to the Phil. Works* (Spedding, I).

minds of Montaigne and Locke the study of nature was the
means to self-growth, the only method of maturing the
senses. To the others this nature-study was the way to
spiritual growth, the surest available avenue to the Divine.
The Sensationalists follow Nature because she alone, they
believe, can perfect the only thing in man perfectable, his
senses. The Supernalists — if I may be allowed so crude
a designation — learn of her because she holds the key,
they maintain, to the mysteries of heaven.

This distinction is fundamental, and cannot be too
strongly emphasized ; for it tinctures the whole history
of education. The attitude of Comenius foreshadowed our
fruitful and expanding system of to-day; that of Locke
culminated in the impossible logic of Rousseau. The epoch
whose dawn Locke witnessed, the era of padding and crino-
line, of wigs and paint, of outward show and inward abomi-
nation, wrought its own destruction in the bloody years
of a century ago. Upon its ruins the doctrine of *Émile*,
whose author was the fatal model of the Jacobins,[1]
rose, and, by a sort of *reductio ad absurdum*, that is, by
awakening hopes and plans which it was powerless to sat-
isfy, gave a wonderful impulse to the "New Education."
But the ethical foundations of that education were laid by
Rabelais, by Luther, and by Comenius.

Between the art and humanity of Greece and the humanity and art of the Renaissance, a thousand dark years intervened, in which the forces of material freedom were accu-

[1] "Twelve Hundred human individuals, with the Gospel of Jean-
Jacques Rousseau in their pocket, congregating in the name of Twenty-
five Millions, with full assurance of faith, to 'make the Constitution':
such sight, the acme and main product of the Eighteenth Century, our
World can witness once only. For Time is rich in wonders, in monstrosities most rich ; and is observed never to repeat himself, or any of
his Gospels : — surely, least of all, this Gospel according to Jean-

mulating. Between the light of the Renaissance and the illumination of the nineteenth century, the spiritual lapse was shorter, but it was, none the less, a lapse. In it, however, were born mental and moral freedom, the motor forces of modern progress. It was the fashion in those pasteboard days to hide one's real self under a mask of flippancy and affectation. The century followed the mode, and hid its real and mighty forces behind the reckless and brutish stage-show of Versailles. Over this age of frank materialism the sensationalists had, of course, great sway. And, on the whole, their influence was good. They schooled the senses, which the earlier philosophers had left in ignorance; they fed them rationally, where the Church had either starved or surfeited. This diet, and especially this training, were, for three reasons, a necessary preparation for our modern growth: first, they secured to us freedom from that poverty and drudgery which perpetuate brutishness; secondly, they stimulated that love of beauty which must precede a striving after art; thirdly, they aroused that wholesome awe of nature which is fatal to an awe of kings. No schooling in democracy equals that given by a study of the universe. The divine rights of royalty vanish in the presence of the really divine and immutable rights of nature. The influence, then, of those followers of Locke who debased his sense-realism to hideous materialism was not wholly mean and profitless. The doctrine of pure sensation was doomed to fall before the test which it expressly invited, the test of nature. But, in urging the infallibility of the test, it brought men to an intelligent study of phenomena, a study which, in the end, led to a faith sure-founded, whose depth and permanency the old faith in miracle could never have attained.

Jacques." — CARLYLE, *The French Revolution* (Leipzig, 1851), II. 256.

But we have strayed far from the kindly, shrewd, and scholarly gentlemen who, unwittingly, kindled so hot a fire in the world. Montaigne, whose rambling, egotistic, and irrelevant gossip is ever fresh and seldom tiresome, is pre-eminently friendly. What more delightful than to have known him, to have ridden with him on one of his horses that he loved,[1] through the beautiful Périgord that he loved, too! Or what pleasanter than to have sat with him in the tower room that he has described minutely,[2] to have watched him as he turned the leaves of a book, and to have listened as he talked with the full freedom of a mind well stored with anecdote and worldly knowledge. Or, as he paced back and forth in the narrow chamber, planning the essays whose easy flow makes manifest the ripened mind behind them,[3] to have busied ourselves with spelling out the maxims with which he had adorned his walls. What a privilege to have been his companion in Rome during his five months' tarrying there,[4] prowling through the city without a *cicerone*, trusting to his jargon of Italian, concocted in the fashion that he merrily advises.[5] For, while he was by no means learned, he had culture, and he loved Rome and Roman literature only a little less fondly than he loved himself. And had we been thus trans-

---

[1] "I do not willingly alight when I am once on horseback; for it is the place where, whether well or sick, I find myself most at ease. Plato recommends it for health, and also Pliny says it is good for the stomach and the joints." — HAZLITT's *Montaigne*, XLVIII. 134.

[2] *Essais*, Liv. III., Ch. III.

[3] "I know not anywhere the book that seems less written. It is the language of conversation transferred to a book. Cut these words, and they would bleed; they are vascular and alive." — EMERSON, *Rep. Men.*, 160.

[4] See Hazlitt's trans. of *A Diary of the Journey of M. de Montaigne into Italy*, etc.

[5] *Essais*, Liv. II., Ch. XII. (p. 254 of Hazlitt).

planted, our modernity would in nowise have amazed him.
A hearty spectator, he was no lubberly starer at the unknown. His was the well-balanced mind which is at home
anywhere and in any age. "I love temperate and indifferent natures," Florio's quaint translation makes him say.[1]
"Immoderation towards good, if it offend me not, it amaz-
eth and troubleth me, how I should call it. . . . A man
may love virtue too much and demean himself in a good
action." These words are the key to his nature, if, indeed,
a character so frank and so complacent needs a key. In-
temperance was the only vice that roused him to intemperate speech.

Some one calls the *Essays* a proper bedside book; and
rightly. They deal with humanity gowned and slippered,
rid of the shamming of to-day, careless of the pretence of
to-morrow, poised in a waking dream of irresponsibility.
We all of us need, even more than we like, this undress
period, this mental nakedness, stripped of the trappings of
conventionality. No one puts us so gently into this mid-
night state as does this rational, whimsical country-gentle-
man, not over-nice in his language, not over-strait in his
morals, but just in his human estimates. A homely, helpful philosopher, abounding in friendliness, in wit, in
charity.[2]

Such a nature, too, was Locke's. But he was no closet
philosopher. Despite the hysterical estimate of Michelet,[3]
education owes little, it seems to me, to Montaigne, beyond
what he did for it in inspiring Locke and Rousseau. We

---

[1] *Essayes*, XXIX., Vol. II. 36.

[2] See his quaintly apologetic analysis of himself in the *Essais*, Liv.
II., Ch. XVII., *De la presumption*.

[3] In *Nos Fils:* " . . . qu'il " (Locke) " est faible, sec, pauvre, loin,
et de l'ampleur de Rabelais, et de la vigueur de Montaigne ! De ces
grands hommes à lui, quelle chute ! " etc., p. 187.

shall consider, later and together, the two treatises of Education, — that of Montaigne addressed to the Countess of Foix, that of Locke written for Mr. Clark. Their weight is much the same. But behind Montaigne's fragment we have nothing beyond his essays, — gay, shrewd, garrulous, — except the lovable man himself. Behind Locke's hasty notes, on the other hand, we have the great *Essay concerning Human Understanding*, we have its posthumous sequel, the *Conduct of the Understanding*, we have those monuments of free thought, the *Letters on Toleration* and the two *Treatises of Government*, and we have the experience of a learned man busied to his latest day in matters of public welfare.[1]

A consumptive through inheritance, Locke was a lifelong invalid. His entire career was dominated, active and fruitful though it was, by the necessities of constant self-nursing. He came of a good middle-class family in easy circumstances, and was reared in a strong but liberal Puritanism. Sent to Westminster School, he found it, as were all the public schools of his day, the abode of savages. Baited, pummelled, and made utterly wretched by these manly little heathen, he gained a hatred of gregarious education which never forsook him. A student at Christ Church, he obtained, without trouble, his master's degree, and, with a view to caring for his "crazy body," studied medicine there. After some diplomatic service abroad, he obtained a scholarship, that carried with it a pension and a residence in the college until such time as he should choose to marry.

[1] The first *Letter on Toleration* appeared in Latin, at Tergou, in 1684 ; the *Essay concerning Human Understanding*, although begun in 1671, was not published until 1689 ; the *Treatises of Government* were issued, for political effect, in 1690 ; while the *Conduct of the Understanding* was not published until two years after Locke's death.

While at Oxford, Locke met the first Earl Shaftesbury, then Lord Ashley. That nobleman, being the victim of an internal abscess, was, in the absurd fashion of his day, "drinking the waters." In some slight service connected with his Oxford potations, Locke came under his notice, interested him, and, within a few years, was domesticated with him. He saved Ashley's life by draining the abscess, and was made, thereupon, physician to his lordship. But he soon became more than this. His offices grew to embrace, also, those of secretary, tutor, and confidential adviser.[1]

But, as we know, Shaftesbury fell, rose again for a fleeting period, was led into Monmouth plottings, fled to Holland, and escaped the scaffold by dying in his bed. The interval of six years between Shaftesbury's two terms of power — times when he required the constant service and counsel of his factotum — was passed by Locke chiefly on the Continent, where he travelled, studied at Montpellier, and acted as tutor to a rich young Englishman. After Shaftesbury's final downfall, it was necessary, for Locke's safety, that he should flee to Holland. There, in rather

---

[1] When it is a question of marrying the Earl's only and sickly son, it is to Locke that the delicate mission of wife-hunting is entrusted. He negotiates successfully, and to general satisfaction, for the hand of the Lady Dorothy Manners. His hovering care of this young couple and of their eldest son, who, as the third Earl Shaftesbury, was to be the famous author of the *Characteristics*, and whose education was placed wholly in his hands, is both pretty and droll. He stays at home and minds this noble baby, while its parents go a-visiting ; in the Earl's absence, he takes care of the household ; when the Earl, as Lord Chancellor, goes forth in state, Locke walks bareheaded by his coach's side. To these various, and, with our present conception of him, humble duties, he brings the true dignity of the philosopher, being equally ready to compose letters of state or to help in the guiding of the great Cabal.

a timorous way, he dodged about, avoiding the proscription that the Dutch, we imagine, would have been slow to obey. We find him now at Amsterdam, again at Utrecht, and finally at Rotterdam, everywhere making friends among the learned whom Holland had gathered into asylum, and, best of all, finishing the great essay on the *Understanding*. In 1686 and 1687 he has strange visitors at Rotterdam, and makes secret journeyings thence. These, in the following year, are explained when the successful Revolution calls William of Orange to England, and Locke, a few months later, follows, an honored courtier, in the Princess's train. Thenceforward, so far as his health permits, his life is fortunate and active. He has offers of embassies and other posts of dignity which he is too ill to accept actively and too honest to take as sinecures. He writes, in a letter of earlier date,[1] to a friend who urges him to marry: —

"My health, which you are so kind to in your wishes, is the only mistress I have a long time courted, and is so coy a one that I think it will take up the remainder of my days to obtain her good graces and keep in her good humor."

This uncertain mistress was, too truly, the ruler of his later life, which was spent, so much of it as was possible, in London, the rest at Oates, in Essex, where he sought refuge from cold and fog with his close friends, the Mashams.[2] At their house he died, serenely and cheerfully, as he had lived. He wrote in Latin his own epitaph.[3]

"Stay, traveller: near this place lies John Locke. If you ask what sort of man he was, the answer is that he was contented with his modest lot. Bred a scholar, he used his

---

[1] In June, 1677, to Dr. John Mapletoft. See **Fox** Bourne, *Life*, I. 369.

[2] See Fox Bourne, *Life*, Ch. XII. (II. 212).

[3] King, *Life*, 266.

studies to devote himself to truth alone. This you may learn from his writings; which will show you anything else that is to be said about him more faithfully than the doubtful eulogies of an epitaph. His virtues, if he had any, were too slight for him to offer them to his own credit or as an example to you. Let his vices be buried with him. Of good life you have an example, should you desire it, in the gospel; of vice, would there were none for you; of mortality, surely (and may you profit by it) you have one here and everywhere. That he was born on the 29 of Aug. in the year of our Lord, 1632, and that he died on the 28 of Oct. in the year of our Lord, 1704, this tablet, which itself will quickly perish, is a record."

A summary as true as it is modest. His writings do exhibit him, not as Montaigne shows himself, confidential through very garrulity and self-conceit, but simply, naïvely, because, through enthusiasm, he put himself into them, and because that self was pure, single, and manly. The world, having grown better, permits of the existence, now, of many men like Locke. In the days of the Stuarts and Louis XIV. they were rare. We may believe, then, that no small part of Locke's influence was founded upon his possession of the homely virtues of honesty, sincerity, and simplicity. These characteristics cemented, without doubt, the friendships that his fame and learning brought. But he was much more than a good man, rare in his generation. That he was a physicist of no mean ability, the nature of his friendship with Boyle, Leibnitz, Huyghens, and Newton shows. That he was a physician of insight far above the common, the public praises of his close friend, Sydenham,[1]

---

[1] "Nôsti præterea, quam huic meæ methodo suffragantem habeam, qui eam intimius per omnia perspexerat, utrique nostrum conjunctissimum Dominum Johannem Lock; quo quidem viro, sive ingenio judicioque acri et subacto, sive etiam antiquis (hoc est optimis) mori-

testify. He was a theologian, too, of such power that Limborch and the Dutch divines sought his counsel. Finally, as a philosopher and statesman, he ranks among the greatest in England.

In all these departments of learning he wrote somewhat extensively, although the years of his authorship were the last of his life. Our aim calls for an examination of only a limited range — the *Essay concerning Human Understanding*, that on the *Conduct of the Understanding*, his *Thoughts on Education*, and a fragment entitled *Of Study*. The last two, although nominally of directest value to school work, are, broadly speaking, of less importance than the great *Essay*. The *Thoughts* materially influenced methods of teaching, but the *Essay* changed the foundations of education itself.

Locke devotes the first of the four books of his *Essay*[1] to a proof of his proposition that the mind possesses no innate ideas. He premises that the mind, using a comparison suggested by Aristotle's *Tabula rasa*,[2] is "white paper," or employing a more vivid simile, —

bus, vix superiorem quenquam inter eos qui nunc sunt homines repertum iri confido, paucissimos certe pares." Quoted by Brown, *Spare Hours*, 3d ser., 42.

[1] The *Essay concerning Human Understanding* has been the centre of so much discussion, holds, in fact, so conspicuous a place in English literature, that it is with much hesitation I venture to discuss it. It is, however, essential to an understanding of Locke's place in education.

Not until this chapter was in press was I able to see Professor Fraser's splendid edition of the *Essay*. This, in its *Prolegomena* and notes, is a mine of valuable and scholarly commentary.

[2] " The " (Aristotle's) " metaphor is not to be pressed as though it implied a purely empirical account of thought and knowledge. The comparison refers simply to one point, and it is misused when taken as an equivalent to Locke's white paper or other sensualist similes. All

"Methinks the understanding is not much unlike a closet wholly shut from light, with only some little opening left, to let in external visible resemblances, or ideas of things without."[1]

Upon this blankness, as upon fair wax, impressions are made, or into this vacancy, as into an empty room, sensations enter from the external world. "In experience," Locke declares, "all our knowledge is founded, and from that it ultimately derives itself."[2] This is pure materialism; and had Locke limited himself to this narrow position, had he not permitted, as we shall see, exceptions to this rule of knowledge, either he must soon have given up his essay, or he must have been led into demonstrations and assertions wholly contrary to his real belief.

Fortunately, not only was he inconsistent, not only did he use the term "innate" with great license, but he at once proceeded to endow the mind with that activity which, just before, he had distinctly denied to it. The mind is not inert, he asserts, but, upon receiving sensations from without, "turns its view inward upon itself and observes its own actions about those ideas it has," (and) "takes from them other ideas, which are as capable to be the objects of its contemplation as any of those it received from foreign things."[3]

In other words, man, as he imagines him, is capable

---

that Aristotle means to bring out by his comparison is that just as a sheet of paper may be regarded as containing *a priori* and implicitly all that will be written on it, so similarly the intellect or reason may be viewed as implicitly containing its objects, *which like itself are rational.*" — EDWIN WALLACE, *Aristotle's Psychology* (Cambridge, 1882), 103.

[1] *Essay*, Bk. II., Ch. XI., § 17.
[2] *Essay*, Bk. II., Ch. I., § 2.
[3] *Essay*, Bk. II., Ch. VI., § 1.

of inward as well as of outward sensation. More than this, he is able to analyze internal sensations and to educe others from them. Allow to the mind this power to reason about itself, and its wonders are explained. But whence this power? Locke does not say; still less does he try to reconcile its existence with his rejection of innate ideas. He neither acknowledges nor analyzes the power which transmutes sensation into thought. In his eagerness to maintain his proposition that the mind is but a bundle of experiences, he will not see that his position is untenable. Valiantly does he close his eyes, admirably does he expand his wilful premise, boldly does he enter upon the demonstration of good and evil, of liberty and faith, of infinity and eternity. Not until the ninth chapter of the fourth book is he brought finally to bay.[1] Here he comes to a point where he must definitely answer the question, How do I know that I am? He sees plainly that no outward, no inward sensation — as he limits them — can give a satisfactory reply. He understands that upon the reality of the *ego* the whole logic of his sensational doctrine rests. And, thus confronted, he does not hesitate to sacrifice consistency to faith. "Let us proceed now," he begins,[2] mentally bracing himself, "to inquire concerning our knowledge of the existence of things and how we come by it. I say then, that we have the knowledge of our own existence by intuition." Thus far his statement is consonant with his theory, for he has limited intuition to the mind's act of agreement with its ideas. But, growing bolder, he continues,[3] "We perceive it so plainly and so certainly that it neither needs or is capable of any proof; for nothing can be more evident

---

[1] This book was evidently written, however, earlier than the other three.

[2] *Essay*, Bk. IV., Ch. IX., § 2.

[3] *Ibid.*, § 3.   See also Bk. IV., Ch. XVII., § 14.

to us than our own existence. . . . If I doubt of all other things, that very doubt makes me perceive my own existence,[1] and will not suffer me to doubt of that. . . . Experience then convinces us that we have an intuitive knowledge of our own existence, and an *internal, infallible perception* that we are."

Alas for fallible humanity and the doughty Mr. Locke! Have we followed him through hundreds of pages, wherein he tells us that there are not, can not be, must not be, innate ideas, only to find that we ourselves know that we are through an internal, infallible perception? Has he devoted one entire book to showing, in masterly fashion, the use and abuse of words only to lead us, himself, into this verbal pit? In acknowledging the infallibility of even one sensation, he has sacrificed his logical premise, but he has saved his soul. The God that he educes while denying innate ideas, is a mere mathematical formula, a finite series to infinity. The Deity whom he acknowledges after he has granted the existence of infallible intuition, is the God of the agnostic, as certain as he is incomprehensible.[2]

---

[1] Cf. Descartes's famous proposition, *Cogito ergo sum.*

[2] Cardinal Newman, looking only at the relentless logic of sensationalism, says, rightly from that point of view (*The Idea of a University defined and illustrated;* London, 1889, 319) : "Locke is scarcely an honor to us" (meaning England) "in the standard of truth, grave and manly as he is." But Locke himself, knowing himself, and that his knowledge was higher than his reason, writes (*An Examination of P. Malebranche's Opinion of Seeing All Things in God,* § 52) : "I . . . content myself with my ignorance which roundly thinks thus : God is a simple being, omniscient, that knows all things possible ; and omnipotent, that can do or make all things possible. But how he knows, or how he makes, I do not conceive : his ways of knowing as well as his ways of creating are to me incomprehensible ; and, if it were not so, I should not think him to be God, or to be perfecter in knowledge than I am." See *ante,* 97.

I have made this long digression, partly to enter a plea — poor enough — for an author who is unjustly under the ban of atheism, but mainly to show that the fallacies in his reasoning, fundamental as they are, seriously affect questions of higher ethics only. It is enough for ordinary pedagogic use that we try to understand the mind and the growth of the minor morals. We need not deal with primal causes or with ultimate problems of faith and free-will. We may avail ourselves, in short, of Locke's reasoning, and of his results, without concerning ourselves with the truth or error of his premises. This pedagogics has done, greatly to its profit and advancement.

Accepting, therefore, Locke's theory merely as a working hypothesis, we have, in the last three books of his *Essay*, an admirable treatise on psychology, the first formal discussion of modern times, and one that profoundly influenced the progress of education. Let us look at its main arguments.

Having proved, as he believes, that the mind is originally blank, Locke shows that it can be furnished in two ways only: through sensation — that is, through the impress of outward phenomena upon the senses; and through reflection — that is, to use his own words, through "the notice which the mind takes of its own operations and the manner of them."[1] From sensation and reflection, singly or combined, result ideas, and upon ideas the progress and history of the mind depend. Locke tries, though not always successfully, to separate *ideas*, which are the images given by sensation and reflection, from *qualities*, which are the actual essences or natures of the idea-exciting phenomena.[2] Qualities are, of course, beyond our comprehension.

[1] *Essay*, Bk. II., Ch. I., § 4.
[2] See *Essay*, Bk. II., Ch. VIII., § 7 *et seq.*

From simple ideas, he maintains, the mind produces by combination,— that is, by a process akin to that of the calculus,— ideas of space, of duration, and even of infinity and eternity. Complex ideas, involved and multiform as they are, he asserts to be but combinations and associations of simple ideas, "bottomed,"[1] to use a favorite word of his, in a simple sensation, in a simple reflection, or in a sensation and a reflection combined.[2] In the third category he places pleasure and pain and their derivatives, good and evil. Complex ideas, he says, may be comprehended under three classes, *substances*, *modes*, and *relations*, or, roughly speaking, ideas of things, ideas of action, and ideas of comparison.

We cannot follow him into the maze — which he yet makes reasonably clear — of the classification of ideas. But this sorting and naming lead him, farther than he had primarily expected, into the discussion of words, which are the expression of ideas. He devotes, therefore, the entire third book to an analysis of language. With righteous wrath he shows the vain subtleties of the scholastics to be but foolish quibbling. "Notwithstanding these learned disputants, these all-knowing doctors," he exclaims,[3] in an outburst against them, "it was to the unscholastic statesman that the governments of the world owed their peace, defence and liberties ; and from the illiterate and contemned mechanic (a name of disgrace) that they received the improvements of useful arts. Nevertheless, this artificial ignorance and learned gibberish prevailed mightily in these last ages, by the interest and artifice of those, who found no easier way to that pitch of authority and dominion they have attained, than by amusing the men of business and

[1] Cf. *Conduct of the Understanding*, §§ 42, 43.
[2] *Essay*, Bk. II., Ch. XII. *et seq.*
[3] *Ibid.*, Bk. III., Ch. X., § 9.

ignorant with hard words, or employing the ingenious and idle in intricate disputes about unintelligible terms, and· holding them perpetually entangled in that endless labyrinth."

Defining very exactly the use of words and the nature and causes of their abuse, he thus sums up[1] man's duty to his tongue: —

"1st. Every one should take care to use no word without a signification, no vocal sign without some idea he had in his mind, and would express by it.   2nd. The idea he uses a sign for should be clear and distinct; all the simple ideas it is made up of, if it be complex, should be settled.   3rd. These ideas must be accommodated as near as we can to the common signification of the word in its ordinary use. It is this propriety of speech which gives the stamp under which words are current, and it is not for every private man to alter their value at pleasure."

In the fourth book, he proceeds to the demonstration of knowledge, which he limits unwarrantably by defining it as nothing but the perception of the agreement or disagreement of any two ideas.[2] He soon finds it necessary, as I have shown, to acknowledge the existence of "infallible intuition," and, thenceforward, his argument wavers, clutching first at his material, then at his spiritual, logic.

It is unreasonable to ask for a flawless treatise, however, in the seventeenth century, upon so elusive a science as psychology. The point attained to-day is not so high that Locke's seems very far below it. Crude, insufficient, and self-contradictory as he often appears, the marvel is that he was not more faulty.

These major things, at least, his *Essay* did. It proved

[1] *Essay*, Bk. III., Ch. XI., § 8 *et seq.*
[2] *Essay*, Bk. IV., Ch. I., § 2.

and established the positions of earlier educational reformers, by reaching their conclusions regarding the discipline and the capabilities of the mind through a scientific though empirical reasoning ; it showed the possibility and necessity of applying laboratory methods to the investigation of mental phenomena, thereby inaugurating that tremendous advance which has come to the educational ideal through the study of psychology; it demonstrated a fact which had been almost unknown or neglected, that accuracy and clearness, both in thought and in speech, are prime factors in the solving of all human problems ; finally, it established the compass of the mind, on the one hand defining the limits of mental competence and, on the other hand, opening up new fields wherein the mind could profitably exercise itself.

Locke's main emphasis was upon common-sense. His chief object in dealing with the human mind at all was to bring it down to a level where it might be examined, where its competence to this investigation, its incompetence to that speculation, might be clearly shown. The subtleties of the Schoolmen, the chimeras of the alchemists, the jargon and fictions of the pre-Renaissance philosophers, all arose, mainly, from ignorance of the true limits of the mind. So long as this ignorance existed, just so long would these barren parasites eat up the substance of knowledge, deform its image, and hinder its growth. Locke simply continued that warfare against "Idols" which Bacon had begun. More than this, he examined and described the "New Instrument" which Bacon vainly sought to discover and disclose. Still more, in showing the limitations of that "Instrument" in certain directions, he made plain its enormous powers in other paths hitherto hardly suspected.

In this single essay Locke crystallized the work of two hundred years, and framed the skeleton of scientific education. The true pedagogic way, before him a matter of vision and speculation, was by him established as a matter of definite experiment and research. Investigating scientifically the action of the mind, he reached conclusions agreeing with the *a priori* theories of Rabelais and Comenius. The "New Instrument" of Bacon Locke showed to be the searching mind itself, ordered and developed. Object-teaching, the inductive process, self-activity, all those pedagogic helps at which the earlier reformers had guessed, Locke, from the nature of the mind, showed to be fit and necessary tools of teaching. As the typical book of a new era in education, as a distinct and active first-cause in philosophical thought, the *Essay* is colossal.

The *Conduct of the Understanding*, which follows naturally upon the *Essay*, is built upon less formal lines. Short and pithy, it invites study, even by those to whom the lengthy *Essay* is too much. A sentence from it here and there will serve to show Locke's vigorous style.

"We are of the ruminating kind, and it is not enough to cram ourselves with a great load of collections; unless we chew them over again, they will not give us strength and nourishment." [1]

"It is undoubtedly a wrong use of my understanding to make it the rule and measure of another man's." [2]

"General observations drawn from particulars are the jewels of knowledge, comprehending great store in a little room; but they are therefore to be made with the greater care and caution, lest, if we take counterfeit for true, our loss and shame be the greater when our stock comes to a severe scrutiny." [3]

"God has made the intellectual world harmonious and beautiful without us, but it will never come into our heads

[1] § 20, *Reading.*   [2] § 23, *Theology.*   [3] § 25, *Haste.*

at once. We must bring it home piecemeal, and there set it up by our own industry, or else we shall have nothing but darkness and a chaos within." [1]

We are ready now to examine Locke's *Thoughts on Education*, and, in connection with it, Montaigne's essay, *De l'Institution des enfans*. Both of these were written "to oblige a friend," and Locke's was published to oblige other friends. Therefore they are written *ad hominem*, and are limited to the problem of how to educate a gentleman. The common people were beneath notice in the sixteenth and seventeenth centuries, except by men of Luther's robust temper. "Knowledge, madam," writes Montaigne,[2] with a courtly mental flourish towards his correspondant, the comtesse Diane de Foix, "is a great ornament and a tool of marvellous worth, especially to those of your exalted station. Truly, it fails of its right use in low, base hands; it is more eager to lend its aid in the conduct of a war, in the ruling of a nation, or in the practice of diplomacy, than in bolstering dialectics, in arguing a law suit, or in compounding pills." Says Locke,[3] in the Epistle Dedicatory: "The well Educating of their Children is so much the Duty and Concern of Parents, and the Welfare and Prosperity of the Nation so much depends on it, that I would have every one lay it seriously to Heart, and . . . set his helping Hand to promote every where that Way of training up Youth, with regard to their several Conditions, which is the easiest, shortest, and likeliest to produce virtuous, useful, and able Men in their distinct callings ; tho' that most to be taken Care of is the Gentleman's Calling. For if those of that Rank are by their Education once set right, they will quickly bring all the rest into Order."

---

[1] § 37, *Presumption.*   [2] *Essais*, Liv. I., Ch. XXV., ¶ 9.
[3] *Thoughts*, p. lxiii.

It would have been superhuman for these men, bred as
they were, to have condescended to the public school.
Their horizon includes only the tutor as educator, and the
gentleman as pupil.[1]

But Locke's ideal teacher fills a *rôle* quite opposite to that
of Montaigne's. Both, in Montaigne's words,[2] "would
. . . choose a tutor whose head is well tempered rather
than well filled. Require both qualities in him, but of the
two, rather manners and understanding than learning."
But Montaigne is fearful of the warm and tender atmosphere of home, and would use the tutor at once as a shield
from the indulgence of parents and as a guide to lead boys,
open-eyed, into the wicked world. "I should like to have
the pupil," he says,[3] "begin to travel in his infancy, especially — thereby killing two birds with one stone — into
neighboring countries where his tongue, while it is yet
supple, may be formed to new languages." Locke, on the
other hand, regards the tutor as a screen to ward off mun-
dane contamination, and as a map of society to point out
pitfalls to the child without tearing him from the shelter
of home to expose him to the temptations of the world.
"'Tis *Virtue* then, direct *Virtue*," he maintains,[4] "which
is the hard and valuable part to be aimed at in Education.
. . . This is the solid and substantial Good which Tutors

---

[1] Locke's abhorrence of the endowed school was life-long. "Take
a Boy from the Top of a Grammar-School," he says (*Thoughts*, § 70),
"and one of the same age bred in his Father's Family, and bring them
into good Company together, and then see which of the two will have
the more manly Carriage, and address himself with the more becoming
Assurance to Strangers. Here I imagine the School-Boy's Confidence
will either fail or discredit him; and if it be such as fits him only for
the Conversation of Boys, he were better to be without it."

[2] *Essais*, Ch. XXV., ¶ 11.

[3] *Ibid.*, ¶ 19.

[4] *Thoughts*, § 70.

should not only read Lectures and talk of, but the Labour and Art of Education should furnish the Mind with, and fasten there, and never cease till the young Man had a true Relish of it, and plac'd his Strength, his Glory, and his Pleasure in it; . . . therefore, I cannot but prefer breeding of a young Gentleman at home, in his Father's Sight, under a good Governour, as much the best and safest way to this great and main End of Education ;" . . . (but) "I must here take the Liberty to mind Parents of this one Thing, viz. That he that will have his Son have a Respect for him and his Orders, must himself have a great Reverence for his Son." [1]

The two authors agree in strongly endorsing a thorough physical training. Locke's own sufferings taught him the value of a sound body, and he advocates early and continued hardening. "Use your children as the honest Farmers and substantial Yeomen do theirs. . . . Most Children's Constitutions are either spoil'd, or at least harm'd, by Cockering and Tenderness;" [2] and he lays down, for guidance,[3] these "few and easily observable Rules: Plenty of open Air, Exercise, and Sleep, plain Diet, no Wine or Strong Drink, and very little or no Physick, not too warm and strait Clothing, especially the Head and Feet kept cold, and the Feet often us'd. to cold Water and expos'd to wet."

Montaigne is no less strenuous for a rude training as a means to perfect health. Locke, more apt to self-denial than the pleasure-loving Gascon, makes, at this point, an obvious analogy.[4] "As the Strength of the Body lies chiefly in being able to endure Hardships, so also does that of the Mind. And the great Principle and Foundation of all Virtue and Worth is plac'd in this: that a Man is able

[1] *Thoughts*, § 71.   [2] *Ibid.*, § 4.   [3] *Ibid.*, § 30.   [4] *Ibid.*, § 33.

to deny himself his own Desires, cross his own Inclinations, and purely follow what Reason directs as best, tho' the Appetite lean the Other Way."

Assured of the sound body, they strive, secondarily, for the sound mind. This they secure by *cultivating the understanding.* "Children must be treated as rational creatures," says Locke.[1] "Let him know that he knows," says Montaigne, and, continuing, "It is the understanding which sees and hears. Learn, if you can, to manage a horse, a lance, a lute, or your voice, without practice; but that is what those would have us do who would teach us to think and speak without giving us practice in speaking and thinking."[2] Says Locke, pursuing the same idea, "I can no more know a thing by another man's understanding, than I can see by another man's eyes. So much I know, so much truth I have got; so far I am in the right, as I do really know myself; whatever other men have, it is in their possession, it belongs not to me, nor can be communicated to me but by making me alike knowing; it is a treasure that cannot be lent or made over."[3]

This is the true spirit of education. This is the principle that Montaigne partially, Locke fully, enunciated. The details into which they expanded it are of little moment. They are antiquated, of course, but so are the details of John's education of yesterday in regard to Henry's education of to-day. Education is a mobile art, eternally in flux. If the groundwork of principle be but secure, the *minutiæ* of its application will develop spontaneously with each pupil taught. Cultivate the divine understanding within the child, going to nature for guidance and inspiration, — that is the spirit of the rational education

---

[1] *Thoughts*, § 54.   [2] *Essais*, Liv. I., Ch. XXV., ¶ 16.
[3] *Of Study.* See King, *Life*, 106.

which was preached by both these men. "Do not imprison the boy," pleads Montaigne; "do not abandon him to the rage and gloom of a fanatic pedagogue. Do not curb his spirit by binding him down to a hell of work, in the fashion of the age, fourteen or fifteen hours a day, like a porter." . . . "This great world . . . is the mirror into which, to know ourselves, we must look. Let this be my scholar's book. To him a closet, a garden, the table, and his bed, solitude, society, morning and evening, all hours will be the same, all places will be his school. Play, even, and exercise, will be no small portion of his studying, — racing, wrestling, music, dancing, hunting, riding, and feats of arms. . . . It is not a soul, it is not a body, that we are training; it is a man."[1]

"When I consider," says Locke,[2] "what ado is made about a little Latin and Greek, how many years are spent in it, and what a noise and Business it makes to no Purpose, I can hardly forbear thinking that the Parents of Children still live in fear of the School-master's rod, which they look on as the only instrument of Education; as a Language or two to be its whole Business. . . . What, then? say you, would you not have him write and read? Not so, not so fast, I beseech you. Reading and Writing and *Learning* I allow to be necessary, but yet not the chief Business. Learning must be had, but in the second Place, as subservient only to greater Qualities. . . . Secure his Innocence, cherish and nurse up the good, and gently correct and weed out any bad Inclinations, and settle him in good Habits. This is the main Point, and this being provided for, Learning may be had into the Bargain, and that, as I think, at a very easy rate."

Both these humane men regarded with horror the cru-

---

[1] *Essais*, Liv. I., Ch. XXV., ¶ 38.   [2] *Thoughts*, § 147.

elties that made torture-chambers of the schoolrooms. "Away, I say," Montaigne cries with unwonted vehemen'ce;[1] "away with violence and force. . . . Approach one of our schools. You hear only screams and children beseeching and masters drunk with rage. What way is this to arouse an appetite for learning in these tender and timid minds, to present this horrid image of it, armed with whips? Iniquitous and shameful spectacle! . . . Decorate our schoolrooms with flowers and leaves, not with bundles of bloody rods." Locke is no less severe in his denunciation; but, on the other hand, he avoids the worship of rewards as an incentive to learning, that mistaken cult which has proved so great a bane to sound education.

As to the details of instruction, both are advocates of strict and careful method, believing it to be a principle of exceeding importance. Latin they would teach as a modern language is imparted, by daily speech and practice. Montaigne gives[2] an extremely interesting account of the experiment tried by his father upon him, permitting him to hear no language except Latin until he had passed his sixth year, even the servants being compelled to address him in that tongue. Locke eagerly accepts this method, and hopes, by its adoption, to save years of study to the child, years that he would fill up with geography, astronomy, chronology, anatomy, geometry, and some parts of history. Locke's attitude towards history is vacillating and whimsical, quite other than that of Montaigne, who commends it strongly provided it be rightly taught, not as a chronicle of war, but as a record of human experience. Locke has no patience with the prevailing fashion of requiring pupils to write long moral themes, and to compose bad Latin verses. Rather would he devote this time to a modern language, or

[1] *Essais*, Liv. I., Ch. XXV., ¶ 41.   [2] *Essais*, Liv. I., Ch. XXV.

perhaps — for he expresses distrust, even of the "incomparable Mr. Newton" — to natural philosophy. Greek he boldly discards, as a waste of time for any except scholars. Finally, he would have boys taught all the manly arts, as, for example, fencing, wrestling, riding, and dancing, and, wonder of wonders, he would have all young gentlemen learn at least one trade. In this he forestalls the later · apostles of manual training as, in another place, he makes general prophecy of the kindergarten. "I have thought," he remarks,[1] "that if Playthings were fitted to this purpose, as they are usually to none, Contrivances might be made to teach Children to read, whilst they thought they were only playing. . . . Children, if you observe them, take abundance of Pains to learn several Games, which, if they should be enjoined them, they would abhor as a Task and Business."

There is much more in these *Thoughts* of Locke's. Especially are the sections on regimen, on family relations, and on the management of children, wise and helpful, though abounding in what to us learned moderns are mere truisms. No one with even a slight interest in questions of education, but will be glad to have read these homely, rough notes of this wise old bachelor inspired to the training of other men's children.

But to return to Montaigne. He, too, rejects the Greek and Latin taught by the humanists as "fine acquisitions which we buy too dear." Languages, learned naturally, he approves, and any other study that tends to a broad humanity. Philosophy, he asserts, is the beginning and end of education; not the thorny wrangling of the schools, but a real philosophy, a real love of wisdom. "Cultivate an honest curiosity to inquire into everything," he writes.[2]

---

[1] *Thoughts*, § 150.   [2] *Essais*, Liv. I., Ch. XXV., ¶ 26 and 30.

"Among the liberal arts begin with the art that makes us free. All serve in some way, as does everything about us, towards our instruction, but choose first that which aids us most directly."

Freedom and self-reliance, those are the watchwords of these two marvellously "modern" men. Expansion, real education, drawing out, widening out, that is the burden of their preaching; and voices in the wilderness theirs were! Narrowness, bigotry, flippancy, inertia, were to reign until Rousseau should come, and even his voice was to fall upon deaf ears in England. Perhaps Montaigne had visions of this long night of self-absorption, peopled by folly and fanaticism, when he wrote:[1] "We are contracted and shut in by self, and our vision extends no farther than our noses. Socrates, being asked whence he came, did not answer, from Athens, but from the world. He, whose imagination was richest and broadest, claimed the universe as his dwelling-place and held acquaintance, friendliness, and relationship, with humanity; not like us, who look only downwards. When the vines are nipped, in my village, by the frost, my priest thinks the wrath of God is upon the human race, and believes that the pip has seized the cannibals. . . . When it hails upon our heads, the whole universe seems swallowed up in storm. We all of us fall unwittingly into this error, an error of great and evil consequence. But he who gazes, with right perspective at this mighty image of our mother, Nature, in her simple majesty, who discerns in her aspect her limitless and inexhaustible variety, who sees himself therein, nay, not only himself, but an entire kingdom, as nothing greater than the marking of a point, he alone views things in their right proportion."

Again he writes:[2] —

---

[1] *Essais*, ¶ 28.   [2] *Ibid.*, ¶ 33.

"The signal mark of wisdom is unruffled joy. She calms the tempests of the soul, and teaches hunger and fever how to laugh, not by means of imaginary epicycles, but through plain and normal reason; her end is virtue, who is not, as the scholastics say, seated on the top of a high mountain, rough and inaccessible; those who have sought her declare, on the contrary, that she dwells in a fertile and flowery plain, with all good things around her; and that the journey thither, if one but go aright, is through shady paths, turf-carpeted, and filled with fragrant blossoms."

CHAPTER VI.

THE JANSENISTS AND FÉNELON.

THE CHILD HAS A HEART TO BE DEVELOPED.

THE ROMAN CATHOLIC CHURCH ; THE REFORMATION ; THE RE-FORMATION
IN THE CHURCH OF ROME ; LOYOLA ; THE ORDER OF JESUS ; ITS
MAIN PRINCIPLES ; ITS ATTITUDE TOWARDS EDUCATION ; THE "RATIO
STUDIORUM "; ITS METHOD AND AIMS ; THE JESUIT EDUCATION ;
ITS DEFECTS ; ITS ADVANTAGES ; ITS MORAL BASES ; THEIR FALSE-
NESS ; THE JANSENIST CONTROVERSY ; ITS RESULTS ; ITS LEADERS ;
PORT-ROYAL ; THE JANSENIST EDUCATION ; ITS FOUNDATIONS ; ITS
INFLUENCE ; THE "LITTLE SCHOOLS "; THEIR SPIRIT ; THEIR
METHODS ; CONTRASTED WITH THE JESUIT SCHOOLS ; THE TEXT-
BOOKS ; THE COURT OF LOUIS XIV. ; FÉNELON ; TUTOR TO THE
"LITTLE DAUPHIN "; HIS METHODS ; HIS WRITINGS ; INFLUENCE
UPON HIM OF PORT-ROYAL ; MADAME DE MAINTENON ; SAINT-CYR ;
ITS INFLUENCE UPON EDUCATIONAL GROWTH.

HAVING considered the phase of educational reform
which was coincident with the Protestant movement, we
must go back to the beginning of the seventeenth century,
in order to study that important, but too often despised,
factor in educational growth, the Roman Catholic Church.
The Reformation was not the cause, it was one of the
effects, of an extended moral awakening, and the sudden
and marked advance in educational ideals which followed
it was its brother, not its child. Europe was seeking freedom in every direction, whether in religion, in government,
or in thought, and this particular phase of growth, though
different in its results, was not less marked inside the

Church than outside. While the Reformation gave free growth to tendencies which for years had been straining at the bonds of Rome, it none the less emancipated that Church itself, securing to it a strength and a buoyancy which, through its own corruption, had been fast disappearing.

Although Luther drew from the Church of Rome much of her best material, he tore away, at the same time, the incubus of corruption which had been perverting and destroying the Catholic body. The upheaval within the Church differed from that without, however, in that the new faith accepted the spirit of democracy, while the old not only clung to feudal principles, but re-founded itself upon a military hierarchy.

When the smoke lifted from the battle-field of schism, and the Roman Church could seek the causes of her defeat, it was plain that failure had arisen chiefly from lack of organization, or, rather, from an antiquated organization weighed down by a burden of corruption. Recognizing this, had she proceeded to adapt herself to new conditions, had she re-formed herself upon broad lines of humanity and freedom, creating a great commonwealth of Christianity, she might have done much towards averting further schism and checking disaffection. She chose, instead, clutching at immediate power, to put herself upon a military footing, to fight for her lost supremacy, and, more than this, to carry a war of aggression into new territory. Fortunately for her, having made this choice of action, she found sprung up in her midst a body of picked warriors, a standing army of the faith, trained by a man peculiarly fitted to the task. Ignatius Loyola, the roystering soldier of the Emperor, had been transformed,[1] by a seeming mira-

---

[1] For a graphic account of Loyola's conversion see Ranke, *Hist. of the Popes*, I. 181. Cf. Hughes, *Loyola*, 19.

cle, into an austere, an invincible, an indispensable soldier
of a military Church, and by him, twenty years after
Luther separated from Rome, the Society of Jesus had
been founded.[1] This is not the place to follow the history
of this extraordinary body of religious soldiers who, with
numbers never exceeding twenty-five thousand,[2] held for
so many years the stronghold of the Church, dictated European policy, moulded kingdoms, conquered nations, and
controlled the Holy See itself.[3] Such devotion, such sin-
gleness of aim, such absolute obedience, such supple diplomacy, have seldom been combined in the history of mankind.
Nothing short of a power mightier than all these forces
together — the spirit of freedom — was able to destroy the
dominion of the Society of Jesus.

I do not presume to analyze the complex problem of the
growth of the Jesuits, of the means they used to secure and
keep their ascendency in Europe,[4] but, so far as I understand them, it seems to me that their astonishing success
arose chiefly from their grasp of the fact, earlier than

[1] By the bull of Paul III., *Regimini militantis Ecclesiæ*, dated
Sept. 27, 1540.

[2] "In 1749, when the Society seemed, externally, at the height of
its prosperity, it counted, in thirty-nine 'provinces,' 22,589 members."
— HUBER, *Jes. Orden*, K. V. 217.

[3] In addition to the usual three vows (poverty, chastity, and obedience), the Jesuits take a fourth vow of absolute devotion to the See of
Rome. From this has arisen their power in the Church.

[4] It is difficult, in dealing with the Order of Jesus, to keep a middle
course between the absurd panegyrics of its own writers and the
equally absurd denunciations of its opponents. While finding it
impossible to rid myself of prepossession towards the anti-Jesuit
writers, I have given no credence to the violent statements of those
authors who avail themselves of the libellous *Monita secreta* — an
obvious literary forgery — to build up, by hyperbole and insinuation,
a monstrous indictment against the Jesuits.

others, that systematic education can fashion men into almost any mental or moral shape. Not only did Loyola see that, to create a zealous and aggressive organization, he must make his Order a camp under military law, but he understood that, to prolong the spirit of zeal — which, in the face of immediate danger to the Church, it had been easy to arouse — the habit of obedience, the spirit of self-interest, the belief in the reality and the necessity of the Jesuit idea, must be instilled into and made an integral part of the plastic mind of youth. Devotion to the Church, he saw, must be made, by a definite and organized plan, the goal of education.[1] It must be made a habit, a very breath of life, hostile to the poisonous influence of schism, to the prevalent spirit of historical and scientific research, to the *Zeitgeist* of intellectual questioning.

But he was astute enough to perceive that the day for slavish devotion had gone by, to realize that enthusiasm for the Order of Jesus must come from a sense of power, that its solidarity must be the joyful cohesion of advancing conquerors. He fostered, therefore, a consciousness of strength, but took care that this feeling should rest upon a far different basis within the Order than without. His clergy, he determined, should be made truly learned,[2] that they might have the firm sense of power which knowledge alone can give. The education of the laity, on the contrary,

[1] The fourth part of the *Constitutiones* and the *Ratio Studiorum* are saturated with this spirit of devotion. Everything must be done "*Ad Majorem Dei Gloriam*"; that is, to the glory of God as interpreted by the Order of Jesus. Literature is to be expurgated, philosophy is to be restricted, theology is to be limited, so that nothing inimical to the tenets of the Order shall be brought to the attention of impressionable youth.

[2] To this end they are allowed to mingle in secular affairs, to read heretical writings, and, in general, to lead a freer life than is permitted to other religious.

was to be made elaborately superficial, in order to give them that vanity of learning which is the best safeguard against real thought and progressive study. By inflating the secular mind with vapors of false attainment, he not only stifled dangerous speculations, but he created a medium favorable to the influence of the astute minds of the clergy. Perhaps this is not, baldly, the conscious goal of the Jesuits, but their instructions concerning education have, I am convinced, this general tendency.

It is maintained[1] that the Order of Jesus is indifferent and, indeed, hostile towards popular education — that to this spirit is due its restriction of teaching to the secondary schools and universities. While it is evident that its policy would be easier of maintenance among an ignorant people, still I cannot but find, perhaps unjustly, a deeper reason for its neglect of primary instruction. It appears to me that, with characteristic keenness, Loyola secured his ends without instilling the spirit of his Order into children; he perceived it to be better to take youth at the impressionable period of early adolescence in order either to fill it with the half-mystic, half-military spirit of Jesuitism, or to puff it up with a vapor of sham learning. He wasted little energy, therefore, upon primary instruction; but bore

---

[1] For example, by Compayré: "A permanent and characteristic feature of the educational policy of the Jesuits is, that, during the whole course of their history, they have deliberately neglected and disdained primary instruction. The earth is covered with their Latin colleges ; and wherever they have been able, they have put their hands on the institutions for university education ; but in no instance have they founded a primary school. . . . The truth is that the Jesuits neither desire nor love the instruction of the people. . . . The ignorance of a people is the best safeguard of its faith, and faith is the supreme end." — *Hist. of Ped.*, 142. Cf. *Doct. de l'éd. en France*, I. 170 *et seq.* See, in this connection, the Order of Aquaviva, Feb. 22, 1592, "*De non admittendis pueris ad Scholas*"; Pachtler, *Rat. Stu.*, I. 311.

with the whole force of his teaching-machinery upon the transition period of growth, upon that critical time when the grasp of instinct is loosening, and that of reason is as yet weak. By this concentration of energy the Order accomplished tasks which, in a broader field of teaching, might have been impossible.

I have spoken of Loyola's plan as though it were the sum of the Jesuit education. He was, indeed, the author and promoter of their system of teaching; but for more than fifty years, the wisest and subtlest minds of the Society discussed, tested, and compared its details, adding to it, modifying it, and strengthening it, as occasion taught them,[1] until, under Aquaviva, the fifth general of the Order, it took final shape in the *Ratio Studiorum*, which is, to-day, substantially the rule and practice of the Jesuit teaching.[2]

---

[1] The fourth part of the *Constitutiqnes*, that relating to education, was begun in 1540. The first draft of the *Ratio Studiorum* was published in 1584, but it was not until 1599, after criticism, discussion, and trial throughout the "Provinces" of the Order, that it was formally promulgated. As the *Ratio* is verbose and is, in the main, simply an amplification of Part 4 of the Constitution, I have, in general, referred to the latter authority, using the edition of Pachtler.

[2] "That all the modifications have not altered the *essentials* of the *Ratio* appears from the letter which the general of the Order, P. Beckx, addressed in 1854 to the Austrian Minister of Worship, wherein he designated the *Ratio* as the rule (norm) to whose unalterable principles the Order holds fast and must hold fast, and which can be amended only in detail to meet the exigencies of the times. He specifically declares that the chief end of the Humanistic education is the formal culture of the mind, and opposes the unwarranted extension of science-teaching into the gymnasia. 'The gymnasium must remain what it is proper for it to be, a gymnastics of the mind, consisting, not so much in material as in formal culture, not at all in the gathering together of multitudinous, heterogeneous knowledge, but in the right, natural, and gradual unfolding and improvement of mental power.'" — HUBER, *Jes. Ord.*, K. VII. 373. Cf. letter of Father Root-

The foundation of the Jesuit system of education rests, without question, upon the development of the individual so far as he is related to the Society, the entire suppression of the individual so far as concerns himself. The child, in their scheme, is not to be brought to his own perfection, but is to be moulded into a symmetrical and unchangeable pillar of the Jesuit Order. He is to become, not a human temple, but an infinitesimal fraction of the Church Jesuitical. Relentless is the military axiom that the discipline of the army must rest upon the absolute effacement of the individual. Seeking this military perfection, the Jesuits studied the child, perhaps as he had never before been analyzed, but they utilized their knowledge of him, not to raise him to his highest independent development, but simply to employ his strength — and his weakness, too — in the service of their Order.[1]

Not content, however, with self-perpetuation by the education of their own priests, the Jesuits strove, with wonderful success, to gain control of all instruction.[2] Using a rigorous spirit of selection in the choice of its own members, the Society laid a guiding hand upon all secular education and created for the Church, thereby, a great militia, with rank and file so thoroughly drilled in the Jesuitical tactics, with soldiers so bent to the Jesuit will, · that they

haan on the revision of the *Ratio* in 1832 ; Pachtler, *Rat. Stu.*, II. 228 (translated in Hughes, *Loyola*, 289 *et seq.*).

[1] " What gave the teaching of the Jesuits all its power was absolute obedience, which they strove to obtain through a sort of voluntary self-effacement on the part of their pupils. The latter lived in an atmosphere of minute and untiring surveillance. . . . The supreme art of the Jesuits was in making their captives love their prison." — DOUARCHE, *L' Univ. de Paris et les Jés.*, 159.

[2] " In 1710, the Jesuits directed the theological and philosophical teaching in more than eighty universities." — HUBER, *Jes. Ord.*, K. V. 217.

could be depended upon to fight blindly, and therefore passionately, upon the side of the Catholic Church.

This being granted, it is easy to see why their educational process is what we find it to be, — mere acquisition, real on the part of the Jesuits themselves, false on the part of the laity whom they control. Their course of study for those outside the priesthood is little more than the scholastic training,[1] stripped of its sombre garment of controversy, and wrapped in a graceful cloak of elegant disputation, a gauzy mantle of grammatical trifling. The barbarity of the Schoolmen, dreary as were their metaphysical disputes, is preferable to this shallow elegance, in which the soul of learning is bartered for empty and mellifluous words, in which the spirit is killed by the very perfection of the letter.

Their linguistic training had none of the vigor and earnestness which made the study of the ancients, in itself not very fruitful, a living impulse towards the Renaissance. Their pupils read extensively in the Greek and Latin authors, covering the entire field of philosophy, rhetoric, history, and poetry; they disputed concerning them, imitated them, aspired towards their perfection; but always it is a question of form, never of substance.[2] In expurgating

---

[1] *Const. S. J.*, IV. 14. "In Logica et Philosophia Naturali et Morali et Metaphysica doctrina Aristotelis sequenda est; et in aliis Artibus liberalibus et in commentariis tam hujusmodi auctorum quam Humaniorum Litterarum, habito eorum delectu, nominentur ii, quos videre discipuli, quosque ipsi Præceptores præ aliis in doctrina, quam tradunt, sequi debeant. Rector autem in omnibus, quæ statuerit, procedet juxta id, quod in universali Societate magis convenire ad Dei gloriam judicabitur." — PACHTLER, I. 58.

See, also, *Decret.* XXXVI., *Congr. gen.* XVI. 1 (Pachtler, I. 104); and *Rat. Stu.*, Reg. Prof. Phil., § 20 (p. 80).

[2] "Originality and independence of mind, love of truth for its own sake, the power of reflecting and of forming correct judgments, were

the classics, the Jesuit teachers were right; in extracting and epitomizing them to the point of desiccation, they were, it seems to me, wholly wrong. And this error came from no excess of zeal; it arose, rather, from a fear that if the pagan authors were given in unmutilated form, the pupils would suspect that wisdom and virtue had been born earlier than the foundation of the Catholic Church. To make the pagan authors heralds and prophets of Christianity was, avowedly, the aim of the Jesuit leaders.[1] To do this, it was necessary to take them to pieces and to suitably re-arrange the fragments before this perverted image could have its desired effect upon the pupils.

Their philosophical and theological teaching, too, was given at second-hand. Even Aristotle, too strong intellectual meat for these moral sucklings, must be diluted through Jesuit commentators; while, in theology, the Vulgate and St. Thomas must serve as screens to the Sacred Books.[2]

Finally, their system rests upon a distrust, almost a horror, of reasoning and research.[3] Theirs is not an edu-

not merely neglected — they were suppressed, in the Jesuits' system."
—QUICK, *Ed. Reform.*, 51.   See, also, P. Beckx, quot. p. 129.

[1] "These authors must be interpreted in such manner that, although profane, they all may become the heralds of Christ." — JOUVENCY, *Magistris scholarum inferiorum S. J. de ratione discendi et docendi.* (Paris, 1711), 176.   (Quot. by Compayré, *Doct. de l'éd.*, I. 189.)

[2] Cf. *Ratio*, 43 and 48; *Regulæ Prof. sacræ Scripturæ* and *Regulæ Prof. Scholasticæ Theologiæ.*

[3] " In iis etiam, in quibus nullum fidei pietatisque periculum subest, nemo in rebus alicujus momenti novas introducat quæstiones; nec opinionem ullam, quæ idonei nullius 'auctoris sit, iis, quæ præsunt, inconsultis; nec aliquid contra Doctorum axiomata communemque scholarum sensum doceat: sequantur potius universi probatos maxime Doctores et quæ, prout temporum usus tulerit, recepta potissimum fuerint in Catholicis Academiis." — *Ratio (Reg. Prof. sup. fac.)*, 38.

See, also, Ordinances of P. Oliva (1687) and P. Tamburini (1706)

cation of to-day for to-morrow; it is one of yesterday concerning subjects and modes of thought long dead and cast aside.

On the other hand, the Jesuit teaching was the first methodical instruction which had been organized on a great scale. Having a definite, though bad, object in view, it kept strictly to the path leading to that end. It never wandered or wasted time, but marched to its futile goal in military order, without hesitation or shadow of wavering. It must have been this orderliness and sureness of aim which attracted Bacon and drew from him praise that he could nowhere so unfittingly have bestowed. In so far, their system of education was superlatively good and, very rightly, served as a model for all time. Since their advent teachers have wandered and stumbled, and, indeed, still grope and clutch, but never since the supremacy of the Jesuit education have there been absent from the minds of the trainers of children some conscious aim — false or true — and some method — foolish or wise — of fulfilling that aim. Comenius, whose chief pedagogic merit, as we have seen, lay in his insistence upon method, undoubtedly drew all his inspiration, in this particular, from the *Ratio Studiorum*. The wide difference in result came from the different spirit of its application.

A certain good principle existed, too, in the Jesuit system of lay punishment.[1] By it the priestly teacher was

against the teachings of Descartes and Leibnitz. (Pachtler, *Rat. Stu.*, III. 121 and 122.)

[1] "Propter eos, qui tam in diligentia suis studiis adhibenda quam in iis, quæ ad bonos mores pertinent, peccaverint, et cum quibus sola verba bona et exhortationes non sufficiunt, Corrector, qui de Societate non sit, constituatur, qui pueros in timore contineat et eos, quibus id opus erit, quique castigationis hujusmodi erunt capaces, castiget." — *Const. S. J.*, IV. 16.

kept above the horrid details of the rod, which, even with them, was the accepted medicine for human depravity in those cases where persuasion and argument had failed.

In questions of health the Jesuits were wise and careful. They required early and regular hours of going to bed, a full and nourishing diet, short hours of study,[1] and much exercise and play in the open air. An excellent spirit of gayety and comradeship pervaded their teaching. The priests took part in boyish games, encouraged healthful and innocent amusements, and initiated those elaborate theatrical performances which, in their day, were famous.

On the whole, then, the instruction given by the Jesuits was, in itself, not bad. It was superficial, frivolous, and conduced to the making of "great boys, not men"; but it was methodical, cheerful, and painstaking. The *education* given by the Jesuits was, on the other hand, wholly bad; first, as I have shown, because it totally suppressed the individual, robbing the child of his birthright of character; secondly, because it used bad pedagogic tools — prizes, decorations, and elaborate rewards,[2] and bad methods of moral pressure — spying and tale-bearing;[3] and, thirdly, because the spirit of the Jesuits, a spirit which by no possibility could have failed to permeate their teaching and

[1] "Id tatem peculiari cura animadvertum erit, ut temporibus valetudini corporis incommodis Scholastici non studeant; ut somno, quantum temporis satis sit, tribuant; et in laboribus mentis modum servent." — *Const. S. J.*, IV. 4.

[2] See *Rat. Stu.*, "Regulæ communes Professoribus classium inferiorum." (P. 114 of the ed. of 1635.)

[3] "A pupil could rid himself of certain punishments by denouncing another, and every pupil had to have a rival to watch and denounce him. Moreover, the plan of studies makes denunciation a duty, and every pupil is constituted, by this duty, a spy upon his fellows." — PAROZ, *Hist. univ. de la Péd.*, 136.

debauch their pupils, was wickedly casuistic.[1] Combat as they may the minor errors of the *Provincial Letters*, the testimony which Pascal there brought against them is too strong to be disproved. Their doctrines of "probability," of "intention," of the "justification of the means by the end," may have been necessary to carry out in their way the conquest upon which they had entered; they may honestly have believed that the salvation of mankind depended upon the success of their efforts;[2] the results, from their point of view, may have sanctified the doctrines; but the holders of such beliefs are not fit for the bringing up of youth; a body of men, however earnest, which advances by such arts must miserably fail in education, no matter how brilliant may be its teachers, or how apparently successful may be its schools. Whether or not it explicitly taught these doctrines, so long as it maintained them the Order was immoral, the education which it gave was sure to be bad, the pupils whom it taught were bound to be perverted.

It was against this cardinal immorality, and against its

[1] See the *Provincial Letters*, especially the fourth and fifth. Against the Jesuit contention that their evil casuistry, if it ever existed, is a thing of the past, we have the testimony, among others, of Cartwright (*Jesuits*, Part II. 145 *et seq.*), and of Bert (*La morale des Jés.*) who quote from modern Jesuit writers of standing and popularity, and show that immoral casuistry still forms a part of the Order's pedagogy. The whole question is one of evidence, and, to me, the weight of it is against the Jesuits.

[2] "Their object is not to corrupt manners ; that is by no means their design. But neither is their sole object the reforming of them ; that would be impolitic. This is their aim : they have so good an opinion of themselves as to believe that it is desirable and, indeed, essential to the good of religion that their influence shall be extended everywhere, and that they shall control all consciences. . . . Having to deal with persons of every condition and nationality, they must have casuists to suit the diversity." — PASCAL, *Prov. Let.*, V. 87.

propagation as Christianity, that, it seems to me, the Jansenist movement arose in protest. Ostensibly, the battle between the Jesuits and the Jansenists was fought over issues centring around the famous Five Propositions concerning Divine Grace.[1] None but the subtlest of theologians could presume to argue upon these propositions; and, had they been the real ground of the quarrel, the discussion, doubtless, would have confined itself to the wrangling doctors then so plentiful. But I venture to assert, after as full a study as my theological ignorance has permitted, that the real difference between these factions of the Church lay much deeper than the interpretation of these Five Propositions and the occult distinctions between *fait* and *droit*.[2] There were present, of course, the political forces which entered into all theological controversies, but, greater than

[1] Beard (*Port Royal*, I. 247) records the Five Propositions "in all their original obscurity" as follows: —

"I. Some commandments of God are impossible of performance to just men, according to their present strength, even though they be willing and striving to perform them; and the grace which would make these commandments possible is also wanting to them.

"II. In the state of fallen nature, no resistance is ever made to internal grace.

"III. In order to produce merit or demerit in the state of fallen nature, liberty from necessity is not required in man, but liberty from constraint is sufficient.

"IV. The Semi-Pelagians admitted the need of prevenient internal grace for all actions, even for the beginning of faith; and they were heretics, inasmuch as they would have this grace to be such as the will of man could either resist or obey.

"V. It is a Semi-Pelagian error to say that Christ died or shed his blood for all men, universally."

Cf. Ste. Beuve's treatment of the Propositions (*Port-Roy.*, II. 103).

[2] See Pascal, *Prov. Let.*, XVII. and XVIII. The famous distinction was first made by Antoine Arnauld in his *Second Letter to a Duke and Peer*, published in 1655. See Beard, *Port Roy.*, I. 254.

these, were the moral forces that permitted of no other outcome than the martyrdom, if we choose to call it so, of the Port Royalists. To the lay mind their doctrine of grace was essentially that of Calvin,[1] and I cannot but think that, upon the common ground of moral responsibility, the two beliefs were identical; therefore, the Jansenist movement was, to all intents and purposes, a protest against the essential immorality of the Jesuits, just as the Lutheran movement was a protest against the real immorality of the Papacy. Their theology was Calvinistic, but their spirit was fundamentally Lutheran.

The Jansenist uprising may be said to have produced a fivefold result — first, in the tremendous theological controversy relative to the efficacy of Grace, the echoes of which still linger; secondly, in the revival of asceticism and the birth, within the Church of Rome, of that hyper-conscientiousness which Calvin had engendered in the Protestant fold; thirdly, in the advent of woman as a power in spiritual leadership; fourthly, in a revolution in literary style, based upon the ascetic simplicity of Port Royal and perfected in the *Provincial Letters* of Pascal; fifthly, in a reform in the spirit of Catholic teaching, to bring it into harmony with the world-force acting without the Church.

[1] Gibbon, although scarcely a competent witness, says, cleverly (*Decline and Fall*, etc., III. 215): "The Church of Rome has canonized Augustine and reprobated Calvin. Yet as the real difference between them is invisible even to a theological microscope, the Molinists are oppressed by the authority of the saint, and the Jansenists are disgraced by their resemblance to the heretic." In the valuable discussion of the controversies regarding predestination and grace in Le Clerc's *Bibliothèque Universelle* (T. XIV. 157) we read: "In regard to free-will and the efficacy of grace, the principal difference existing between them" (the disciples of St. Augustine) "and the Protestants, consists in the fact that the Augustinians, imitating their master, pick their phrases much better than Luther and Calvin."

With the literary revolution that sprang from Port Royal
we need not concern ourselves; with the labyrinthine theological discussion and the swarm of books and pamphlets
which it evoked I am not competent to deal, even were
the study productive of anything except utter bewilder-
ment.[1] It is in the new *rôle* given to women by this
heresy, and in its reform of education, that we are interested.

The greatest leader in this struggle, not for a new faith,
but for a purer, simpler faith, and a direct, unflinching
standard of morality, was the Abbot of St. Cyran.[2] He
and his close friend, Jansen, Bishop of Ŷpres,[3] resting their
faith upon the teaching of St. Augustine, from which the
Church had drifted into Semi-Pelagianism,[4] steeped themselves in his writings, and, after a lifetime of study, Jansen
wrote a Calvinistic exposition of him, called the *Augustinus*. Meanwhile M. de St. Cyran had found, in the Abbey
of Port Royal, which was under his spiritual charge, a marvellous woman, "Mère Angelique " Arnauld. Under his
guidance she brought to an even higher standard of devotion this abbey, which, coming to it as a young girl, she
had already transformed from a lounging-place of court
ladies into a real house of prayer and good works. Furthermore, by sheer force of her extraordinary will, she
gathered about her the larger part of her family, its men,

[1] To gain an idea of the literature of the controversy, see the list of
more than three hundred writers, most of them voluminous, given in
the *Dict. des Jansenistes.*

[2] Jean du Vergier de Hauranne, born at Bayonne in 1581, died, after
five years' imprisonment, in 1643.

[3] Cornelis, "son of Jan," was born, of peasants, in Holland in
1585. His *Augustinus* was not published until after his death (of the
plague), in 1638.

[4] For the "*sentiments*" of the Semi-Pelagians, see the *Bibliothèque Universelle* of Le Clerc, VIII. 221.

under the leadership of Antoine Arnauld, establishing a monastery upon the fervent and ascetic rule which she had instituted at Port Royal. When we remember that this family of Arnauld was one of the great intellectual families of France,[1] that its members who forsook the world at the instigation of this masterful woman were its greatest figures, and that those whom they gathered about them were lights of the French court only less shining, we can understand how stern was the rebuke given by their simple and God-fearing lives, and how instinctive was the dread of them which arose among the Jesuits, arch-casuists as they were, and open supporters of the prevailing standards of morality. Richelieu, too, had his private grudge against Jansen,[2] and was only too glad to further the charge of heresy brought by the Order of Jesus against the *Augustinus.* M. de St. Cyran, of course, supported the orthodoxy of the treatise, and his devoted spiritual flock at Port Royal sustained him. The Abbot was imprisoned, and the Port Royalists were subjected to intermittent persecution. When this persecution was at its height, and the Five Propositions were under examination and probable condemnation by the Holy See, there arose a new champion for Port Royal, one who brought the controversy out of the cloister and the antechamber of the court into the light of popular interest and enthusiasm. When the cause seemed most hopeless, Pascal published the *Provincial Letters,*[3] and inaugurated, not only a new era in the Catholic Church, but an epoch in literature.

[1] For the Arnaulds, see Ste. Beuve, *Port-Roy.,* Liv. I.; and Book I. of Beard's *Port Royal;* also, Tollemache, *French Jansenists.*

[2] On account of his *Mars Gallica,* a violent attack on the Cardinal's policy.

[3] See the over-dramatic account of their origin in Ricard, *Prem. Jan. et Port-Roy.,* 366 *et seq.*

Blaise Pascal and his sister Jacqueline[1] are among the extraordinary figures of history. He, a marked scientific genius, she, one of the most poetic of natures, both threw themselves into the Jansenist controversy with the zeal and consuming self-sacrifice of the martyred saints. Both died at an early age, destroyed by the flames of their own ardor, but not until they had changed the whole face of the controversy in which their part was so conspicuous. Around them and the Arnaulds the supreme interest of Jansenism centres; but hundreds of other minds, the most brilliant in France, fill the scene of Port Royal, and make the study of this heresy, wholly apart from its theological side, one of the most fascinating of the world's smaller dramas. Unfortunately, we cannot pursue it. In spite of the brilliancy of the Port Royal group, in spite of the power and popularity of the Arnaulds, in spite of the sacrifice of the two Pascals, the Jansenist uprising was quelled, and its adherents were driven into the Netherlands. The Jesuits outwardly triumphed, and had still before them their most prosperous years; nevertheless, a handful of exiles, to most men merely a name, to many men a byword and a hissing, the Port Royalists had really won the victory. A mortal blow had been given to the Order of Jesus by the fourth *Provincial Letter*.

A recent Jesuit writer[2] points with some complacency to the fact that the men of the Reign of Terror were the first generation for two hundred years that had been denied the privilege of a Jesuit education. Rather ought he and his to hide their heads in shame that two hundred years of

---

[1] See Cousin's brilliant monograph regarding her.

[2] Hughes, *Loyola*, 20. Cf. Crétineau-Joly (T. IV., Ch. III. 210). "It was not while they" (the Jesuits) "occupied the Collège Louis-le-Grand that the Robespierres, the Camille Desmoulins, Frérons, Talliens, Cheniers, and so many such, attended."

Jesuitical control could not end otherwise than in the Reign of Terror. We are accustomed to say that Rousseau lighted the torch of the French Revolution; perhaps we ought rather to assert that it was kindled, more than a hundred years earlier, by Angelique Arnauld, and the fierce recluses, all soul and conscience, who hovered like accusing angels over the self-doomed monarchy.

To interpret the work of the Jansenists in education it is essential to understand their attitude towards children. Holding the doctrine of foreordination, though in softer form than that of wrathful Calvinism, their feeling towards their pupils was one of immense and tender yearning. Believing salvation ordained for only certain pre-selected lambs, they nevertheless besought it, fervently, for all their flock, and mournfully prepared each little soul — which they shuddered to think destined for eternal wrath — for the rare possibility of everlasting bliss. This enfolding, womanly tenderness of the men of Port Royal,[1] their intense sympathy for these innocent victims of Divine vengeance, is one of the great *human* pictures of history. There is something profoundly pathetic in these stern monks, self-torn from earthly affairs, self-separated from love and domesticity, warming within their hearts their little charges, and trying, clumsily, to create a sort of home for them. A sad hearth, perhaps, with cruel Divine *in*justice ever impending; but, still, a better home than the worldly ones from which they came, in that it held human sympathy for the children and in that it strove towards their comprehension and development. "I would you could read in my heart," said M. de St. Cyran,[2] "how great is my affection

---

[1] See the conversation of De Saci reported by Fontaine (Ste. Beuve, *Port-Roy.*, III. 416).

[2] Ste. Beuve, *Port-Roy.*, III. 398.

for children." Said one of his disciples regarding him:[1]
"M. de St. Cyran's love, being catholic and universal like
his faith, brooded these little lost souls and, since Jesus
Christ shed his blood for their salvation, he could but
think himself blessed in giving his life to succoring them."
This brooding love inspired him with the idea of the
"Little schools." He did not live to establish them, but
his followers founded them in harmony with his teachings
and wholly in his spirit.[2]

This attitude towards children, though sixteen centuries
old, was a new one to the modern world. Seldom before,
since Jesus taught it and made it a fundamental part of
Christianity, had this spirit towards children been exhibited;
never before had it been shown in a way so marked and so
impressive. It held the germ of a complete ethical revolution. The Protestant leaders in education had possessed
themselves, in a measure, of this sympathetic quality;
Comenius especially had understood its power in the training
of the young; but it remained for these ascetics of Port
Royal to show the womanly tenderness, the feminine self-
projection into the plane of infancy, that are the bases of
true education. This is the attitude in which we try to
put ourselves to-day; it is the heart of the Froebelian
movement; but is it always present in our systems of
teaching? We have taken children out of the shadow of
avenging Deity, but, in so doing, have we always secured
to them the atmosphere of sympathy which is the essential
moral nourishment of childhood, and of which these stern
and pessimistic monks were so wisely lavish? There was
nothing of the sentimental in their treatment of children;
still less was there a trace of effeminacy in the Jansenists,

[1] M. de Ste. Marthe. Quoted by Ste. Beuve, *Port-Roy.*, III. 412.
[2] See the interesting summary of the principles of their pedagogy
given by Ricard, *Prem. Jan. et Port-Roy.*, Ch. IV., § 2.

whose very nuns were virile. But to the men of Port Royal was given that till then unknown stimulus of feminine influence necessary to the development of a natural plan of education. The "Little schools" were controlled by the monks of Port Royal, but the rulers and leaders of the moral struggle for which Port Royal stood were, it is evident, the nuns. France, having been the first to give her women intellectual freedom, was also the first to give them their rightful place as moral leaders. The influence of such women as those of the Hôtel de Rambouillet, on the intellectual side, had been immense,[1] and had carried France far ahead of her sister nations. That of the women of Port Royal was to be greater still, for it was to bring about the moral regeneration of Europe. Such forces as this of Jansenism are, humanly speaking, slow. The Jesuits, with their false morality, were to have nominal power for still another century; Pompadour and Du Barri were yet to sully the throne of France; and the *philosophes* were to possess, for a time, all literature; but after these the *carmagnole* was to be danced; the women of the people were to knit on the Place de la Révolution; the Year One was to be proclaimed; and out of this horrid travail were to be born the free man, the free woman, and the free child.

From womanly sympathy with and feminine comprehension of the child sprang the Jansenist education. The revolt against Jesuitical casuistry was but another form of it. Angelique Arnauld hated untruth and scorned subterfuge. She taught her women to hate and scorn them too. Fixing on these lines the direction of the Jansenist movement, she gathered about her, as all great moral souls ever

---

[1] " . . . in the elegant *salons* of the Italian Hôtel de Rambouillet, the national speech took on suppleness and grace, unhappily spoiled by affectation ; in the desert of Port Royal, it learned strength and masculine energy." — RICARD, *Prem. Jan. et Port-Roy.*, 304.

have done and ever will do, the scattered forces of morality, and inspired the abbesses who succeeded her to stand out against the Jesuits. With four loyal bishops,[1] a handful of monks, and a still smaller group of nuns, Port Royal did battle with Mazarin, with France, with Rome itself, — and won.

The schools of the Jansenists, modestly — perhaps not ingenuously — called "Little schools," existed less than twenty years, and during much of that time led a precarious life. Held sometimes at Port-Royal-in-the-Fields, sometimes in private houses, during a few years of comparative prosperity in Paris, they were feeble things, and in them were trained, altogether, a mere few hundred children. They seem indeed "little" beside the prosperous, well-ordered institutions of the Jesuits, crowded with the French *noblesse*. But their spirit, as we shall see, soon dominated France, their text-books became models even for their enemies, and their spirit — slowly but absolutely — changed the course of education.

It is for this spirit that we owe our chief debt to the Jansenists. Their methods of teaching and their text-books were simply its embodiment. Their war against the Jesuits, in which that body received its death-wound, was but an irresistible impulse from it. Their martyrdom in defence of the Five Propositions, which, so far as the nuns were concerned, were vain theological quibbles, was a part of the same steadfastness in the cause of truth. In their relations with children this spirit took the form of absolute sincerity, scrupulous fidelity, a single eye to the child's own best development, the cultivation of everything good in him and the suppression of everything evil, and a constant tender watchfulness over him. Add to these the

---

[1] See Beard, *Port Roy.*, II. 189 *et seq.*

sympathy that was inspired by their doctrine of Divine grace, and we have the explanation of the immense power of the Jansenist influence in education.[1]

The Jesuits had in view little more than grace, polish, and a vain, superficial learning; the Jansenists aimed at solidity, thoroughness, and the humility of real knowledge. The Jesuits studied language in order to attain elegance, the Jansenists in order to give full meaning to the truth. The Jesuits studied the classic authors from the outside, weaving over them an arabesque of grammatical cobweb; the Jansenists studied them through and through, reverencing their beauty of thought more than their finish of form. The Jesuits clung to the scholastic torture of making, even with infants, the study of Latin the beginning of all learning; the Jansenists built up their teaching upon the mother-tongue,[2] thereby not only smoothing the stony road to learning, but redeeming the beautiful French speech from its disgraceful bondage. The Jesuit teaching was bookish, pedantic, and syntactical; the Jansenist was conversational, natural, and free from many of the barbarities of scholasticism. Finally, strange as it may appear, the Jansenists accepted the enlightened opinions of Descartes, which the Jesuits rejected, based their teaching in matters of science and philosophy upon his, and gave thereby a strong impulse to the progress, within the Church, of Baconian principles.

We may say, too, that with the Port Royalists began the evolution of the text-book as a tool of teaching. Books for pupils had not been wanting, and the scholastics had heaped volume upon volume into mountains of well-nigh worthless learning. The Jesuits, also, had prepared many books adapted to their ways and ends of teaching. But

---

[1] See Ste. Beuve, *Port-Roy.*, Liv. 4me. ; and Beard, *Port Roy.*, II. 132 *et seq.*

[2] Cf. Ricard, *Prem. Jan.*, Ch. IV., § 5.

neither the ponderous works of the Schoolmen nor the warped puerilities of the Society of Jesus were real text-books, — they were not, that is, perfect and articulate skeletons for the teacher to flesh-clothe.   It remained for *Messieurs de Port-Royal* to produce true text-books; not flawless ones, indeed, but soundly planned, and built upon such lines that growth and expansion could safely rest upon them for many years to come.

Three names are conspicuous in connection with the text-books of Port Royal, — Antoine Arnauld, to whom the *Geometry* as well as the plan, and a large share of the execution, of the *Logic* are due; Lancelot, most modest of self-effacing Jansenists, who wrote the grammars and, with Arnauld, the general treatise on grammatical science; and Nicole, not of the inner brotherhood of Port Royal, but one of the hardest and most fertile workers in their cause.   We cannot examine the writings of these men; indeed, the study of dead text-books is a melancholy quest ; enough to know that they are based upon Port Royal principles. The authors use the mother-tongue as the vehicle of study — Greek, for example, being divorced from Latin ; they avail themselves largely of *viva voce* methods, and languages are taught, to a remarkable degree, through conversation.   The child is treated as a rational and dignified being, and as one having a definite law of development, worthy of consideration.   In short, the spirit of these writings is broad, honest, earnest, far-seeing, and Cartesian.[1]

Says Paroz, in his *Histoire Universelle de la Pédagogie:* [2] "If France had carried forward the educational work begun by Port Royal, she would be almost two centuries farther forward.   The whole of the eighteenth and the first third of the nineteenth centuries were chained to barren theories

---

[1] See Beard, *Port Roy.*, II.   [2] 158.

in philosophy and economics; it is only within a very few years that good educational books have again begun to appear in France, taking up the thread where Louis XIV. broke it." A generalization true in so far as it is not contradicted, as all broad statements must be, by specific exceptions.

Thus the two tendencies — that of the Jesuits towards evil, that of the Jansenists towards good — wrestled within the Church and the latter, in its very defeat, overthrew the former. But aloof from this contest, however they may have been affected indirectly, stood the mass of Roman Catholics, sympathizing as little with the casuistry of Jesuitism as with the heresy of Jansenism. This majority could be affected only by an impulse from the court. Although a priest-ridden age, that of Louis XIV. until Madame de Maintenon's ascendency, was far from being a fanatical one; and the king was little disposed to continue that regency of the Church which, previous to his majority, had been the normal condition in France. His death, however, would probably restore ecclesiastical dominion. Immense significance attached, therefore, to the choice of tutor for his son the Dauphin and his grandson, the Duke of Burgundy, called the "Little Dauphin." For the former duty was selected Bossuet, the awful Bossuet, whose orations we admire and never read; for the latter was chosen, in due time, Fénelon.[1] Around these two men gathered court factions, for upon one or both of them, if the old order returned, would rest the government of France whenever death should remove the *Grand Monarque*. But death delayed in cutting short so unique a career, and both the Dauphin and his son died before their ancestor, leaving

---

[1] François de Salignac de la Mothe-Fénelon was born at the Château de Fénelon (Périgord), Aug. 6, 1651, and died at Cambrai (virtually in exile), Jan. 7, 1715.

poor France not only at the mercy of a regency, but in the hands of men far different from either the honest, though autocratic, Bossuet or the mild and saintly Fénelon.

Long before the "Little Dauphin's" death, however, Fénelon had brought himself into conflict with his old master, Bossuet, and with the court, by his unwise zeal in supporting the notorious Madame Guyon and her doctrines of modified Quietism.[1] What may have been Fénelon's real position in this affair, what political intrigue may have been brought against him, we need not inquire ; sufficient that his connection with this schismatic transcendentalism banished him from court to the safe seclusion of his Archbishopric of Cambrai and separated him from his beloved royal pupil. His educational work was done, however; overdone, I fear, since he had not only curbed the headstrong and passionate nature of the boy, but had transformed him into a morbid zealot kept only by royal pressure outside the cloister.[2] But this result came rather from the intensity than from the ill-direction of his training. The tutor's ambition had overleapt itself, but its leap was rightly aimed. There must have been power in the method

[1] Madame Guyon's doctrines are set forth, principally, in the *Moyen court de faire oraison* and in the *Explication du Cantique des cantiques*. It seems to have consisted, mainly, in the attainment of a state of passive ecstasy : —

" L'abandon parfait, qui est le clef de tout l'intérieur, n'excepte rien, ne réserve rien, ni mort, ni vie, ni perfection, ni salut, ni paradis, ni enfer. L'âme ne se sent plus, ne se voit plus, ne se connaît plus ; elle ne voit rien de Dieu, n'en comprend rien, n'en distingue rien ; il n'y a plus d'amour, de lumières, ni de connoissance." — *Livre des Torrents* (Quot. by La Bruyère, *Dial. sur le Quiét.*, 612 and 630). For Fénelon's connection with this heresy, see Brunetière, *Nouv. études crit.*, II. 27, and Upham, *Madame Guyon and Fénelon.*

[2] See La Harpe's *Éloge de Fénelon* (*Œuv. Comp. de Fén.*, X. 386) ; also Saint-Simon. (Quot. by Janet, *Fénelon*, Ch. III. 41.)

as well as strength in the man to have overcome such a nature as that of the "Little Dauphin," — headstrong, passionate, self-indulgent, — transforming it into that of a pious prig.

Most persons have read *Télémaque*, many the *Fables* and the *Dialogues of the Dead*. In all these Fénelon's plan is clear; it is mainly one of teaching by indirection. It is an attempt to instruct, especially upon the ethical side, through the use of narrative, and to surprise the pupil with a sort of climax of moral truth. All these books, especially the *Fables*, were composed to provide for certain necessities of the Prince's training, and they are by no means general pedagogic treatises; rather are they models upon which every teacher who wishes to follow Fénelon's plan must build new fables, new dialogues, and new romances suited to his several pupils. To us, in these days of literary sub- tility, when the value of the moral is in proportion to its obscurity, these teachings of Fénelon seem painfully obvi- ous. Too marked indeed, even to Louis, was the lesson given by *Télémaque* ; and, however innocent Fénelon may have been of a definite attempt to satirize his reign, the old king was undoubtedly glad to seize upon his Quietist leanings as an excuse for removing him from the court. But the book itself could not be put out of the way so easily. Together with the *Dialogues* and the earlier treatise *On the Education of Girls*, it had a marked effect upon both the political and the educational growth of France. Through these books, quite as much, perhaps, as through the writ- ings and text-books of the Jansenists themselves, did the Port Royal influence make headway. For Fénelon, in his spirit, was a thorough Jansenist. Good Catholic and loyal subject though he was, he had imbibed, unconsciously enough, the atmosphere of the Port Royal schools, and his teaching as well as his books were permeated with it.

His method of education is Jansenist in that it regards the child as an entity to be fully developed by rational methods, and one to be individually studied, so that the methods may be adapted to him. It is Jansenist in that it is gentle and sympathetic, and is scrupulous in its regard for simplicity and truth. Even its indirection, which savors of duplicity, and which Rousseau later developed into real deceit, is with Fénelon merely the expression of the necessity of adapting one's self to the child, of treating him with conversational freedom, and of using his ordinary, daily life to teach eternal truths. The *Fables* are kindergarten stories, "writ large" and distinctly labelled with their moral.

"Show them," says Fénelon,[1] speaking of the relations of the ideal teacher to his pupils, "the utility of the things you teach; . . . else study will seem to them abstract, barren, and hard. What use is it, they will say to themselves, to learn all these things which no one talks about and which have no relation to our actions? . . . One must always show them a definite and pleasant end to sustain them in their work, never attempting to compel them by hard and unreasoning authority."

"Never assume," he continues,[2] "except in extremity, an air of command, frightening children. . . . You will close their hearts and sear their consciences, without which education will be fruitless. Make them love you; let them be at ease with you, and not afraid to have you see their faults. To reassure them, be indulgent to those who wear no disguise before you. Appear neither astonished nor irritated by their evil propensities; on the contrary, pity their weaknesses." And again:[3] "Often it is a question only of not harassing children, of busying one's self in their

---

[1] *De l'éd. des filles (Œuv. Comp.,* VI. 26).   [2] *Ibid.*   [3] *Ibid.*, 107.

vicinity while watching them, inspiring them with trust, replying clearly and intelligently to their little questions, taking advantage of their natural disposition to acquire, correcting them patiently when they make mistakes or do wrong." Quotations might easily be multiplied to show the liberality and modern spirit of the gentle Archbishop.

Through Fénelon, then, whose orthodoxy and loyalty, until the unhappy affair of Quietism, were unquestioned, and who, after his banishment to Cambrai, was bitter, so far as bitterness was possible to him, in persecution of the Jansenists infesting his see, the influence of Port Royal was brought into the fold of the Church and established there at the very moment when the cause of Jansenism appeared most hopeless, and the triumph of Jesuitism seemed forever assured.

It is a singular spectacle, this of Fénelon, himself virtually an exile because of his heresies, vigorously pursuing other heretics, unjustly banned as he was, and for opinions closely akin to his. And more singular still is the figure of Madame de Maintenon, self-appointed missionary to His Most Christian Majesty, deadliest enemy of Jansenism, and of Fénelon, too,[1] adopting, in her school at St. Cyr, the educational ideas of both, and giving deep and permanent root there to those principles of enlightened liberty, the fruitage of which all of them — Jansenists, Fénelon, and Madame de Maintenon — would have united in condemning. Nevertheless, in the commonplace and rather vapid course of study at St. Cyr,[2] — that school for girls which,

[1] After his connection with Quietism. Before that time he was one of her trusted advisers.

[2] There were two distinct phases, during Madame de Maintenon's lifetime, in the very interesting and historically instructive experience of St. Cyr. In the first, the school was approximately secular, its pupils produced the *Esther* and *Athalie* which Racine wrote especially

next to his Majesty, received the largest share of Madame de Maintenon's attention, — is to be found, it seems to me, the germ of the wide educational opportunities now open to women.[1]

The nuns of Port Royal, strong as they were, and helpful as was their influence upon the teaching work of the monks, had not courage sufficient to make their schools for girls anything more than most rigid convent schools ;[2] but their zeal and sincerity, shaped by Fénelon in his educational work, and trained by Madame de Maintenon in her school for girls grew, in time, into the vigorous tree of feminine education, whose roots are in the public schools, and whose branches are pushing steadily upward into the rare ether of the universities.

for them, and its spirit was that of the lay schools of the Jesuits. In the second, through a sudden revulsion of feeling on the part of its founder, St. Cyr assumed a conventual aspect, and, while nominally more completely under Jesuit control than before, became, in fact, more closely akin to the Jansenist schools.

[1] See the very interesting comparison of Fénelon and Madame de Maintenon with Rousseau, in Girardin, *J.-J. Rousseau*, II., Ch. XII.

[2] See Jacqueline Pascal's *Réglemènt pour les enfants*, given in Faugère, *Let. de Jac. Pascal*, 228.

CHAPTER VII.

ROUSSEAU.

THE CHILD HAS A SOUL TO BE KEPT PURE.

HIS INFLUENCE ; HIS CHARACTER ; THE "CONFESSIONS" ; HIS CAREER ;
HIS WRITINGS ; ROUSSEAU AND LOCKE CONTRASTED ; THE INTER-
DEPENDENCE OF RELIGION AND EDUCATION ; THE FUNDAMENTAL
IDEAS OF THE JANSENISTS AND OF ROUSSEAU ; VIGILANCE ;
"ÉMILE" ; ITS PRINCIPLES ; THEIR ORIGIN ; ÉMILE'S EDUCA-
TION ; ITS DETAILS ; ITS FALLACIES ; ITS TRUTHS ; ITS INFLUENCE.

MADAME DE STAËL redeems a commonplace preface to
her immature *Letters on Rousseau* by one happy phrase.
She characterizes Rousseau[1] as "Him who has succeeded
in making a passion of Virtue." With feminine instinct,
she has seized a subtle fact missed by more learned critics.
So far as epigram can go, she has probed the mystery
of this weak man's power. Rousseau taught little that
was new; he borrowed unblushingly from books that he
affected to despise;[2] he was an egotist, often illogical, not
seldom insincere. How, then, did he and his books sway
this rigid world so that it still trembles? Here in America
he inspired the form of our Declaration of Independence
and the doctrines of our Democratic party.[3]   In France his

---

[1] *Œuv. Comp.*, I. 4.

[2] See, *e.g.*, the denunciations of Cajot, *Les plagiats de M*r* J. J. R.
de Genève sur l'éduc.*

[3] Especially through *Du contrat social*. Many of Rousseau's ideas
originated, however, with Locke, upon whose writings Jean-Jacques
drew freely.

absurdest paradoxes were law and gospel to the Jacobins. *Émile*, an unpractical treatise merging into a tiresome romance, is the one book on education of which none will hesitate to say, " Here begins an era in social development." Yet it contains scarcely an idea that is not already in the Greek and Latin literatures, in Rabelais, Montaigne, or Locke. Whole passages even, if we put faith in his detractors, are taken bodily from obscurer writings.

Why, then, is this stream of borrowed thoughts to-day a living force, while its creative springs are choked and half-forgotten? Something more than we now superficially see in the ideas, something more than we now pityingly learn of the man, must have belonged to Rousseau and to his books. Madame de Staël, it seems to me, has discerned this *something*, and has crystallized it in her phrase. Rousseau had the power — the only power that could make headway in his time — to raise virtue out of its usual place as a duty, out of its lower rank as an instinct, into the effective position of a passion. This moral enthusiasm of his, spreading through France, through Europe, and into America, became the greatest single force that modern history has known.

The Jesuits had preached a perfunctory, self-seeking virtue; the Jansenists, those "Christians who weep," had taught a true but hopeless and unattainable morality; the *philosophes* had gravely dissected the corpse of virtue, dead at their hands; the *femmes d'esprit*, singeing their wings in the candle of the court, had made epigrams upon the ten commandments in the intervals of breaking them; and the common people, the only real practisers of morality, had lived rightly in obedience to an instinct not far above the animal. It remained for Rousseau to quicken this objective virtue, this plaything of society, this groping of the people, into a vital passion, hurrying all — priests, philosophers, women, and dumb millions — into the vortex of revolution.

Himself a living emotion, Rousseau, during the few intense years of his literary productiveness, rose far above ordinary hysteria into a divine ecstasy, wherein his weak body and sensual mind often misled him, wherein he confused erotic with celestial visions, wherein he blindly battled, uncertain of his real aim; but through which he swayed France and made history.

I have no intention of reviewing that lesson in mental pathology called the *Confessions*. Rousseau's love of paradox led him, undoubtedly, to picture himself in evil, as he believed himself to be in everything, unlike all other men. To this conceit of singularity we owe the paraded frankness that none the less offends because prurient ignorance masquerades as innocence. To a study of *Émile*, however, the *Confessions* are a necessary footnote. They show the forces that, for forty years, caroused and quarrelled within him before Rousseau reached serious manhood, and was ready to utter truths strong with the bitter strength of self-abasement.

These confessions, the only published self-analysis pathologically complete, make plain the fatal defect of their author's moral structure. He was cursed with an inherited weakness of will which was fostered by mal-education. This champion of freedom was morally slavish. His imagination alone soared heavenward; he himself burrowed, inertly, in the dark places of earth.

A motherless boy, of a highly emotional temper, of a moral habit that lacked reactive force, he is brought up in a Calvinistic atmosphere by a weak father and an indulgent aunt. With a training exaggerating his natural defects, he is bound, at an early age, to uncongenial tasks, and, shirking them, is branded as a blockhead. He is of the stamp of man that does not struggle against odds, finding it so much easier, for the moment, to claim the Bohemian privilege of flight. A trifling incident[1] — the locking of the city gates while he is outside the walls of Geneva — gives him the necessary excuse, and he breaks loose from society in his sixteenth year, to enter it again only after his thirtieth year.

He crosses the Swiss border into Savoy, is received into the fold of the Church, as was the friendly custom towards Protestant vagabonds, — who found this a pleasant alternative to starvation, — is sent, for dogmatic training, to a vivacious little animal, Madame de Warens,[2] and leads with her and her chaotic household a pseudo-idyllic, kennel-poetic existence, in which he finds the happiness that prolonged youth and postponed responsibility give to weak and dreamy natures. He wanders in and out of her life, now into Italy, now into France, and back again to the arcadian bower of her farm-house *Les Charmettes*. One guesses that he fancied himself a modern Gil Blas, the echo of that immortal scamp is so distinct. But it is a *bourgeois* echo. Rousseau is too often a lackey in spirit, however exalted his sentiments; while Gil Blas, frankly servile, has yet a manliness of spirit, as well as a sense of humor, that save him from degradation.

On the other hand, Rousseau's love of nature is as deep and beautiful as it is rare. He has that feeling for the sublimity and dignity of the external world which, in the growth of materialism, has become almost a lost sense. This, and his unconquerable youthfulness, redeem these years with Madame de Warens from mere swinishness.

In his thirtieth year this idyl ends; he leaves *Les Char-*

---

[1] *Conf.*, Liv. I. 38 ; Morley, *Rousseau*, Vol. I. 28.
[2] *Conf.*, II. 44 ; Morley, I. 47 (Ch. III.).

mettes, goes to Paris, and plunges disastrously into political life, following an embassy to Venice.[1] Returning, he takes to himself a stupid and evil wench, Thérèse Le Vasseur,[2] and assumes, in a measure, the long-avoided burdens of society. The curse of weakness, however, has yet to fall upon him. Not content with escaping his share of neighborly duty, he shirks parental obligation, and sends his five children, against the pleadings of poor, ignorant Thérèse, to the foundling hospital.[3] This is the sombre background against which play the fires, celestial or volcanic, of the remainder of his ill-poised life.

In his fortieth year his intellect, or, rather, his emotions, for his genius was nervous rather than intellectual, dissever themselves from his baser side, and, in ten years of exaltation, of sensual tumult aggravated by bodily pain, he produces his four great books, — the *Discourse on Inequality*, *The New Heloisa*, the *Social Contract*, and, finally, *Émile.*[4]

In this period of exaltation, almost of emotional insanity, it is not Rousseau, lover of the wretched Thérèse, ungrateful dependent of Madame d'Épinay,[5] sickly worshipper of Madame d'Houdetôt, who speaks. It is some far higher voice using him as those better men, the Hebrew prophets, were used, as an emotional mouthpiece, unworthy otherwise than through exquisite keenness of intellectual vibration to be the herald of liberty. He was, to change the metaphor, the instrument with which some divine Orpheus chose to

[1] *Conf.,* VII. 286 ; Morley, I. 98.
[2] *Conf.,* VII. 321 ; Morley, I. 104.
[3] *Conf.,* VII. 335 ; Morley, I. 118.
[4] The *Discourse on Inequality* was published in 1753, *The New Heloisa* in 1761, the *Social Contract* and *Émile* in the spring of 1762.
[5] Grimm's Madame d'Épinay ; Madame d'Houdetôt was Madame d'Épinay's sister-in-law. See *Conf.,* VII., VIII., and IX.

tame the wild beasts of sensuality, greed, and vanity that were devouring the patient people, those people who, fired by the same strains, were soon to turn, and, with a cruelty taught by centuries of injustice, to rend their devourers.

Reaction followed the publication of *Émile*. The nervous strain had been too intense. Exasperated by unceasing physical pain, hounded on all sides, — by the priests because of his heresy, by the philosophers because of his theism, — driven even from Switzerland,[1] haunted, we hope, by the ghosts of his lost children, tried beyond measure by the unamiable and unfaithful Thérèse, Rousseau grew irritable and suspicious. This wretched condition may have been insanity,[2] the sad death to which it led may have been suicide.[3] What matter? Rousseau's paradoxes, that supreme paradox, his life, must remain enigmas until we learn the true relationship of mind to body, of soul to mind. It is vain to attempt to reconcile the man and his work, to try to explain how Jean-Jacques could write grandly of unpractised virtues. Many times, indeed, his sentiments, pure in expression, exalted in form, are plainly pasteboard, especially when they are used to mask his own misdeeds. But, in a far greater number of instances, his language is indubitably that of sincerity, of earnestness, of belief, — the language, indeed, of inspiration.

It is interesting to compare Rousseau with Locke, his avowed master in matters of education. Both were of a weak constitution, both suffered from painful chronic disease. But physical ills chastened Locke to serenity, temperance, and sweetness; while similar sufferings drove

---

[1] For the persecution of which Rousseau was a victim, see Morley, II., Ch. XI.

[2] Cf. Brunetière, *Études crit. sur l'hist. de la lit. fran.*, IV. 325. (*La folie de J.-J. Rousseau.*)

[3] Cf. Musset-Pathay, *Hist. de J.-J. R.*, I. 269.

Rousseau to irregularity, irritability, and a moroseness ending in mania. But, curiously enough, Locke preached a materialism inconsistent with his devout, unselfish practice; while the rebellious and unclean Rousseau, by his unswerving and hopeful theism,[1] made himself almost the sole bulwark against the atheism of the philosophers. From him, in part, sprang the healthful religious reaction that Rome and Geneva had been equally powerless to arouse. The exemplary Locke was the chief agent in establishing a pernicious doctrine of despair from whose consequences Europe was saved, in no small degree, by the evil Rousseau.

The movement of educational thought, it is evident, follows closely the changing phases of religious belief. Around the past, present, and future of childhood, religion centres itself, and it must therefore link itself with that natural modifier of evil and conserver of good, education. As the religious value and dignity of the child increases, so will the care of his education become of greater moment. The manifestations of this law, often obscure, are clearly apparent in the educational ideals of Comenius, springing, as they did, from his pan-Christian aims.[2] They are equally evident in the system of the Jesuits, founded upon a devouring ambition of ecclesiastical power. We have seen[3] a striking example in the dominant idea of the Jansenists,

[1] See *Profession de foi du vicaire Savoyard*, in *Émile* (Liv. IV. 295). "Though I be born on a desert island, though I see no other man than myself, though I never learn what once was done in a corner of the world; if I exercise my reason, if I cultivate it, if I make good use of the simple faculties which God has given me, I shall learn of my own impulse to know Him, to love Him, to love His works, to desire the good that He wills, and to fulfil, for His sake, all my duties upon earth. What can all the learning of mankind teach me more?" (p. 348.)

[2] See note, p. 92.

[3] See p. 141.

whose doctrine of grace compelled them to watch the child
unceasingly, lest, led astray by his evil nature, he break
the slender thread holding him to salvation.   Rousseau, no
less solicitous, based the necessity of vigilance upon an
opposite belief.   He feared from without what the Port
Royalists dreaded from within.   To him, good was natural,
and evil external; to them, evil was natural, and good not
only external but supernatural.   In other words, the Jansenist teachers believed themselves to have in keeping souls
lost from ˙the beginning, and to be saved only through
Divine intervention; while Rousseau believed the teacher
to guard souls saved from the beginning, and to be lost only
through human perversion, — antipodal creeds which reached
the same end in securing to the child a watchfulness that
is the price of education no less than of liberty.   This lesson
of pedagogic vigilance was a contribution to educational
progress second only to Rousseau's chief gift, the inspiration of moral fervor.

   Jean-Jacques's central idea, in his sleepless care of Émile,
is to keep the boy unspotted from the world.   He conceives
a soul not unlike Aristotle's image of the mind,[1] — a
smoothed tablet upon which Nature is to write the laws of
morality.   But it is a tablet upon which vice makes deeper
impress than virtue.   "Ignorance is not fatal," he declares,[2] "but error is."   Nature, Rousseau believes, is infallible.   She will develop virtue and knowledge in all
children, provided we shelter childhood so that her processes are neither disturbed nor distorted.   Nature has her
own ways of teaching; our duty is fulfilled when we allow

   [1] See *ante*, p. 106.
   [2] *Émile*, III. 171.   " Souviens-toi, souviens-toi sans cesse que l'ignorance n'a jamais fait de mal, que l'erreur seule est funeste, et qu'on
ne s'égare point par ce qu'on ne sait pas, mais par ce qu'on croit
savoir."

her freely to exert her influence. This mental *laissez faire* is Locke's doctrine of sensationalism carried, in the direction of free play, to its extreme. It does not involve, however, a derived doctrine of materialism; for Rousseau is steadfast in his acknowledgment of an inward power of moral discrimination, which he calls conscience.[1]

Taking, then, as his basis of belief, the assertion that every child is innately perfect, that good is from Nature and evil is from Man,[2] he finds the task of the teacher to be an actively negative one. The tutor must not teach the pupil, he must not attempt to directly mould his growth, but he must so hedge him about that evil shall enter only as he wills, and only in definite and well-directed sequence. This sequence is determined by the grouping of the child's development into three distinct periods. In the first, extending from birth to the age of twelve, he is to be made a perfect physical being; in the second, extending to the age of puberty, he is to be made a critical or understanding being; in the third, beginning with puberty, he is to blossom into a social and emotional man. Before taking up this plan of education, let us see upon what it is based.

In Rousseau's day the type of human perfection was the noble savage. By so far as the primitive state of man was attained, in that measure, it was believed, did humanity approach the ideal state of Eden. This noble savage, existing in some fair Pacific isle or on the banks of the Orinoco, was a favorite puppet of the eighteenth century. His was perfect happiness. Vice was unknown to him,

[1] "There is in the depths of the soul an innate principle of justice and of virtue through which . . . we judge our actions and those of others as good and bad, and to this principle I give the name, conscience."— *Émile*, IV. 324.

[2] "Ôtez nos funestes progrès, ôtez nos erreurs et nos vices, ôtez l'ouvrage de l'homme, et tout est bien." — *Émile*, IV. 315.

despair was a stranger, and death came only as ripeness comes to the fruit, the proper climax of a life of sunshine. The worship of this mythical savage was not unnatural. His naked freedom seemed the only sort possible in the hard and evil political conditions, the false and diseased social relations, preceding the great revolutions. Rousseau, an emotional vagabónd, thirsty for the spring of eternal youth with its primitive and irresponsible pleasures, could scarcely fail to join in the idealization of this untrammelled savage. He went still farther, and imagined the peasant, without aspirations, without emotions except of sense, without social obligations and conventionality, to be a kind of savage, placed in the midst of civilization to neutralize its evils. He idealized the peasant, extolled his passive virtues, and gave him a social weight that had no small effect in bringing about his subsequent freedom. Adopting this ideal wild man and his tamed prototype, the peasant, — both so different from their squalid and debased originals, — Rousseau reached the unwarranted conclusion that, since the natural man is perfect and the civilized man is vile, nature must be the true source of virtue. Therefore, he argued, Émile's education should be from nature, and the boy should be brought into contact with man only at the latest possible day, at the evil hour when that cursed relation can no longer be postponed.

This prime error gave birth to many others, and, in the very beginning, forced Jean-Jacques to alienate his model pupil from society and even from his kindred, in order to secure for him the necessary atmosphere of freedom. It forced him to make Émile an orphan, and to place him absolutely in the power of a tutor who should mould fate for him up to the very door of matrimony. A sad paradox, that impelled Jean-Jacques, after celebrating the holiness of the married state, after painting, in *The New Heloisa*, so exquisite a picture of home life, after arousing public opinion against the cruel baby-farming universal among the wealthier French, to destroy Émile's home and to consign him to the barren affections of a celibate tutor. By an added paradox, an odd perversion that limits Rousseau's system to bounds almost as narrow as those set by Montaigne and Locke, Émile is well-born and wealthy, — fortunate, therefore, in the very accidents which Jean-Jacques despised. But obscurer passages, as well as other educational writings of Rousseau, show us that these limitations are not to be permanent; they are unessential when all men shall be, or shall have been, Émiles. This first figure, this educational model, is a modified creation, an amphibious being, suited to the slime of the old order of things, as well as to the free air of the new. When his likeness shall have so multiplied as to create a society of Émiles, then the tutor will merge into the parent,[1] and rank and riches will expand into the rank of intellect and the riches of mutual helpfulness.

For Rousseau is distinctly an individualist-socialist; that is, he believes in the absolute mental and spiritual independence of man, but not in his social freedom. Fondly as he dreamed of the idyllic state of savagery, he was both too wise and too tame to refuse the idea of social obligation. "There is much difference," he says,[2] "between the natural man living in the midst of nature and the natural man dwelling in the social state. Émile is not a savage to be banished to a wilderness; he is a savage made to live in

---

[1] "The true nurse is the mother, just as the true teacher is the father. . . . The child . . . will be better brought up by a judicious though narrow father than by the most competent tutor in the world; because zeal supplies talent far more readily than talent supplies zeal." —*Émile*, I. 20.

[2] *Émile*, III. 221.

cities.   He must know how to make a living, to profit by
•his neighbors, and to live, if not like them, at least with
them."

The absolute freedom of his pupil is to end, therefore,
as soon as dawning manhood proclaims him a social creature.   At that moment, forsaking his pasturage in the free
field of nature, he is to be harnessed to the car of mutual
obligation and to be fastened with a yoke that only death
can throw off.   But, in the truly social state that is looked
forward to in the *Social Contract*, this yoke is of the lightest.

Behold, then, Émile, galloping in absolute happiness,
through the formative years !   He is an animal, pure and
simple, knowing no law except the inexorable "Hold!" of
circumstance, no guiding voice but the "Come!" of his
inclinations.   "Nature," Rousseau says, "cannot err," and
so long as she does not impose her automatic veto, the child
is right in doing as he pleases.   But — and this is a very
important limitation — this pure state of nature is encom-
passed by the impure state of man.   The sway of nature
cannot be absolute unless the child be isolated in a thrice-
guarded fold of ignorance.   This, however, is impossible.
No defence but has its vulnerable point.   A time must come
when knowledge of evil shall have taken full possession.
The innocence secured prior to that time can be little more
than artificial, maintained by sleepless vigilance.   To this
police task the tutor is chiefly to apply himself, serving as
a shield to the child, and, as the pupil develops, admitting
him, in elaborate and roundabout ways, to ever greater
acquaintance with evil.

Rousseau gravely lays bare much of the machinery, cum-
brous enough, of this artificial naturalism.   The spectacle
would be comic were it not haunted by the shadows of the
five children whose honest eyes would have shamed him
out of his folly of deceit.   In no place is his ignorance of

real children so apparent; in no part of *Émile* does his total lack of humor lead him so far astray. The theatrical tricks exhibited with such pride are so tawdry, so ridiculously inartistic, that it would be a dull child indeed who should fail to laugh them into oblivion. This pedagogic charlatanism needs no argument of refutation other than that given by Rousseau himself, who condemns old methods of teaching because they foster deceit, and yet bases his own system upon elaborately acted lies. What, we wonder, would be Émile's reverence for Jean-Jacques after he should have discovered, as any real child would, the strings that pulled the moral puppet-show, pretending to be a drama of real life?

Rousseau's deification of the untutored savage led him into another fallacy, a scorn of books.[1] Himself a book-spawner, a diligent reader in his special paths, an accused plagiarist, this scorn is, at least, humorous. It is a pity that the faculty of laughing at himself was not given to Jean-Jacques. It would have spared him much laughter from the rest of humanity. Indeed, it is a misfortune for even a genius to take himself too seriously. Remembering the mountains of useless books and the silly worship of the modest hills of good books, he sweepingly denounces all literature for youth, excepting one volume, *Robinson Crusoe*.[2] "Well-ordered brains," he says,[3] "are the surest preservers of knowledge;" but he forgets that books are the medium of exchange between these brains, that they are the common money into which present riches and past treasures of human growth and discovery are transmuted to serve as an inheritance for posterity and a common fund for mankind. He would deprive a child of this ready-made

---

[1] "I hate books; they teach one only to talk of things about which one knows nothing." — *Émile*, III. 194.

[2] *Émile*, III. 195. [3] *Ibid.*

fortune, and would make each brain create for itself, out of
the sphinx-like earth, all science, all art, and all philosophy. He would make each new-born being an absolute and
independent microcosm. "Let him not learn science, let
him invent it," he rather sententiously remarks.[1] And
again,[2] "The scientific air kills science." . . . "Émile
will never know optics. He will never have dissected
insects: he will not have counted the spots on the sun:
he will know neither microscopes nor telescopes. Your
learned pupils will deride him. They will not be wrong;
because, before using these instruments, I mean that he
shall invent them, and you are right in believing that that
will not be early."[3]

Rousseau is seldom inconsistent in the parallels he draws
between the childhood of the individual and that of society. Without formal purpose of comparison, he discovers
between these two embryonic states analogies that bear
directly upon his theories. Unfortunately, he could not,
even had he wished, study primitive man, and he had
deliberately forfeited the daily lessons given by a growing child. His savage, therefore, no less than his Émile, is
a creature of the imagination. Reasoning from this half-
known child to this unknown savage, he has little difficulty,
of course, in deducing a parallel order of natural development in harmony with his preconceived ideas. He finds his
imaginary child mentally self-sufficient and unsocial, and
there are children so unfortunately born; ergo, man is by
nature solitary and independent; ergo, society is artificial.
He finds the thoughts of the child to be simple and sense-
limited, as, superficially, they are; hence man is not, by
nature, a reflective being, and subtlety is the offspring of
civilization. He sees the child free from sentiment and

[1] *Émile*, III. 173.   [2] *Émile*, III. 183.   [3] *Émile*, III. 223.

complex emotions, — a most unwarranted observation; [1] — *ergo*, the passions of savages are limited, like those of beasts. Finally, he denies to the child the capacity to reason, and limits the savage to the narrow horizon of immediate physical deduction.

Scientific observation of mental processes, and patient study of primitive peoples, long ago exploded these false premises; but Jean-Jacques honestly maintained them, and, reasoning backward in his vicious circle, reached the conclusion that, since the savage has no new instincts except those invited or compelled by circumstance, so the child's development must await the pressing urgency of nature. From this springs his thesis that the social instinct arises only with the passions, that it must be defended from an earlier awakening, and that the time of its expansion should be, as long as possible, deferred.

To make good his conception of society as a secondary condition, not a primitive law, of mankind, he accepts Hobbes's doctrine of selfishness,[2] and bases the social instinct upon self-love. "When the power of an expanding soul," he says,[3] "identifies me with my neighbor, then I wish to spare him suffering only that I may not suffer; I interest myself in him through self-love, and the basis of" (the Golden Rule) "is in nature itself, that fills me with a desire for happiness in whatever place I feel a consciousness of myself. . . . The love of man derived from the love of self is the principle of human justice." Upon this rather uncertain foundation rests the glowing benevolence devel-

---

[1] "Je n'ai jamais rencontré de personnalité plus profonde que chez les enfants," says, with truth, Mgr. Dupanloup. *L'Enfant* (Paris, 1874), 22.

[2] See Thomas Hobbes, *Phil. Rudiments concerning Government and Society* (Vol. II. of Eng. Works, London, 1841), Ch. I.

[3] *Émile*, IV. 257 (note).

oped in Émile.   It has no root in philanthropy, but springs
wholly from self-love, which, to render inadequately the
carefully distinguished phrase of the French, is an outgrowth
of self-regard, the first instinct of the new-born child.   The
law of self-preservation involves this self-regard, which, as
it becomes conscious, must grow into self-love.   At puberty
it expands into love of offspring, and, according to Rousseau, must develop, under the stimulus of emotional self-
projection, into a love of mankind, or philanthropy.   Thus,
by one of those clever transformation scenes, — not to say
stage-tricks, — in which Jean-Jacques was fertile, he out-
witted the materialists.   Granting their premise of human
selfishness, he made this very selfishness the father of
philanthropy.

Ingenious as is this reconciliation of hostile theories, it
led to the gravest of Rousseau's errors, the postponement
of all ethical teaching, all social knowledge, all moral habit
until puberty;[1] and to the parcelling out of the child's life
into well-defined stages.   It is true that the first twelve
years of life are, mainly, animal; it is true that in them
the body is the main object of care, and that, without this
care, all later education will be a mockery; but it is equally
true that, in certain directions, these are the great acquisi-
tive years.   More than this, childhood is free from that
subtle foe, *ennui*.   There are many essential tools of the
intellect that can be secured only by a treadmill repetition

---

[1] "The end that should be sought in the education of a young man
is to form his heart, his judgment, and his mind, and that in the order
named.   Most masters, pedants especially, regard acquisition and the
heaping up of information as the only object of a good education, forgetting that often, as Molière says: —

"'A wise fool is a greater fool than an ignorant fool!'" — *Projet
pour l'éduc. de M. de Ste.-Marie* (*Supp. à la Collection des Œuv. Comp.
de J.-J. Rousseau*, Paris, 1782, III. 13).

of effort. Only either the dull or the exceptionally patient mind can experience this monotony without rebellion, except in this early exuberance of force, when the high heat of eager youth helps wonderfully the slow blows of dull repetition. Rousseau recognizes this truth so far as it applies to mechanical skill, and, rightly, demands that in these early years the child's senses shall be thoroughly and accurately trained; but he does not perceive — or his theories will not permit him to perceive — that there is a mechanism of the intellect, a mechanic art of the mind, skill in which must be secured, if ever, in these first years, when the child is patient of everything except idleness, and is ready, when tired of one monotonous task, to put his whole energy into another. This childhood time, moreover, by an extension of the preceding argument, is that in which are formed either good habits, the friendly chains, or bad habits, the torturing spurs, of passion. Jean-Jacques thinks himself a foe to habit, and, while under this impression, says,[1] "The only habit that a child ought to acquire is that of contracting none." This freedom from habit, he believes, is a necessary accompaniment of liberty, forgetting that he only has time to be free whose actions are, by the aid of habit, so nicely adjusted that, in the larger things of life, he can act unhampered by petty, drudging details of mere existence.

Rousseau's aim, in these first twelve years, is, he says,[2] "not to gain time but to lose it." Time is inexorable, however, and the art of social living must be acquired; must be gained too, so far as concerns its conventional signs and common stock of knowledge, before the tumultuous years following what Rousseau calls the second birth, — the birth of sex. He crowds, therefore, into the two or more

---

[1] *Émile*, I. 39.   [2] *Émile*, II. 75.

years following the twelfth, so much of this conventional acquirement — the ordinary teaching of the schools — as he approves, believing that the fallow years preceding will have made a soil so strong and weedless that this short time will give a harvest as rich, nay, far more rich, than is the tangled garden-growth of the usual school-planting.

It is not worth while to follow his rather vague pruning of the pedagogic tree. As, in the first period, the question always to be asked is, What are the dictates of Nature? so, in this second stage, the question is, What are the dictates of utility? "Of what use is it?"[1] — that is the shibboleth by which to decide whether or not a subject shall enter the boy's range of study. Jean-Jacques refrains, wisely, from limiting the word utility, and avoids, thereby, a trap of definition set by his own hands.

Putting aside, then, this minor matter of a choice of studies, and accepting as true Rousseau's picture of a boy brought to his twelfth year by his system of negative activity, we may, nevertheless, question the wisdom of crowding this task of study into years which are truly, as Rousseau maintains, the years of greatest relative strength, but which are, no less, years in which the poise of the expanding nervous system is easily overthrown. Furthermore, to open for the first time, simultaneously with the dawning of the passions, the wide and bewildering prospect of social and emotional life, is, to say the least, a hazardous trial of human nature, even if one concedes, as is difficult, the perfect moral balance inhering in a child brought to his fifteenth year with no principles of action beyond self-regard and immediate utility. With here a fatal tendency to paradox, Rousseau has denied to the moral nature that even and co-ordinate growth which, he sees, is

---

[1] *Émile*, III. 187.

essential to right physical development. He imagines his orphaned puppet, Émile, a moral Harlequin, changing, *instanta,* his entire mental and spiritual garb.

Having touched upon these major fallacies of Rousseau's, I will not presume to discuss minor flaws, about which there may be a wide diversity of opinion. Let us turn again, rather, to the more congenial study of the strength of his book. In doing so, it must not be forgotten that our debt to Rousseau is not to him as an originator[1] He was, rather, a concentrator of a class of ideas that had wandered, without definite lodgement, for two hundred years. If, into a saturated solution of certain salts, we let fall one tiny last drop, instantly the liquor solidifies. The slow drops added to the point of saturation count as nothing before this final magic one. Such a last drop in the changing constitution of society were the writings of Rousseau. His cry of liberty really brought freedom; therefore this successful voice drowns the murmur of the tens of thousand earlier voices that had cried in vain. His call for freedom found the world ready to respond. Especially in education was his time most opportune. The very year of *Émile* was that of the expulsion of the Jesuits. Something must be found to supply their place in the domain of teaching. The political ferment was such that any change, be it only radical enough, was welcome. The wide spreading of materialism had produced a swarm of visionaries praying for a prophet. Even the enmity of the "Philosophers," of the Calvinists, and of the Churchmen — each body, in its way, fuming, arguing, and thundering against the book — was, vulgarly considered, a marvellous advertisement. *Émile*

---

[1] "Rousseau at least invented new form, and that is well known to be often as great an exploit as the discovery of new matter." — MORLEY, *Rousseau*, II. 198.

flashed over Europe in a blaze of excitement, leaving an impress of one kind or another in every fibre of civilization.

But it had more solid grounds of influence than mere fortuitous ones. I have already attempted to show the main foundation of its power, which was its supreme aspiration towards virtue. But Rousseau went farther than to stimulate vague yearnings. He proved that virtue springs from liberty and is, in its turn, the parent of liberty, of the only real freedom that man knows. *Émile* begins with this idea, and, through its wandering paradoxes, clings to this thread of principle. Others had preached, and would continue to preach, the rights of man; some, even at that early day, had proclaimed the rights of women; Rousseau championed the rights of the child, — the right to his mother's breast, the right to his father's guidance, the right to a home, the right to free physical and mental development, the right to innocence, the right, finally, to be happy. *see 208*

In this advocacy of freedom, especially in this plea for happiness, *Émile* did incalculable service to education. With all his capacity for personal, and often deserved, unhappiness, Rousseau had the true measure of real happiness, for he found it to lie not in the multiplication of our wants but in the discipline of our desires. In this direction, Émile is consistently educated to a mental and physical stoicism that laughs at the sieges of ill-fortune, knowing itself garrisoned and victualled for a lifetime of assault. "There are two sorts of dependence," says Rousseau,[1] "upon things, which is natural; upon men, which is artificial. Dependence upon things, there being no question of morality, does not interfere with liberty or engender vice; dependence upon men, being contrary to order, propagates

[1] *Émile*, II. 65.

every vice and mutually depraves the master and the slave."
From this is deduced his method of education. "Make the
child dependent solely upon things," he continues. "Experience or weakness should supply the place of laws. Grant
nothing to him because he asks it, but only because he
needs it. . . . Let him feel his liberty both in his actions
and in yours. . . . In receiving your help with a sort of
humiliation, let him look forward to the time when he can
dispense with it, and when he will have attained the honor
of taking care of himself."[1] "Let him know only that he is
weak and you are strong. . . . Let him feel early, on his
proud neck, the heavy yoke that nature puts upon man, the
hard yoke of necessity under which, for discipline, all must
bend; let him see this necessity in things, never in the
caprice of man; let the curb that restrains him be force, not
authority. . . . Finally, there is no middle course; either
you must require nothing at all of him, or you must compel
him to absolute obedience. The worst of all educations is
to leave him vibrating between his will and yours, disputing
ceaselessly with you as to which is the master."[2]

This is not, as might appear at first, a grim doctrine of
necessity, cousin-german to the philosophy of despair.
Rather is it an added plea for that early happiness which
Rousseau believed was the right of every child. "Men, be
humane," he pleads,[3] " . . . Love infancy; abet its play,
its joy, its affectionate instincts. . . . Why will you fill
with bitterness and grief these first, short years which will
never return to him any more than they can come back to
you? . . . Why do you add to his inevitable ills, without
being sure that the present sorrows are a draft upon the
future? and how will you prove that these bad instincts
which you pretend to correct are not a product of your

[1] *Emile*, II. 65.   [2] *Emile*, II. 73.   [3] *Emile*, II. 57.

senseless education rather than of Nature? Wretched foresight, that renders a human being actually miserable upon
the hope, well or ill founded, of some time making him
happy."

First, freedom for the child; then, happiness; or, indeed,
both first; since they are, Rousseau believes, correlative,—
the unhappy child not being free, nor the enslaved child,
happy. Freedom and happiness secured, the next essential
of education is action. Freedom is a birthright; happiness,
a birth-privilege; action, a birth-duty. The child may
demand of us the right to be untrammelled and to be guarded
from sorrow; we, in turn, may require of him the duty of
doing. Rousseau's fervor in preaching the gospel of action
would almost persuade us that he himself was never a
drone; his strenuous plea that Émile shall, even from
infancy, feel the weight of social obligation, makes us half
forget the forty selfish years of Jean-Jacques's life. He
saves himself by a sophism. "Out of society," he says with
complacency,[1] "the isolated man, owing nothing to any one,
has a right to live as he chooses." Doubtless, he believed
himself entitled to this right, confounding lawlessness with
isolation and counting his obligations to Madame de Warens
and to other Bohemian benefactors as nothing. "But," he
continues,[2] "in society, where, of necessity," (man) "lives
at the cost of others, he owes in work the price of his
support. This rule admits of no exception. To work is a
duty which social man cannot shirk. Rich or poor, high
or low, every idle citizen is a knave."[3] Following this
dictum with a rhapsody upon manual labor, he changes the
ground of his argument to that of utility, and makes an

---

[1] *Émile*, III. 209.   [2] *Ibid.*

[3] "Temperance and work are the two true medicines for man:
work sharpens his appetite, and temperance prevents him from abus-
ing it." — *Émile*, I. 29.

extraordinary prophecy regarding the aristocracy of France, so soon to be striving, with clumsy fingers and dull brains, to earn their daily bread. Ascending to a higher plane, he continues, "But it is of less consequence that he learn a trade merely that he may have a trade, than that he may conquer that prejudice which despises labor. You, you say, will never be reduced to earning your living. Eh! so much the worse, so much the worse for you. But, no matter. Work, then, not from necessity, but for glory. Lower yourself to the laborer's level in order to rise above your own. To rule fortune and fate, begin by making yourself independent of them."

"I insist that Émile shall learn a trade," he repeats.[1] "An honest trade, at least, I hear you say? What is that? Is not every trade which is of public use, honest? I would not have him an embroiderer, a gilder, or a varnisher, like Locke's gentlemen pupils; I would not have him a musician, an actor, or a maker of books. . . . I would prefer him to be a shoemaker rather than a poet; I would rather have him pave highways than make porcelain flowers. . . . So let us choose an honest trade, remembering that there is no honesty without usefulness." What untold mischief has this fantastic doctrine of utility wrought! What a host of beautiful things, material and spiritual, have been sacrificed on this altar of the useful! To how narrow and hard a path has it confined the divine feet of Liberty, and with what chains of gold has it dragged her down! Slowly, but very slowly, is this path widening to include within its borders all good things, are these fetters dropping off to free Liberty from her last tyrant, commercialism.

But we are not concerned with the remote consequences of a utilitarianism whose immediate tendency was a health-

---

[1] *Émile*, III. 211.

ful reaction against a false philosophy. The tonic of pure utility was necessary to a society which valued a man in proportion to his idleness and folly. The dignity of labor was a new lesson that the aristocracy, spelling out as a pastime, under Jean-Jacques's tuition, were soon to learn, painfully, under the bitter rod of hunger. This doctrine of utility gave a new basis to education. How widely different has been the educational ideal since Rousseau preached this gospel, I need not point out; let us see, however, his development of it.

"To live, is the trade I mean to teach. On leaving me," (my pupil) "will be, I intend, neither a magistrate, nor a soldier, nor a priest; he will be a man."[1] . . . "Remember, the spirit of my school is not to teach the child many things, but to never let any save right and clear ideas enter his mind. If he know nothing, no matter, provided he be not deceived, and I put truth into his head merely to save it from the errors that, otherwise, would enter . . . Reason, judgment, come slowly; prejudices rush in pell-mell; it is from them that he must be saved."[2] . . . "The proper study for man is that of his surroundings. So long as he knows himself only on the physical side, he must study himself through his relations to things; that is his childhood task; when he begins to feel his moral being, he must study himself through his relations to men; that is his life-work."[3]

". . . When I see a young man, in the period of his greatest activity, limited to studies that are purely speculative, and then, later, thrown without a shadow of experience upon the world and into affairs, it seems to me that reason and nature are equally offended, and I am no whit surprised that so few know how to conduct themselves.

[1] *Émile*, I. 11.   [2] *Émile*, III. 177.   [3] *Émile*, IV. 230.

What mischievous spirit impels the teaching of so many useless things while the art of action counts for nothing? They pretend to fit" (children) "for society, and they teach each one as though he were to pass his life meditating in a cell or arguing in the air." [1]

"Of the knowledge within our reach, a part is false, a part is useless, a part serves to foster pride in him who possesses it. The small portion that really contributes to our well-being is alone worthy of the study of a wise man, and, consequently, of a child whom one would have wise. It is not a question of knowing everything, but only what is useful." [2] Rousseau takes pains to show us, however, that his aim is a higher one than mere bread-winning. The trade of living that he would teach is the "Plain living and high thinking" of Wordsworth. [3] "If I have made myself understood," he says, [4] in summing up his discussion of manual training, "it must be seen how, by means of physical exercise and manual labor, I lead my pupil, insensibly, to a taste for reflection and meditation, to balance in him the idleness that would result from his indifference to public opinion, and from the dormancy of his passions. He must work like a peasant and think like a philosopher, in order that he may not be as lazy as a savage. The great secret of education is to make the exercise of the body and that of the mind serve always to relieve each other."

Still other two great truths that men have been slow to recognize did Rousseau teach. The first, that no learning is real and enduring which does not spring from a desire to learn ; the second, that acquisition which comes from rivalry and prize-hunting is not only false, but morally unsound. "I would rather a hundred times," he says, [5]

[1] *Émile*, IV. 275. [2] *Émile*, III. 171.
[3] See, "O friend! I know not which way I must look."
[4] *Émile*, III. 218. [5] *Émile*, III. 194.

"that Émile should learn nothing, than that he should learn
through rivalry or vanity.   Only, every year, I shall mark
the progress that he will have made; I shall compare it
with that to be made next year. . . .   I shall thus excite
him without making him jealous of any one.   He will wish
to surpass himself; well and good.   I see no wrong in self-
emulation."

Rousseau's Émile, then, is a young man vigorous, free,
happy, alert, unashamed, with no false notions, with many
true ones.   He loves mankind because he respects himself.   He is jealous of none, afraid of none.   He is as
innocent as he is manly; as enthusiastic as he is level-
headed.   He is full of sentiment without sentimentality,
of love without brute passion.   He is a cheerful companion
to himself, a wise teacher to his children, an unselfish
member of society, a far-seeing unit of the state, a tolerant
citizen of the world; in short, in the full sense of the word,
he is a *virtuous man.*

However strongly we may doubt the adequacy of the
means, we cannot doubt the perfection of the ends of Émile's
education.   In making society conscious of the wisdom and
importance of these ends, Rousseau began a new era in
education.   More than a hundred years have passed; the
world has progressed, but it has moved along the lines that
Rousseau indicated.   The problems of education are receiving ever greater thought, but the goal is still that at which
Rousseau aimed.   The world-Émile is still evolving, slowly,
with many slips and discouragements, but his ends are still
those which Jean-Jacques saw, and, in his wild, paradoxical way, forced mankind to see.

CHAPTER VIII.

PESTALOZZI AND FROEBEL.

Senses, Heart, and Soul must be educated together.

PESTALOZZI, PERFECTER OF ROUSSEAU ; LOVE ; THE USE OF FANATI-
CISM ; PESTALOZZI'S CAREER ; "LEONARD AND GERTRUDE " ; HIS
SYSTEM ; YVERDUN ; HIS PEDAGOGY ; HIS PRINCIPLES ; HIS METH-
ODS ; HIS SPIRIT ; "ANSCHAUUNG " ; HIS INFLUENCE ; FROEBEL ;
CONTRASTED WITH PESTALOZZI ; FROEBEL'S AIM ; HIS PRINCIPLES ;
THE KINDERGARTEN ; THE TRUE FROEBEL ; THE FALSE FROEBEL ;
THE "EDUCATION OF MAN " ; THE RESULT OF FROEBEL'S WORK.

At last the scale of education is complete. The harsh
discord of mediævalism, thrown into wild promise of harmony by Rabelais, was modulated, by slow tonal changes,
until, with Rousseau, there remained only the dissonant
note of isolation. This, Pestalozzi, the perfecter of Rousseau, threw out. Replacing it by the true tonic, *love,* he
sounded the full major chord of education. Upon this we
are building, with many pauses, with many false notes,
with many useless repetitions, the symphony of human
perfectibility which, in centuries, may become harmonious
with the music of the spheres.

Dating from the Renaissance, one reform after another
had slowly made way against human inertia, until, in
Émile, was shown the ideal individual education. It remained only to adapt this impossible, selfish training to the
normal conditions of the social state, in order to begin the
work of expansion which is taking place to-day. This

adaptation Pestalozzi achieved by bringing into educational processes the elements of sympathy, of interdependence, of spiritual harmony, or — in one word — of love.

This vital Pestalozzian basis of education, love, had been half seen by many earlier reformers. Comenius especially had rightly founded his school within the mother's arms, and had expanded it continuously therefrom into universal knowledge. But his voice cried in a mental wilderness to ears not yet fine enough to heed a doctrine so simple and sublime. It required more than two centuries for the truths which he uttered to penetrate from the high level of his inspiration to the lower — which is, however, the permanent and effective — level of popular understanding. And this slow ethical permeation was not enough. The common mind had to be awakened, had to be made aware of the vitality of truths which, unconsciously, it already held. To such ends the order of mind called fanatic is created, and cries its startling message to the world. As the slow drilling of the rock is fruitless without the sudden shock of powder which lays bare in an instant the hidden work of years, so all moral reforms must be consummated by the noisy work of fanaticism.

Johann Heinrich Pestalozzi, born at Zürich in 1746,[1] had, to a marked degree, the fanatic temper. An only child, brought up in semi-isolation by a widowed mother and a doting servant, he imbibed from them the feminine ethical sense — a quality so different from the masculine.[2]

[1] For the details of Pestalozzi's life, see Von Raumer, *Gesch. der Päd.*, II. 365 (trans. in Barnard, *Amer. Journ. of Ed.*, III. 401) ; and, especially, De Guimps, *Pestalozzi* (trans. by J. Russell).

[2] This ethical sense — whether we esteem it to be inherent or induced — has been, it seems to me, the chief element in determining that the growth of humanity should be upward rather than downward. Experience leads men, usually, towards conservatism in ethical

Ungainly, odd, a butt for stupid wits, he passed through a fiery ordeal that seared him forever against the sting of ridicule. Unpractical and self-forgetting, he entered upon life with that spirit of optimism, that disregard of consequences, without which fanaticism is impossible. Finally, his career — which was essentially constructive — fell upon a time of reaction from revolution, when the mad desire for tearing down had been succeeded by an equal rage for building up, when social speculations found ready belief, and schemes, no matter how monstrous, for creating a new heaven and a new earth seemed possible and easy.

Bred to the law, Pestalozzi early recognized his total unfitness for it. He turned, as have other unplaced geniuses, to the pursuit of farming, with a vague hope, perhaps, of finding at the great heart of nature the sympathy and comprehension which humanity denied to him. But her heart, too, was cold, and — more momentous — her bosom was unyielding, even of daily food. In five years he had exhausted his small resources, had reduced his wife and child to want, had failed utterly in agriculture, and had succeeded scarcely better in human farming; for the beggar children, whom, in his intense and uncalculating philanthropy, he had brought to his fallow fields, rewarded his loving efforts with ingratitude and petty crimes.

The history of the eighteen years following this failure at Neuhof [1] — the years between 1780 and 1798 — is the old

endeavor, towards acquiescence in evil, towards, in too many cases, pure cynicism. This tendency would soon induce in humanity a distinct slackening of moral effort were it not that each new generation remains, through its formative years, in an atmosphere that is created by women, and that is by them charged with those ethical beliefs, aspirations, and, if you please, chimeras which are the foundations of moral progress.

[1] Neuhof was a tract of about one hundred acres of barren, clayey land. near Birr, which Pestalozzi, backed by a Zürich firm, had pur-

one of genius struggling to assert itself, of a voice with a message for humanity striving to make itself heard above the roar of commonplace. The chief tangible fruit of this bitter time was the book *Leonard and Gertrude*.[1] Read this, and see how puerile it is, how too obvious are its moralities. Read it a second time, and note how earnest it is, how exact and accurate are its peasant scenes. Read it yet again, and recognize in it the outpouring of a rare soul, working, pleading, ready to be despised, for fellow-souls.

The picture shown in *Leonard and Gertrude* is very crude. Everywhere is visible the rough hand of the painter, a strong, untiring hand, painting an eternal image, of which this in paper and print is the merest sketch. It is a madonna which he paints, a mother-picture, in which the wife, by right of her love, stands supreme, saving the husband, protecting and ennobling their children. Gertrude, a village mason's wife, whose horizon extends no farther than the feudal baron and his little tenantry, has no higher ambition than to keep her husband sober and to bring up their children in the love of God. Her pleasures are as sorry as her griefs. But mean as is the picture, it is a symbol of the one great, overmastering fact of education; it is a demonstration that the true training of childhood radiates from motherhood, and should find its centre, no matter how widely it may be extended, in parental respon-

chased, and on which he had attempted, on a large scale, the cultivation of madder. Failing in this, and virtually tied to the estate by the large and expensive house which he had erected on it, he tried, with almost grotesque results, to convert his farm into a juvenile place-of-refuge.

[1] Miss Channing's abridgment (in translation) of this book preserves its spirit while avoiding the tedium and irrelevancy of Pestalozzi's style.

sibility. This was Pestalozzi's supreme idea; this he strove for, for this he kept himself poor and mean, for this he lived his life as he did, a sacrifice to the orphaned and outcast, an aspiration to give them that which he felt was the one essential thing in human life, — love.

This we must never lose sight of, for this *is* the Pestalozzian "system." Disfigured by imitators,[1] smothered, even in the founder's own experience, by restless experiment and his unhappy lack of balance, formalized into a dry-as-dust method by petty minds, the inner aim subsisted, the aim to make fatherhood and motherhood the active centre of education. Indeed, the chief fault of Pestalozzi's later teaching, wherein, as was pithily said, he succeeded chiefly in "mechanizing education," arose from his mistaken belief that the whole process might be brought, by a proper system, within the four walls of the home. "The parents' teaching," he makes a peasant in *Christoph und Elsa* say,[2] "is the kernel of wisdom, and the schoolmaster's business is only to make a husk over it." And again, in his own person, he declares,[3] in the address delivered on his seventy-third birthday, "The only sure foundation on which we must build, for institutions for popular education, national culture, and the elevation of the poor, is the parental heart, which, by means of the innocence, truth, power, and purity of its love, kindles in the children the belief in love."

Long before this, he had written, in his *Letters on Early Education:*[4] "The mother is qualified, and qualified by the

---

[1] England especially, in the early part of the century, was liberally supplied with "Pestalozzian institutions" of a most dreary and profitless sort.

[2] Barnard, *Pest. and Pest.*, Pt. II. 153 (*Sämmt. Schrift.*, Bd. 12).

[3] Barnard, *Pest. and Pest.*, Pt. II. 178.

[4] Quoted by Quick, *Ed. Ref.*, 356.

Creator Himself, to become the principal agent in the development of her child; . . . and what is demanded of her is · a *thinking love*. . . . It is recorded that God opened the heavens to the patriarch of old and showed him a ladder leading thither. This ladder is let down to every descendant of Adam; it is offered to thy child. But he must be taught to climb it. And let him not attempt it by the cold calculations of the head, or the mere impulses of the heart; but let all these powers combine, and the noble enterprise will be crowned with success. . . . Maternal love is the first agent in education. . . . Through it the child is led to love and trust his Creator and his Redeemer."

"It was," he says,[1] referring to *Leonard and Gertrude*, "my first word to the heart of the poor and forsaken. It was my first word to the heart of those who stand in God's stead towards the poor and forsaken. It was my first word to the mothers of the country, and to the mother-heart which God gave them that they might be towards their own what no creature on earth *can* be in their stead."

And we must never forget that this first word is his last word, and the word that he strives always to utter through his writings, through his fantastic teaching, and even in those last humiliating years when, no longer master of himself or of his house, he drove his old followers from him, and countenanced a teaching which was, indeed, a husk of his rich first-harvest.

Leonard and Gertrude brought him fame and prediction of success as a novelist. Other things he wrote, many things he did, in these sad eighteen years; but this hard experience was preparation time only. Not until the age of fifty-five did his life really begin; the preceding thirty years of manhood were intellectually prenatal, the bitter

---

[1] Quoted by Von Raumer, *Gesch. der Päd.*, II. 386.

gestation-term of genius. "For thirty years," he wrote[1] to Zschokke, "my life has been a desperate struggle against most frightful poverty. . . . Do you know that for thirty years I have wanted the bare necessities? Do you know that until now I have kept out of society, away from church, because I had neither clothes nor money to buy them? O Zschokke, do you know that I am the laughing-stock of the passers-by because I look like a beggar? Do you know that more than a thousand times I have had to forego my dinner, and at noon, when the poorest even were sitting at table, I have been bitterly devouring a crust on the highway? Yes, Zschokke, and to-day even I am struggling with painful poverty; . . . and all this to come to the help of the poor through the triumph of my principles."

Unnecessary pain, much of it; and, except as the bitter trial deepened the power of his love and capacity for self-sacrifice, impotent years. He himself recognized this. "Gray-haired, I was still a child," he wrote to Gessner,[2] referring to the time of the French occupation of Switzerland; "I was not only deceived by every knave, I was hoodwinked by every fool, and believed in the good faith of any one who appeared before me and spoke fair words. Nevertheless, I knew the people and the sources of their savagery and degradation, and I desired nothing more than that these sources be stopped and their evil effects arrested; and the 'new men' of Helvetia,[3] who were not content with so little, and who did not know the people, soon found that I was not suited to their use. These men, in their new position, like shipwrecked women, believed every straw to be a mast

---

[1] Quoted by Paroz, *Hist. univ. de la Péd.*, 310.

[2] *Wie Gertrud*, etc. (*Sämmt Schrift.*, V. 10). See trans. in Barnard, *Pest. and Pest.*, Pt. II. 187.

[3] The French officials who were trying to remodel Switzerland into the "Helvetian Republic."

on which the republic might be rescued; but me, me they took for a straw not fit to sustain a cat.

"Without knowing it, without wishing it, they did me good, more good than any men have ever done me. They restored me to myself and left me nothing, in the amazement caused by their shipwreck, except to say, as I had said in the first days of their confusion, 'I will turn schoolmaster.' For this I found confidence. I became a teacher. . . . Stanz had just burned down, and Legrand begged me to make this place of misery the first scene of my undertaking. I went; I would have gone into the farthest clefts of the mountains to come nearer to my aim; and now, in truth, I did come nearer. But think of my position! Alone, destitute of all tools of teaching, alone! — superintendent, bursar, steward, and even maidservant, in a half-ruined house, — surrounded by ignorance, disease, and unwonted things of all kinds. The number of children increased, by degrees, to eighty; all of different ages, some of good origin, others from the ranks of beggary, and all, with a few exceptions, wholly ignorant. What a task! Imagine it; to educate these children. What a task!

"I attempted it, and stood in their midst; I uttered various sounds and made them imitate them; whoever saw it was struck with the effect. Truly it was a meteor that flashes through the air and vanishes. No one understood its nature. I did not understand it myself. It was the result of a simple, psychological idea which had been revealed to my inward consciousness, but which I myself was far from clearly understanding."

In this characteristic way does he describe this point in his life, this epoch from which dates his fame. "I will turn schoolmaster," he said, and, standing before a beggarly rabble of orphans, he uttered sounds, knowing not why he uttered them. But, in an invisible and illimitable circle around those beggar children sat the civilized world listening to hear, through those aimless syllables, the Heaven-sent message which was to redeem education.

The school at Stanz, fortunately for Pestalozzi, whose health was quite unequal to such hardship, was short-lived. The French again entered the town, the pupils were dispersed, and Pestalozzi secured the enforced rest upon which his very life depended.

Restored in body, he undertook primary teaching in the schools of Burgdorf, where his vagaries and his total unfitness for the duties of an instructor, judged by common standards, won him little esteem. Short experiences in independent teaching — fortunate at Burgdorf and unfortunate at München-Buchsee — were followed by his removal to Yverdun to establish there, in 1805, the famous institution which grew to be less a school than a pedagogic pulpit, to which pilgrims from every corner of the world flocked to listen and be taught.

The Yverdun school existed twenty years, and it was not until 1825, two years before Pestalozzi's death, that it went wholly to ruin, and he retired to Neuhof. But, every year, new and more bitter dissensions arose between him and his assistants; every year the institution drifted farther and farther away, not merely from harmony, but from its old educational ideals. As one or another of the assistants, each a specialist, gained a temporary ascendency, the teaching took on a mathematical hue, a geographical hue, or a linguistic hue, until, at last, it showed only the dull monotone of the routine schools of pre-Pestalozzian days. But meanwhile, and most fortunately, the spark of inspiration had been carried away from the atmosphere of the school itself into every part of Europe and even into America, there to kindle fires which no poisonous breath of dissension from Yverdun could extinguish.

Perhaps there has never been a poorer teacher, of any fame, than Pestalozzi.[1] Without steadiness, without patience, without definite method, his schools, as schools, were shamefully inadequate. Whether at Stanz, where he taught, — using the word narrowly, — no one except, reactively, himself; whether at Burgdorf, where he walked in pedagogic clouds, oblivious that he was veiling from the poor children upon whom he poured the torrent of his ideas the sun of understanding; whether, finally, at Yverdun, where, the flood of his incoherency exhausted, he kept his pupils in a noonday glare of publicity, and dried up finally the very springs of their nurture, — everywhere his teaching was a series of experiments, rather than a fixed and definite work. He subjected his boys to endless mental vivisection. He was too eager for results, too enamoured of experimentation, too inflamed with proselyting zeal, to spend much time in weighing his teaching or in calculating its effects.[2] Add to this, that for the last forty years of his

---

[1] Says Krüsi, one of his earlier assistants (quoted by Compayré, *Hist. de la Péd.*, Leç. XVIII. 371), " In the matter of ordinary acquirements and methods of school-teaching, Pestalozzi was inferior to any good village dominie. But he possessed something infinitely beyond that which any course of instruction, no matter how good, can give. He understood what is hidden from most teachers, — the human mind and the laws of its development and cultivation, the human heart and the means of quickening and ennobling it."

[2] "Pestalozzi's teaching," says Compayré (*Hist. de la Péd.*, Leç. XVIII. 367), "was indeed a continual groping, an experiment ever newly begun. Ask him not for formulated ideas, definitely established methods. Always on the alert and in search of perfection, his extraordinary teaching-instinct was never satisfied. . . . His theories almost always followed, seldom preceded, his experiments. Intuitional rather than logical, he himself acknowledges that he went ahead without asking, whither ? . . . He never knew how to profit by others' experiences. He never attained precision in his methods. He complained of not being understood and, truly, he was not."

life he scarcely opened a book, and purposely remained ignorant of what other teachers were striving to do, and it is easy to understand the failure of his schools regarded merely as institutions for instruction. His proudest title, he boasts, is that of schoolmaster. But he never deserved the name, even from his own standpoint. He was not fitted to grasp the petty, daily things of actual instruction. He was made for prophecy, not for drudgery; he was a seer, not a schoolmaster. Like Bacon, he measured the eternal verities, but ignored the infinite little truths of which they are the sum.

Even in the best days at Yverdun, we have proof enough that there was much confusion, much aimlessness, much parrot-work, much vain repetition of names and facts arranged alphabetically, or tagged with mnemonic devices dear to Pestalozzi. But, on the other hand, there was great earnestness, unbounded enthusiasm, and a steady ethical aim in the methods used, crude and mistaken as those methods often were.[1] The institution was essentially a moral one,[2] and it was because of the emphasis of the moral side of education, it was because of Pestalozzi's insistence that boys must be made men first and scholars second, that Yverdun grew to be a shrine of pilgrimage. It was not what he taught or how he taught that attracted teachers from all over the world; it was the spirit in which he

[1] See Herbart's description of a visit to Pestalozzi's Burgdorf school, in *Ueber Pestalozzi's neueste Schrift*, etc. (*Sämmt. Werke*, XI. 47).

[2] " I knew no other order, method, or art, but that which resulted naturally from my children's conviction of my love for them, nor did I care to know any other. Thus I subordinated the instruction of my children to a higher aim, which was to arouse and strengthen their best sentiments by the relations of every-day life as they existed between themselves and me." Quoted by De Guimps, *Pestalozzi* (Russell's trans.), 160.

taught. These teachers went away from Yverdun not much wiser as to educational methods, but infinitely wiser as to educational ends. "The powerful, indefinable, stirring and uplifting effect produced by Pestalozzi when he spoke," says Froebel,[1] "set one's soul on fire for a higher, nobler life, although he had not made clear or sure the exact way towards it, nor indicated the means whereby to attain it. Thus did the power and many-sidedness of the educational effort make up for deficiency in unity and comprehensiveness; and the love, the warmth, the stir of the whole, the human kindness and benevolence of it, replaced the want of clearness, depth, thoroughness, extent, perseverance, and steadiness."

While Yverdun was the resort of kings and philosophers, while it was, for many years, the fashion to send one's children there, the institution was, none the less, the culmination and the counterpart of the beggar schools at Neuhof and Stanz, and the village peasant school at Burgdorf; the tender spirit which ministered to those outcasts was the same which at Yverdun kissed every child who came, took him by the hand, and, leading him into the midst of the pupils, said, "Boys, here is a new pupil; be kind to him, and remember that henceforth he is your brother!"[2]

One searches in vain his letters to Gessner, which Pestalozzi published under the title, *How Gertrude teaches her*

---

[1] *Auto.*, 79. *Gesamm. päd. Schrift.* (Lange), I. 1, 97.

[2] Pestalozzi was a radical as thorough-going as Rousseau, and, with his aggressive philanthropy, would have forced the rich and the competent, could he have done so, to bring about the melioration of the poor and helpless. Therefore, had his fanaticism not emancipated children, we should still owe an immense debt to it for giving an early impulse towards the education and uplifting of the defective and degraded classes.

Children, for clear notions of his educational scheme. He confesses his inability to formulate it, and avails himself of the expositions of his disciples, qualifying them, however, with criticisms and elaborations that but increase our confusion.[1] His fundamental classification is, in itself, a false one, bringing, as it does, all instruction under three heads, — Form, Number, and Language. It is easy to see into what pitfalls so illogical a division must lead. Form and number are, humanly speaking, realities. They are qualities inherent in things; they are tangible and absolute. Language, on the contrary, is extraneous and insubstantial; it is but an arbitrary and varying sign of our impressions. Form and number are impersonal and independent of ourselves. Language is necessarily individual and always in mutation.

It is therefore difficult, and it would be fruitless, to follow the plan of education which Pestalozzi constructs upon this threefold classification. The exposition of it upon which he spent so much labor, the pseudo-philosophy of which he was so fond, have now little value in themselves; they have served their purpose, have done what harm as well as what good it was theirs to do. To many educational monstrosities they have lent a respectable sponsorship;[2] to many a teacher they have been as the Old Man of the Sea. But the spirit upon which they rested stands forth with ever greater distinction and power as the pettinesses extraneous to it are sloughed off.

---

[1] For an exposition of his methods of teaching, see, besides the *Wie Gertrud ihre Kinder lehrt,* von Raumer, *Gesch. der Päd.,* II. 406 ; and Biber, *Mem. of Pest.* (In consulting Biber, care should be taken to separate his own notions from his description of Pestalozzi's methods.)

[2] See, *e.g.*, an article by Miss Martineau ("Pestalozzi," etc.) given in *Littell's Living Age,* LXX. 22.

So vague was his system, even to Pestalozzi, that he failed to distinguish between the eternal and the transitory in his great work. To Gessner he wrote:[1] "If I look back and ask myself, What have I really done towards the progress of education? I find this: I have established the supreme principle of education in recognizing apperception as the absolute foundation of all knowledge; and have sought, by eliminating all individualities of teaching, the true essence of teaching through which the improvement of our species, by following nature, will be brought about. I find that I have resolved all education into three elementary principles" (meaning Form, Number, and Language), "and have determined the special principle through which it would be possible to bring all instruction absolutely under these three heads."

In his New Year's address of 1809 he said:[2] "What I seek is to elevate human nature to its highest, its noblest; and this I do through love. . . . All the capacities for intellect and art and knowledge which my nature holds, I take to be only means for the divine uplifting of the heart to love. . . . Love is the only, the eternal foundation of the training of our race to humanity."

Alas for human blindness, from which not even genius is exempt! That threefold classification which Pestalozzi told Gessner had been established firmly, has long since crumbled away. That vague "uplifting" which, in his New Year's address he said, "I seek," and which he died seeking, he had found and started on its blessed mission to the world years before, among the wretched waifs to whose souls and bodies he ministered at Stanz.

But his false classification, his mistaken details of

---

[1] *Wie Gertrud*, etc. (*Sämmt. Schrift.*, Bd. V. 194).
[2] Barnard, *Pest. and Pest.*, Part II. 176.

method, could not wholly hide his real, eternal principles
even from his contemporaries; through the confusion of his
writings they stood forth; through the disorder and vacillation, the miserable quarrelling at Yverdun, they shone
like stars. The atmosphere of his school, the spirit of his
writings, was that of love, of self-forgetting, of high aspiration. And his instruction, at its best, was worthy of these
virtues. It was thorough, it was individual, it was, in the
highest sense, religious; it was quickening to the moral
as well as to the intellectual nature of the child; it was
gauged to his capacity, it was a logical unfolding,[1] not a
system of instruction. And it was based psychologically
upon APPERCEPTION. Apperception, feeble paraphrase
though it be, is the least unsatisfactory translation of that
key-word, *Anschauung,* around which the pedagogy of both
Pestalozzi and Froebel revolves. *Anschauung* may be defined
as a quickening perception, a perception that registers itself
permanently upon our inner consciousness, and produces
a real and lasting change in our personality. As the
younger Fichte expresses it:[2] "Only that can become the
true and intellectual property of the child and of the man,
which he has thought through and through, and in free per-
ceptive activity brought forth out of himself." It is from
this necessity for *Anschauung* that arises the doctrine of
self-activity which is fundamental to the teaching of Pesta-

---

[1] " ' He seeks to supply all operations of the mind with either data
or heads (*Rubriken*) or main ideas.' (Fischer.) That is to say: he
seeks in the entire world of art and nature the fundamental points,
the *Anschauungsweisen,* the fixed facts which, through their certainty
and universality, can be used as a fruitful means of lightening the
acquisition and consideration of many secondary and related objects."
— *Wie Gertrud,* etc. (*Sämmt. Schrift.,* V. 43).

[2] *The National Education demanded by the Age* (trans. by Emily
Mayer); Barnard, *Kind. and Child Culture,* 321.

lozzi, and which, as we shall see, is pre-eminent with Froebel. It is the now familiar doctrine that, to learn, the child must act, must re-create; and this he must do harmoniously with his inner nature, rhythmically with external nature, and interdependently with humanity. Upon this doctrine rest modern methods of teaching.

"The education acquired from Pestalozzi," writes Madame de Staël, in *De l'allemagne*,[1] "gives every man, no matter what his station, a foundation upon which he can erect, at will, the poor man's hut or palaces for kings."

Upon this foundation the educational systems of Germany, of Scandinavia, of Switzerland, built themselves up. More than two hundred years earlier, Luther and Comenius had given the impulse to the German principalities, but it was Pestalozzi who gave the spirit that unified and quickened the older impulse; from the unity and enthusiasm of the education which he gave to the German states arose Germany herself. We in America followed, as was natural, the models and ideals that England gave us. Upon these we established that system of public education which has been the preservative of the spirit brought across the ocean by the picked men who founded the Republic. To-day we have new problems before us, to which these old standards are inadequate, for which these old methods do not suffice. Fortunately, the spirit of German education has come to us, and is rapidly transforming ours to meet the grave questions that confront us. Back of that spirit is the inspiration of Pestalozzi; but back of him is the spirit of Rousseau and of that French nation which in so many vital advances of civilization has been the prophet of truth, but which in so few has been the recognized and patient apostle.

So completely has the memory of him vanished, that it is

[1] I. 160.

difficult to-day to realize the vogue of Pestalozzi. His name for many years was alike the spark of inspiration and the catch-penny candle of charlatanism. Governments vied with one another in the decreeing of so-called Pestalozzian reforms and in the nursing of self-styled Pestalozzian reformers. And this was natural; it was necessary; it was a part of the appointed work of fanaticism. The sluggish world was beginning to ponder (foolishly in the main), to talk (wildly as a rule), to experiment (aimlessly in the majority of cases), upon educational problems; but enough that it did talk and ponder and experiment. The foolishness and aimlessness were in time to fritter themselves away, leaving a solid residuum of advance towards fuller knowledge of educational ends.

To one of the more rational Pestalozzian schools kept at Frankfort by a certain Herr Grüner, there came by chance, in 1805, a young man of twenty-three who had journeyed from his native Thuringia to study in the city. His name was Friedrich Froebel. He had had a desultory youth, now as forester's assistant, again as a special student at Jena, later as a land steward, and he had made his way to Frankfort in order to add to his already varied, though superficial, knowledge a smattering of architecture.[1] Grüner, recognizing his teaching faculty, offered him a position in the Pestalozzian school; and, from the moment when his class confronted him, Froebel's career was determined. With scarcely an interruption, the remaining forty-seven years of his life were devoted to pedagogic work.

Twice during these years did he visit Yverdun; and, while he found much to criticise, while he failed to see that Pestalozzi had attained the eternal principle of "Unity,"

[1] For the details of Froebel's life, see his *Autobiography;* Frau von Marenholz-Bülow, *Reminiscences;* Schmidt, *Gesch. der Pädagogik*, IV. 238 ; and Bowen, *Froebel*.

still he gained, and himself confesses that he gained, inspiration there that determined in great measure the direction' of his efforts.

One is forced, in justice to both, to place these two
leaders, this master and his pupil, in contrast, so persistently and wrongly have their adherents put them in opposition.   It is true their natures were opposed; their personal
equations contained few like quantities; but the high results for which they strove were in every way similar.
The special forms of their endeavor differed, but the fundamental forms, the formulæ, were identical.   Each made
special application of his theories: Pestalozzi to the neglected infants of mankind, — the outcast, the beggared, the
orphaned; Froebel to the abused infants of men, — the spirit-
ually outcast, the mentally beggared, the sympathetically
orphaned.   But under the aim of each, under the method
of each, under the immediate educational object of each, lay
the eternal principle of the other, that education, be it for
rich or poor, for the intellectually high or the morally low,
must rest upon and grow out of love.

Were any proof needed of the universality of this principle, the opposite ways by which the conviction of it was
forced upon these two men would serve as minor evidence.
Their childhood experiences, those experiences which give
the great moral biases to us all, were antipodal.   Pestalozzi, as we have seen, losing his father in infancy, was
brought up by tender and careful women, who shielded him
too closely.   Froebel, on the other hand, left motherless
and at the mercy of a hateful stepmother, received what
slight care was vouchsafed him from men, all of them, except an uncle with whom he spent four happy boyhood
years, men of a stern, unsympathetic sort.   Yet Froebel,
to whom the blessing was unknown, was convinced, equally
with Pestalozzi, that mother-love is the true basis of educa-

tion. Frau von Marenholz, his most appreciative disciple, testifies [1] that Froebel again and again said, in substance: "The destiny of nations lies far more in the hands of women — the mothers — than in the possessors of power, or of those innovators who for the most part do not understand themselves. We must train women, who are the educators of the human race, else the new generation cannot accomplish its task." "This," she says, "was almost always the sum of his discourse."

But, whether by education or by nature, the mind of Froebel was more masculine than that of Pestalozzi. It was well-ordered and disciplined. It reached its convictions less by divine impulse and more by prosaic reason. Both were pious, but Pestalozzi's possessed the piety of faith, while Froebel's held that of conviction. We may safely make the old distinction between these two men, that Pestalozzi had genius, and Froebel talent; but the small fund· of the latter, by qualities of orderliness and mental thrift, made greater profit than the profuse and scattered intellectual wealth of the former. Such mistakes and abortive struggles as those of Pestalozzi's first fifty years would have been impossible to the clearer, less feverish mind of Froebel; such incoherency as was inseparable from the Swiss reformer was unknown to the more restricted intellect of the German, whose ideas suffer from fancy rather than exuberance; [2] such wretched quarrels as those at Yverdun would have been impossible in the mild atmosphere of Froebel's schools, where the enthusiasm was never of the gusty sort that fans the heat of fervor into the flames of passion. "If I were not afraid of being taken for an idiot

---

[1] Marenholz-Bülow's *Reminiscences* (Mann's trans.), Ch. I. 4.

[2] Froebel's style, however, is more vague and rambling than even Pestalozzi's.

or an escaped lunatic," writes Froebel,[1] "I would run barefoot from one end of Germany to the other and cry aloud to all men." Pestalozzi *would* have run barefoot, and would have gloried in the reputation of insanity: such was the difference between them.

Pestalozzi, the real genius, was unique; he was a sporadic growth, a ferment sent to leaven the doughish lump of humanity. Froebel, on the contrary, was merely a representative of a well-defined class; he was a type — a strongly marked type — of that philosophical spirit which did so much towards the welding of Germany after her humiliation by Napoleon. Practical yet dreamy, scientific yet credulous, analytic yet mystical, filled with fancies, symbols, extravagancies, exuberant in thought and speech, the newborn German nation was like a child, with a child's surplus of strength, a child's ill-balanced imagination, a child's elastic vision, limited to self, yet with sudden illuminating glimpses into eternity. Froebel was the embodiment of this *Zeitgeist*, this exaggeration of yearning, this overestimate of self-promise, this glamour of existence, which characterized the Germany of sixty years ago. If we divorce him from his striking nationality, we lose the key to Froebel's aims. We lose, too, the explanation of the sad havoc which a too literal translation of his figurative and incomplete demonstrations has wrought.

Froebel was first of all a German striving for the redemption of Germany. Inspired by Pestalozzi and gifted with a talent for the probing of first principles, he sought to base German unity upon spiritual unity, upon the omnipotent spirit of unity in nature. This principle of universal harmony he identifies rightly with the all-pervading spirit

---

[1] To Frau Sçhmidt, January, 1847.   See Michaelis-Moore, *Froebel's Let.*, 146.

of love. As all natural phenomena are the outward manifestations of the striving of all things towards unity, so
all ethical phenomena are the outward signs of the inner
striving of the soul towards spiritual unity, towards harmony with God. The task of education, therefore, is to
help the soul in this aspiration towards unity with God [1]
and with His manifestation of Himself in nature. "We
must render perceptible to the child the unity of the
world, absolute existence, the world within; and these in an
earthly, human, childlike, intelligible fashion. Unity must
be perceived in variety, absolute existence in phenomena,
harmony in melody, the soul in the body, — in a word
all things in all things, — and this through many-sided,
harmoniously-active life and work." [2] In these words does
Froebel sum up his principles. Pestalozzi's aim was no
lower, and the educational tool of both these men was that
untranslatable *Anschauung*, that making of knowledge a
part and parcel of one's very being, that mental and spiritual digestion of phenomena. Froebel, however, of an era
somewhat later than that of Pestalozzi, of a receptive habit
of mind, reflecting, as has been said, the extraordinary
German spirit of the dawning nineteenth century, and
assimilating the doctrines of that body of German philosophers whose influence upon educational growth was so great,

---

[1] "Genuine and true, living religion, reliable in danger and struggles, in times of oppression and need, in joy and pleasure, must come
to man in his infancy ; for the Divine Spirit that lives and is manifest
in the finite, in man, has an early though dim feeling of its divine
origin ; and this vague sentiment, this exceedingly misty feeling,
should be fostered, strengthened, nurtured, and, later on, raised into
full consciousness, into clear apprehension." — *Ed. of Man* (Hailmann), 25. *Froebel's gesamm. päd. Schrift.* (Lange), I. 2, 18.

[2] Letter to Frau Schmidt, December, 1840. See Michaelis-Moore,
Froebel's Let., 57.

spiritualized a doctrine which, with Pestalozzi, remained dangerously near materialism. Pestalozzi aimed to make, by his educational process, the outward world a possession of the inward man, to make the "outer, inner." Froebel went further than this, and, not satisfied with making the "outer, inner," aspired also to make the "inner, outer";[1] that is, he aspired not only to bring the world of phenomena into relationship with man, but also to spiritualize material phenomena through man.

It is this endeavor which lies at the bottom of his kindergarten plays; but it is this aspiration, also, which led him into extravagances of subtlety in explaining his educational theories. "I know no more decided enemy of materialism than Froebel," declares his editor, Lange.[2] True; but, in his anxiety to escape materialism, he was betrayed into many absurdities concerning the effect of material upon spiritual phenomena. He would, and did, make the child self-expansive by making him self-active. But, not satisfied with a simple explanation of this beautiful fact, he must needs delve for far-fetched and sometimes grotesque causes for simple effects — effects which are the result, merely, of the satisfaction of energy, of the joy of existence, or, to use his own expression, of the attainment of unity. Without being a psychologist, he gave a psychologic twist to all his theories, and complacently esteemed his will-o'-the-wisps of fancy to be beacon-lights of progress. One

---

[1] ". . . This 'rendering of the inner outer,' is the great Froebelian doctrine of *creativeness*. It is the practical application of the principle of *self-activity*, and, together with the doctrines of *continuity* and *connectedness*, it forms the true heart of Froebel's system. It gives their very life-blood to all the songs and games; and it is the living principle in all the occupations, which without it are mere sticks and stones, and bits of paper." — BOWEN, *Froebel*, III. 54.

[2] Barnard, *Kind. and Child Culture*, 70.

needs but to study his Italian contemporary, Rosmini, who was, indeed, a profound psychologist, and whose theories were parallel to Froebel's,[1] to perceive the shallowness of Froebel's transcendentalism.[2]

This foible of his would be of no consequence were it not that these unsound doctrines have survived and form the whole gospel of many of his disciples, while the deep and everlasting doctrine of their master is forgotten or overlooked. Seldom has a man been at once so fortunate and so unfortunate in his friends. A few — notably Middendorf and Frau von Marenholz-Bülow — have not only interpreted him, but have actually helped him to understand himself. Too many of them, however, have seized upon that in him which was most fantastic, most transitory, most purely local, and have tried to limit him to their elaborations and perversions of these accidental things. Through their mistaken activity, they have succeeded in restricting him to the lesser phase of his work, the kindergarten, and have, in too many instances, so materialized his spirit as to convert it into a pedagogic scarecrow, to excite laughter and derision. Froebel's fancies have too often usurped the place which belongs to his truths. The true Froebel saw "in every child the possibility of a perfect man."[3] He desired (to again use his own words)[4] "to educate men whose feet shall stand on God's earth, rooted fast in nature, while their

---

[1] Compare, *e.g.*, the second and third chapters of the *Education of Man* with Rosmini's *Method in Education.*

[2] Herbart, too, whom I have neglected only because he is of that body of German philosophers which it has been necessary to exclude from the plan of this outline, founds his pedagogics upon a broad and serious philosophy in contrast with which Froebel's psychological fancies seem childish indeed.

[3] Marenholz-Bülow, *Rem.*, Ch. II. 21.

[4] *Auto.*, p. 63. *Froebels Gesamm. päd. Schrift.* (Lange), I. 1, 83.

head towers up to heaven and reads its secrets with steady gaze, whose heart shall embrace both earth and heaven, shall enjoy the life of earth and nature with all its wealth of forms, and at the same time shall recognize the purity and peace of heaven, that unites in its love God's earth with God's heaven." The true Froebel, in this high pursuit, regards the kindergarten as a first step. "Play," he says,[1] "is the first means of development in the human mind, its first effort to make acquaintance with the outward world, to collect outward experiences from things and facts, and to exercise the powers of body and mind." Therefore he uses play, not only to stimulate the budding activities, but to measure and direct the child's individuality.[2] He avails himself of a hitherto unused force and, by harnessing it, vastly increases its power for good. At the same time he leads the child, necessarily, from outer darkness of mental and spiritual neglect, into an atmosphere of sympathy and understanding, bringing to bear upon him, thereby, the power of love; and, thirdly, by magnifying the individuality of little children, he increases, reflectively, the parental consciousness of responsibility.[3]

---

[1] Marenholz-Bülow, *Rem.*, Ch. VI. 67.

[2] " Child's play strengthens the powers both of the soul and of the body, provided we know how to make the first self-occupation of a child a freely active, that is, a creative or a productive, one." — MAREN-HOLZ-BÜLOW, *Rem.*, Ch. XI. 156.

" Up till now there has been no means of ascertaining a man's vocation. To provide such a means is my great care, and is the cause of my devotion to the elaboration of my game system. It is indeed the inmost secret aim I have had in view; and when once it is generally acknowledged, there will begin a new era for the human race." — Letter to Frau Schmidt, September, 1843. See Michaelis-Moore, *Froebel's Let.*, 131.

[3] On this must depend the future, not only of education, but of civilization itself. We are now at such a point of material advance-

The false Froebel, he who, unfortunately, is most commonly preached, is a mechanician, a deviser of graded playthings, a composer of indifferent verses, in which we are asked to see a profound pedagogical system. The playthings, as types, are good; the songs, as suggestions, are worthy of use; but they should remain types and models. Every year in history, every mile in geography, takes children farther away from their literal use. Every child demands, if not new Froebelian *Gifts*, at least a new order in their use; and for every child and every group of children there must be devised new songs, new games, new "occupations." No one could say this more strongly than did Froebel himself in the early days of the kindergarten. It was only when, intoxicated by the success of his *Gifts*, and flattered by the extravagances of his followers, that he forgot that the playthings themselves were transitory, and only the principles which had led him to produce them were eternal. It was then that he lost hold upon the substance of his doctrines, and, grasping these shadows, these toys and rhymes, believed that through them would come the regeneration of the world.

Singularly enough, there came with this hardening of his free spirit into the mould of mechanical routine a change of base similar to that which occurred in the case of Pestalozzi. The old Swiss, in his last, sad years, came wholly under the sway of Schmidt, whom Michelet calls the "cipherer,"[1] and who did, indeed, reduce the Pestalozzian

ment and complexity, the opportunities and incitements towards evil, as well as towards good, have so greatly multiplied, that only in an increased sense of parental duty is there possibility of a spiritual advance in any degree equal to our material progress. Fortunately, this sense of responsibility seems to be rapidly growing.

[1] "Three walls grow up around Pestalozzi. Formalism in three shapes buries him and seals his tomb. The cipherer, Schmidt,

spirit to a kind of mathematical legerdemain. Froebel, too, seemed in his last years, as the development of the *Gifts* bears witness, to lay more and more stress upon mathematics. Already, in the *Education of Man*, he had found a mathematical demonstration or verification of religion,[1] and, in 1847, writing to Miss Howe, he says:[2] "Since order, measure, rhythm, form, size, number, ratio, etc., are on all sides visible and audible, — nay, even they may often also be touched and tasted, — it seems as if everything were pointing to mathematics as the one true way and the one true science of order and knowledge, and, so to speak, the central point of all true perceptions of things." So far towards mechanicalization did his increasing worship of the baggage of his pedagogics carry him. Into far worse depths has a slavish imitation of this baggage-worship led some of his disciples.

A few, however, have kept themselves on the high plane of the true Froebel. Chief among these is the Baroness von Marenholz-Bülow. In her writings and in his own book, the *Education of Man*, the real pedagogic preacher appears, not the narrow being to whom the paraphernalia of the kindergarten are all-important, but the great follower of Pestalozzi, who knew how to shape the vague aspirations, to spiritualize the earthy methods, of the Swiss reformer.

The true Froebel says: "The representation of the in-

becomes the master; thereafter figuring and no longer observation. The German, Niederer, methodical of mind, complicates, with abstruse formulas, rigs up in German dress, the simple, virile ideas of his master, transforming him into a Jena doctor.

"But, worst of all, comes the fatal influence of a reaction to the past. It was reverted to through grammar, through the language-teaching inflicted upon little children." — MICHELET, *Nos fils*, 234.

[1] *Ed. of Man* (Hailmann), 205.

[2] See Michaelis-Moore, *Froebel's Let.*, 254.

finite in the finite, of the eternal in the temporal, of the celestial in the terrestrial, of the divine in and through man, in the life of man by the nursing of his originally divine nature, confronts us unmistakably on every side as the only object, the aim of all education, in all instruction and training." [1]

"All true education in training and instruction should, therefore, at every moment, in every demand and regulation, be simultaneously double-sided — giving and taking, uniting and dividing, prescribing and following, active and passive, positive yet giving scope, firm and yielding; and the pupil should be similarly conditioned : but between the two, between educator and pupil, between request and obedience, there should invisibly rule a third something to which teacher and pupil are equally subject. This third something is the *right*, the *best*." [2]

Thus does Froebel summarize the principles of modern education, principles that began with civilization, that Pestalozzi, for the thousandth time, rediscovered and quickened, that Froebel, imbibing, put in order and made available.

It is still too soon to predict the ultimate effect of the movement in education which, so far as this country is concerned, began with Froebel. We who are in the midst of the slow revolution can measure neither its magnitude nor its results. By it the last serf of civilization, the child, is being made free, and is taking his place in the scheme of the universe as a great, if not the greatest, factor of human progress. By it and through him, man and woman are learning the true significance of life : —

[1] *Ed. of Man* (Hailmann), 16.
[2] *Ed. of Man* (Hailmann), 14. *Froebels Gesamm. päd. Schrift.* (Lange), I. 2, 10.

"Come let us live with our children: then will the life of our children bring us peace and joy, then shall we begin to grow wise, to be wise!"[1]

[1] *Ed. of Man* (Hailmann), 89. *Froebels Gesamm. päd. Schrift.* (Lange), I. 2, 60. (See the whole of this § 47.)

/

CHAPTER IX.

WOMEN IN EDUCATION.

EDUCATION LEADS TO AND FROM THE FAMILY: THE HOME IS
ITS UNIT.

A NEW POWER IN EDUCATION; ITS GENESIS; WOMEN IN ENGLAND; IN
GERMANY; IN FRANCE; THE WOMEN WRITERS; ROUSSEAU'S INFLU-
ENCE; SOPHIE; MADAME DE GENLIS; MADAME NECKER; MADAME
DE STAËL; MADAME NECKER DE SAUSSURE; "PROGRESSIVE EDU-
CATION"; MADAME GUIZOT; ENGLISH WRITERS; GERMAN KINDER-
GARTNERS; OTHER KINDERGARTNERS; THE EFFECT OF THE WOMEN
EDUCATIONISTS; EXPANSION OF EDUCATION; CHILD-STUDY; THE
PRESENT STATUS OF EDUCATION.

BETWEEN Rousseau, educating his Émile by passive
watchfulness and hidden negation, and Pestalozzi, hurrying
his pupils forward by force of enthusiasm and the incite-
ment of association, nearly fifty years intervened. The
half-century that saw this essential change of attitude, and
made the general acceptance of Pestalozzianism possible,
witnessed the rise of a new and indispensable force in education, — that of women. Hannah More had said,[1] in
stately irony: "The rights of men have been discussed till
we are somewhat wearied with the discussion. To these
have been opposed, as the next stage in the progress of
illumination, and with more presumption than prudence,

---

[1] *Works*, IV. 100. Her *Strictures on the Modern System of Female
Education*, from which this is extracted, is, however, very lively, readable, and, in many respects, full of good sense.

the rights of woman. It follows, according to the natural progression of human things, that the next influx of that irradiation which our enlighteners are pouring in upon us will illuminate the world with grave descants on the rights of youth, the rights of children, the rights of babies!" The "progress of illumination," despite those gentlewomen of whom "Mrs." More is so excellent a type, *had* gone on, had emphasized, not alone the rights, but also the real duties of women, and had called the attention of the civilized world to the fact that, for its own safety, it must pay more heed to those rights upon which it had for so many years trampled, the rights of the youth, of the child, and of the infant.

Again we must go to France to see the genesis of the new force. It is true that both in Germany and in England a home-life more genuine than that of France had for a long time existed; it is true, too, that in Germany the influence of Comenius and Luther had produced a system of education much more modern than was elsewhere known.[1] But the German woman, subordinate as she was, could not be a force in civilization until, by the Froebelian movement, she should be exalted into a sort of genius of education; and the English tradition was so wedded to the humanities, the tutor and the endowed school were such sacred and impregnable institutions, that the Englishwoman failed to utilize the enormous uplifting impulse that could have been given by a better home-life.

The position of the Frenchwoman was unique. For two hundred years she had been the controlling power in France. During the seventeenth century the centripetal tendency of French society steadily transformed the tyranny of a royal house into that of a city. Paris grew to be the acknowl-

---

[1] See Barnard, *Nat. Ed. in Europe*, 17 to 340.

edged despot of France; but the politics, the social life, the literature, the art of Paris came, at the same time, under the indirect but absolute dictation of the women. The wife, the mother, the mistress, ruled Paris as Paris ruled France, capriciously and selfishly, but from the æsthetic and intellectual standpoint, fairly well. Their rule showed all the advantages, as well as the enormous defects, of centralization. Whether to its ultimate good or not, France was given by this concentration of its intellectual life, an impetus towards higher civilization that, even to-day, invests her with a certain leadership.

In the eighteenth century, the rule of the Frenchwoman was even greater than in the seventeenth, but this increased dominion had been gained at a fearful cost. The power that she wielded in the earlier century was that of a Madame de Maintenon; in the later, it was that of a Pompadour. From the gallantry of the age of Louis XV. had faded all remembrance of chivalry, and into it the refining influence of democracy had not yet entered. An Oriental brutality in its intrigue had distorted the relations of its men and women, had alienated the latter from their children, and threatened, by this estrangement, to degrade itself into utter license. Materialism and cynicism seemed in full possession until out of chaos came Chaos transfigured in the person of Jean-Jacques, morbidly preaching virtue, and turning frenzied license into an equal extravagance of sentimentalism. After him came the Revolution, with its sudden vision of Hades and its swallowing therein of social parasites. Adversity brought parents and children for the first time together, making them drink in common from the bitter cup of disobedience. There appeared, under these conditions, a new species of *femme d'esprit*, the mother preaching motherhood to her sex. Rousseau had incited women to suckle their children, even in the ball-room, to live with them, even to the point of making the poor babies share the mothers' dissipations. He had led what one might call an orgy of domesticity. But these women preachers who followed him sobered this mad motherhood into one approaching wisdom and unselfishness.

These female evangelists of true education were none of them, if we except Madame de Staël, great women. It was Proudhon who said: "Whenever, in literature, genius, busied with other things, happens to retire, and the feminine element takes the ascendant, then appear the second-rate writers." Certainly, in so far as it is a question of the literature of education, he is right. Genius retired with Rousseau; after him appeared a host of writers, many of them women, who wrote voluminously upon education; but all these women, and all these men indeed, excepting Pestalozzi, were second-rate. What made the rapid advance in educational ideas was not these female writers; it was the "eternal feminine "[1] asserting itself in new ways, and slowly broadening its dominion downward from man adult to man adolescent.

Rousseau leading — or following — the march of events, helped to make this new position tenable; but one could hardly have expected him to take a rational view of woman or of her education. The Sophie[2] whom he trains to be the complement of Émile is not an actuality; she is not even lifelike; she is simply an incident in a masculine career. Indeed, he so far sacrifices artistic proportion and insults

[1] "*Das Ewig-Weibliche.*" See Bayard Taylor, *Goethe's Faust*, II. Note 194.

[2] *Sophie, ou la femme*, is the sub-title of the fifth book of *Émile*. " Sophie must be such a woman as Émile is a man," Rousseau declares (*Émile*, Liv. V., 409) ; but he fails dismally in his attempt to fulfil this opening condition.

his own doctrines as to make her immoral.[1] "The first and most important quality in woman," Rousseau says,[2] "is sweetness. Made to obey a being so imperfect, often so full of vice as man, she must early learn to suffer uncomplainingly even injustice and wrong-doing from her husband. . . . Sharpness and upbraiding serve no end except to multiply the sins and ill-doing of the husband." But to this invertebrate creature he would commit the early education of children, that "first education which, " he rightly says,[3] "is the most important, and which belongs, without question, to women." It was in the mother-heart,[4] however, not in the wife-heart, that the words of Rousseau found lodging, and in a degree we may date from him the rise of woman into her true position.

The first of the distinctly labelled female "educationists " of the new time was that versatile and volatile person, Madame de Genlis. At heart she was of the old *régime*, in which the happy days of her youth had been spent. She loved that silly, puerile life, and describes it[5] with such frankness of affection that we begin to wonder if the Revolution did not swallow up some old world quite alien to ours. But she was French and, therefore, intellectually flexible, and, when the change came, she quickly adapted herself to the new ideas. Borrowing Rousseau's principles, — which, being pernicious, were clearly contraband, — she gave them a *bourgeois* royalist stamp, tried them upon her pupils, the children of *Philippe Égalité*,[6] and found them,

[1] In *Émile et Sophie*, a weak and worthless sequel to *Émile*.

[2] *Émile*, Liv. V. 426.

[3] *Émile*, Liv. I. 6 (note).

[4] See *ante*, p. 184. (Quot. from von Raumer.)

[5] In her memoirs. See, *e.g.*, her description, *con amore*, of the foolish pranks of her early married life.

[6] For adequate sketches of Madame de Genlis, see Ste.-Beuve, *Caus. du Lundi*, III. 15; and Dobson, *Four Frenchwomen*.

thus remodelled, to be perfection.   The more she profited by the Citizen of Geneva, the more loudly she decried him ;[1] but her court edition of *Émile* was not a bad one ; she was a woman determined and successful in making a stir in the world ; and so she did much towards spreading the fashion of maternal responsibility.

Her method of training was not profound; neither was it very consistent.   It was distinctly in advance of the ordinary systems of her day, however, and it succeeded in making a tolerable compromise between the impossible naturalism of Rousseau and that vapid frivolity in education which was the offspring of the time.   She isolated her ideal pupils, her Adèle and Théodore, but she did not forget, as did Jean-Jacques, to isolate their parents too.[2]

What most astonishes one in Madame de Genlis is her literary range and fecundity.   She was fatally ready with her pen, and her plays, her moral disquisitions, as well as her pedagogic romance, *Adèle et Théodore*, are stamped with the garrulity of a half-educated woman too busy, too

[1] " Not to pay one's tutor, not to teach the catechism, not to deny children, not to trouble one's self about them; that is the sum of J.-J. Rousseau's principles."   See the very interesting note (8) at the end of the 83d Vol. (*La Religion*) of the *Œuv. de Madame de Genlis.*

[2] Le baron d'Almane and his wife really exile themselves from Paris, with their two children (aged six and seven years), until Adèle's entrance into society.   In their letters to friends and relatives are developed Madame de Genlis's views on education.   As to her ideal of female education, see *Adèle et Théodore* (Paris, 1825), T. IV. 50 *et seq.*, and the summing up on p. 119: "Ne croyez pas, . . . que mon projet soit de rendre Adèle *savante.* . . .   Je ne prétends que lui donner une connoisance très-superficielle de toutes ces choses, qui puisse servir quelque fois à son amusement, la mettre en état d'écouter sans ennui son père, son frère, ou son mari ; . . . et la préserver d'une infinité de petits préjugés que donne nécessairement l'ignorance."

vain, and too facile to take pains. Madame Guizot said[1] of her that "she always wrote well and never better."

A person of the court, without being in a bad sense a courtier; prodigiously accomplished, as the times went, but fully sensible of the vanity of her education; a prophet to the new no less than an authority to the old order of things, — Madame de Genlis was a factor of importance in the growth of education. While her avowed enmity to Rousseau made her acceptable to the conservative element, her adoption of his principles attached her to the radicals in education. Her pupils, the Orléans children, dull as was to be expected, seem neither to have chilled her enthusiasm nor to have awed her into sparing them a wholesome discipline. In the true scientific spirit, she made their very defects serve the ends of experimentation. Altogether she is an interesting and characteristic figure of the transition time in France.

Quite different from her were the three Necker women, two of whom fill so large a space in the history of the reconstruction of France. These women were distinctly *bourgeoise*. They may be taken as types of the new society that supplanted the old, but they were not of the *bourgeoisie* of Paris; they belonged essentially to Geneva, where theocracy had created a middle class far more advanced, intellectually, and far broader in its sympathies than the mercantile middle-class of the Capital. Madame Necker, perhaps no more clever, certainly not more ambitious, than her overrated husband, had greater tact than he, and possessed, moreover, the high advantage of being a woman. Never acclimated to the feverish atmosphere of pre-revolutionary Paris, — an atmosphere hot with the discussion of problems whose real depths none saw or was capable of

---

[1] Quoted by Ste.-Beuve, *Portraits des femmes*, 232.

seeing,[1] — always a countrywoman in the Parisian sense, she
nevertheless succeeded not only in building up a *salon* from
the heterogeneous material ready to the hand of any skilful
social architect, but in winning an entrance and a recognized place among the remote and all but impregnable fast-
nesses of the old nobility. She and most of her self-
conscious followers were mediocre; the *haute noblesse* were
duller still; but, under circumstances far from favorable,
Madame Necker succeeded in establishing a really brilliant
salon, the last of the old order. She did far better than
this; she created a favorable intellectual soil for her daughter, the future Madame de Staël. The younger woman was
neither mediocre nor Genevese; still less was she really
Parisian ; rather was she European, possessed of a breadth
and tolerance, rare enough at all times, and almost unknown
then in the dweller in Paris. Madame de Staël was no less
alert towards education [2] than towards other topics having
life and contemporaneousness. She wrote sensibly regarding it, and was unusually broad in her grasp and treatment
of pedagogic questions.

But it was Madame Necker de Saussure, a Necker only
by marriage,[3] who was truly and distinctively an "education-
ist." She too was Genevese; more than that, she was a
Calvinist. The agony of the Jansenist breathes through
her prayerful and anxious treatment of educational questions. But she was too sensible to be gloomy, too wise to
be ascetic; her Jansenism, therefore, is healthily modern.
It is not the protection of the cloister, but that of the
home, that she would throw around young girls. She
would keep them in moral safety by discipline, but not

[1] Cf. E. J. Lowell, *The Eve of the French Revolution.*
[2] See, especially, *De l'allemagne* and *De la littérature.*
[3] She was daughter to the famous Swiss naturalist, H. B. de
Saussure.

by the somewhat empty discipline of the convent; rather by the normal pressure of a good home life and salutary home duties. While accepting the naturalism of Rousseau, she is a determined enemy to his doctrine of *laissez faire*, finding the chief fault of education to be "rather negative than positive"; to be in "what is neglected rather than in what is done."[1] She makes education in morals the supreme education, she shapes all teaching to the end of moral growth, but she discards the apparatus and intermediaries that her predecessors had placed around the child, and makes the parents the only — or, rather, the final — sponsors and workers for the child's spiritual progress. With solid reasoning and full understanding she demonstrates the responsibility of parenthood, that responsibility which can never, without hurt to the child, be shirked or delegated; she treats the home relations with that warm sympathy, that sentiment without sentimentality, and that nicety of discrimination which are peculiarly feminine. "It is so truly love," she says,[2] "which produces love in the child, that he possesses an extraordinary tact for discovering it. His preferences, which appear unaccountable, are founded on an inconceivable divination in regard to this point. Ugliness, the infirmities of age, do not repulse him; the most essential services affect him but little; it is love that he wants, love without beauty, without external grace, without even a title to gratitude."

Again she says:[3] "The sway of sympathy over little children is the cause of our power with them. Understanding language very incompletely and argument not at all, we could rule them only by force, if Heaven had not opened to us the way to their hearts. The instinct which compels

---

[1] *L'éduc. prog.*, I. 104 (Ch. V.).
[2] *Prog. Educ.* (Willard's trans.), Ch. V. 175.
[3] *L'éduc. prog.*, I. 200 (Ch. V.).

them to put themselves in harmony with us is the way
chosen by Providence to make them adopt, unconsciously,
our sentiments, and to mould their will upon ours."

Madame Necker de Saussure was a most acute and judicious observer of children. She neglected no smallest trait
of infancy, and drew wise inferences from the commonest
acts of childhood ; but, on the other hand, she was not
over-subtle. While conscious of the immense significance
which may attach, in childhood, to seemingly trivial things,
she did not build up exaggerated and remote explanations
of everything done by the child. She recognized the fact
that children are animals to such a degree that many of
their acts are not only instinctive, but really purposeless.
The infant mind, like any other untrained organ, works in
a bungling and often aimless fashion, and it must not be
held to too strict an accountability.

Madame Necker de Saussure was, then, among the first
to show the importance of child-study, to demonstrate that
this investigation must be carried on among the petty hap-
penings of the nursery, and to prove, therefore, the signal
fitness of women for this task. More than this, she pur-
sued that study in so scientific a way, her reasoning is so
judicial, she was so little carried away by theories or influenced by preconceived opinions, that she forms one of the
safest of guides in this important branch of investigation.

The German observers are, as a rule, too elaborate, too
minute. They lack that scientific perspective without
which just emphasis cannot be placed upon the heterogeneous and often contradictory events of infant and child
growth. Madame de Saussure, without their scientific
training, possessed this wider and clearer vision. This
intuition of the relative value of psychological data is a
peculiarly feminine quality, and was possessed by the last of
the Frenchwomen whom we shall consider, Madame Guizot.

Madame Pauline Guizot,[1] intellectually, was much more than an echo of her husband; she labored zealously and effectively with him upon his *Annales de l'éducation,* and herself wrote — best among many good things — *Lettres de famille sur l'éducation.* These family letters, the imagined correspondence of parents fully conscious of their responsibilities, are not only entertaining and suggestive, but they present and balance very successfully the divergent and sometimes conflicting points of view of the father and of the mother. They deal, therefore, with no small measure of success, with that double, or, indeed, four-sided problem, how the boy and the girl shall be reared by the father and mother jointly, so that there may be entire harmony of action without loss of personal or sexual individuality. These letters are marked by that stamp of sincerity which seizes the mind of the reader, arouses its interest, and makes it active in self-discussion.

Two marked characteristics pervade Madame Guizot's writings, a spirit of intellectual democracy,[2] and a belief in the home. "Of all the theories of education," she says,[3] speaking of the mother, "there is not one equal, I believe,

---

[1] See Ste.-Beuve, *Portraits des femmes.*

[2] " Her favorite idea, her cherished idea, was that the same moral education can and must be applied to all conditions; that under the most diverse external circumstances, under bad and under good fortune, whether designed for a low or a high destiny, a quiet or a feverish one, all men can attain, children must be educated to attain, an ethical development almost identical, — to the same uprightness, the same moral delicacy, the same loftiness of feeling and thought; that the human soul contains within itself that which is equal to every accident, to every combination of human conditions; and that it is a problem only of revealing to it the secret of its strength and of teaching the soul how to use it." — *Une famille.* Extract from preface, quoted by Ste.-Beuve (*Port. des femmes,* 238).

[3] *Conseils de morale,* II. 72.

to the constant force of this gentle care, always on the watch to remedy defects before they become too strong to repress, to propose aims that shall not be too difficult of attainment, to duplicate the little successes which encourage, to foresee even the fear of the fall, so that the pupil, held up before he feels himself stumbling, has faith in the power which sustains him without being aware of the extent of his feebleness which makes that support necessary."

Madame Guizot's educational ideal is placed very high. She has in view neither the duty of the parent nor the self-interest of the child so much as that third *something* to which, as Froebel says,[1] "teacher" (or parent) "and pupil are equally subject — the *right*, the *best.*" No education can reach its highest development until those having it in charge, whether they be parents or teachers, regard it from that standpoint of ultimate human good, and make the training of the child, in the truest sense, a religious act.

Among Englishwomen, until we reach Harriet Martineau, whose *Household Education* is full of good sense, and who, in a way, was the first to popularize the idea, in education, of training to good citizenship,[2] there is no writer upon education who was not either the coadjutor of a literary man, or a schoolmistress politely crying her pedagogical wares. Exception might be made of Miss Edgeworth, whose *Practical Education* is a too greatly neglected book. But she is a propounder of methods rather than of principles, and her teachings are more suggestive than inspiring.

No German woman, of course, wrote upon questions of education until, with Frau Marenholz-Bülow leading the way, the kindergartners began their aggressive and wholesome campaign. Since that day they have been legion, and

---

[1] See p. 205, *ante.*
[2] As, *e.g.*, in her *Illustrations of Political Economy.*

have carried their mission into other countries where seconded — to mention only a few names — by Madame Pape-Carpantier in France, by Miss Shirreff and Mrs. Grey in England, by Miss Peabody and Mrs. Mann in the United States, they have done a noble work in arousing women to a sense of their responsible and indispensable part in forwarding the growth of the educational ideal.

Mediocre, however, as most of the feminine apostles of education were, their preaching was tremendous in its effect. Motherhood began its evolution from merely physical and material functions into the exercise of a spiritual mission. The rights of women began to appear as something more than civil and political ones; they grew to be understood as rights that should fill a wider field; rights that, by liberating the mother intellectually and morally, should, through her, free the child. Rousseau had made clear the tremendous moral *rôle* of the mother, and had incited women to fulfil that *rôle*. But not until the feminine writers dealt with the question was it seen that woman must herself be educated in order to educate her children, that she must have power in order to give dignity to her training, that she must be a partner, not a dependent, in this vital business of mankind, the intelligent rearing of its offspring. She is still far from the attainment of powers that must be hers before she can adequately fulfil those duties which always have been hers, and which, painfully and blindly, she has succeeded in fulfilling; but the path is now open to her; the importance of her position is acknowledged; and it remains only to adapt, in the slow human way, the old conditions to the new ideals.

With the dawning comprehension of what the mother owes to the child, and of what society owes to her, with the conception of education as a home process, a developing of the child by its natural trainers, the parents, in its natural environment, the home, — schools, teachers, and social life being but accessories and aids, — education emerged at last wholly out of the shadow of monasticism, and lost its last bad tincture of mediævalism. The monks in the fifteenth century had made it their task, as teachers, to fit their pupils to the routine, narrow, anti-social, and profitless, which the Church laid down. With the rise of women as a power in education in the nineteenth century began the final stage in that long educational evolution by which these monkish aims are being reversed. Now, through study of the child, through discriminating sympathy, we are making it possible to provide an education that shall be in some degree fitted to the pupil. For centuries the compressive process had been brought to bear upon children; they had been systematically ground down; their real natures had been fettered; their instincts towards divinity had been crushed; and when, despite these weights and chains, they had had force to assert themselves, their independence had been given every manner of ugly name, and their revolt had been attributed to original depravity. Now we are to try the expansive process, letting nature furnish the impulse.

The sins committed in the name of liberty pale before those committed under the guise of education. The school world was filled, in the old days, with the wails of children tortured in body and mind; with the strife of barbarous art contending with outraged nature; with the wrecks of fine souls ruined by mal-education. This battle and destruction had tortured the mothers too. They had seen, and dimly understood, the pain that childhood suffered in this thwarting and distortion of its tendencies; they alone had known, vaguely, the vast gulf set, in so many cases, between the promise of childhood and the fulfilment of youth. For centuries they had accepted this perversion of nature as a necessary evil; they had bowed to the decrees of fate or Providence or the masculine will, and had remained in a double bondage, lashed with the stripes which fell upon their children, sharing the tortures of minds which in their blind worship of custom they were powerless to succor. As the light of greater individual freedom came to them, they began to perceive that it is the mother who knows her child, that it is she who holds the key to education, that this key is love, and that education is a task to be given not to ascetics, but to parents and, above all, to the mother, designed by God to be the developer of the being whom she has borne and suckled.

With the appreciation of this new relationship between mother and child, came a new era to women and to children. The rise of the "motherhood" idea wrought in educational methods a change different in kind from any advance that had preceded it. It was a change not unlike that which came over the study of human institutions when the "dismal science" of political economy flowered, perhaps, indeed, too exuberantly, into that of sociology. Educational theory, on the one hand, came out from the dim chamber of speculation into the light of experience; educational practice, on the other hand, shrank back from the noisy market-place of common trading into the halls of science and art, albeit of an empirical science and an experimental art.

We have seen how great a share Pestalozzi and Froebel took in this awakening of the home-power — that immense social force which had been so nearly dormant; we have seen how the former used sympathy and the latter, play, as instruments in forwarding civilization. Feminine in spirit and harmonious with child-nature as they were, however, they were powerless to extend their principles to their fullest value. They needed the co-operation of women to amend and complete their educational scheme. There arrived a time, perhaps earlier, perhaps later, than their time — human progress is too vast a thing to be fitted to the calendar — when it came to the comprehension of a few women that the kindergarten — or any association of children in mutual helpfulness under sympathetic direction rather than formal instruction — meant more than appeared upon the surface; that it meant the reorganization of the entire educational system, that it entailed an enlargement of the schoolroom to include both nature and society. They began to understand — as Comenius, more than two hundred years earlier, had tried to teach — that the nursery, too, is a school, that education is a process which begins with the first breath and ends only with the last. Pedagogics, they dimly saw, must now be studied from a new standpoint. It must be not an impression upon, but an expression of, the child. The pupil, therefore, not the system of instruction, must be its focal point.

With aims thus readjusted, these women began to understand the minds and bodies of children to be marvellous mechanisms whose adjustment is easily upset, their souls to be winged things which rough handling will destroy, which neglect will cause to fly away. It is the mother's blessed duty, they perceived, to study this mechanism, to preserve its delicate balance, to develop it and its fugitive tenant towards the doing of their best work in the world. Child study was not a new thing; it had been, after a fashion, a branch of science since scientific study had taken its first rude shape; but it had rested upon a purely formal basis, neutral and cold. With the rise of scientific motherhood — to make use of a most barbarous term — child study, while losing nothing in accuracy, gained immensely in sympathy, broadening both its methods and its aims. Its data, no longer bloodless, breathed with the life and vigor, the astonishing moral variety and subtlety, of childhood. Education, touched with Promethean fire, became living and active, filling, as it ought, a large place in human thought and work.

These changes have taken place, of course, only imperfectly, and only in those upper intellectual strata in which all growth must originate, and from which it must filter down to the general mass of mankind. This permeation is now going on, and is producing a bewildering change and stir in the educational world. Everything is in ferment; there seems little but chaos and disputation, groping and oscillation; no goal, no harmony of thought and work. In time we shall see order asserting itself, a true sequence of growth will be fixed upon, the skeleton of right training will be articulated; then we shall begin to realize what a thing this change in the midst of which we are, has been; how profoundly it has altered, or, rather, has helped forward, the course of civilization.

CHAPTER X.

SUMMARY.

THE PROCESS OF GROWTH OF THE EDUCATIONAL IDEAL; THE MIDDLE
AGES; THE RENAISSANCE; THE HUMANISTS; THE NATURAL-SCIEN-
TISTS; THE EDUCATIONAL DEMOCRATS; THE SENSATIONALISTS;
ETHICAL EDUCATION; THE TRUE DATA OF EDUCATION.

THE process of growth in the educational ideal has been
one mainly of simplification. Intricate as our modern
civilization is, it rests, in its highest development, upon
ever simpler principles. Elaboration, far from being evidence of refinement, is a sign of incompleteness. Those
moral attributes, those graces of manner which distinguish
the gentleman and gentlewoman, are singular because of
their naturalness. The refining process through which
good-breeding comes, does not consist in elaboration of
detail, is not made up of a complexity of minor morals
and petty arts; but is, on the contrary, a sloughing off of
extraneous things, of that half-savage husk which, through
inheritance, environment, or lack of teaching, overgrows
commoner natures and hides the real, human kernel of
natural simplicity.

Progress towards a higher standard of education has been
made through an analogous simplification. Nothing could
have been more elaborate, more diffuse, more time-exhaust-
ing, than the empty disputations and vain subtleties of the
Schoolmen. Human nature was almost crushed under a
weight of words. Civilization was sinking under a self-
created burden of useless pedantry. The ignorance and

fear, the social isolation and ceaseless warfare of the early
Middle Ages had given place to such meagre learning as
was possible to men who were self-ignorant, fearful of
research, disputatious, and ill-balanced. Such literature as
had survived was theological and controversial; those who
interested themselves in it at all had no pleasure except in
enlarging its disputations with ever vainer and subtler
arguments. The tyrannical soldiery had no need to learn;
the over-taxed merchants had no time to study; the corrupted priesthood had no wish to know more than the little
that the Church required. Free thought was heresy; experimentation was witchcraft; self-improvement was unhal-
lowed ambition. The spirit of the Brahmin — a desire to
keep themselves a class apart — tempted the few real scholars
to the use of a mystic and obscure learning, of a symbolism
which could be variously interpreted to meet the question-
ings of a jealous and uncertain Inquisition. The Renaissance
reformers, lopping off the false learning, the mysticism, the
windy erudition of this scholastic training, left a solid and
healthful foundation for true study, a basis of real education
which had existed all the time, but which had been lost
sight of under mountain weights of pedantry. These reformers did not create the learning which they made accessible;
classic scholarship lay fainting, not dead, under the pall of
scholasticism; they but revived it and made it again active.

By restoring the classics the leaders of learning awakened
European society to a partial sense of its intellectual poverty and created in it an appetite for fruitful study that, in
time, demanded better mental food than the Schoolmen
were able to provide. In answer to this demand came, not
only the enlargement and expansion of the universities, but
an improved order of boys' school, having for its main
object the study, criticism, and imitation of the classical
authors.

This study, indeed, was little more profitable than the mediæval learning ; but it was at least polished, and it rested upon a foundation more substantial than vain words and empty disputations. More than this, the schools of the humanists, by their emphasis of the literary side of study, made learning fashionable. Education in the Middle Ages had been theological in tendency, and had been confined, almost exclusively, to candidates for the Church. Since these aspirants, as a rule, were the younger sons and weaker brothers of the feudal families, they and their learning, equally, received the contempt of the unlettered, but more fortunate and more powerful, members of society.

Now, however, with the revival of the classics, and with a partial cessation of warfare, learning became, in a measure, necessary to social and political success; the royal and ducal families vied with one another in encouraging and maintaining scholarship; luxury, heretofore barbaric, refined itself into a taste for libraries and museums of art; and the schools and universities became crowded with the rich and nobly born. The wealth of the newly found East and West poured in to support and forward the intellectual revival, and the Renaissance blossomed forth in splendor against a background of mediæval poverty and ignorance.

The improved education made possible by the Renaissance was, however, inadequate and artificial. Its antiquity unfitted it for human needs. It proved to be impossible to shape the learning of Greece and Rome to the enlarged requirements of a Western and more modern society. Education had to be amplified to meet the expanding social and industrial conditions. And this could be properly done only by reversing, in a measure, both the methods and the aims of study. It was found impossible to advance the education given by the classicists beyond the point of mental polish, beyond the narrow limits of linguistic criticism and imitation. The manner of the teaching of these humanists was far ahead of that of the scholastics; but the matter, except in so far as it was enlarged to meet the needs of laymen, was scarcely more valuable than the dry logomachy of the Middle Ages. In Sturm's school, which may be regarded as the model institution of the humanists, little was taught beyond the studies of the "Trivium." Latin and Greek grammar, Latin-German and German-Latin translation, rhetoric, dialectic, the reading of classic authors, the acting of classic plays—that was practically the whole of his school-course. The scholastic barbarians had been routed, but only to leave their tender victims captive to the Greeks and Romans.

The humanists had possessed themselves of the Greek learning, but it was necessary to search nature and man himself, not dusty archives, in order to find and appropriate the true Greek spirit. It was a nature-spirit, but a very limited and feeble one, when compared with that modern nature-spirit to the pursuit of which the growth of modern civilization is due. How to find this spirit, how to question it, how to adapt the knowledge gained from it to the business of life, — these were the next things to be learned. How to learn them was what Bacon, and those who followed him so closely, taught. In this teaching they put the work of education on that broad basis upon which it rests to-day. While it is difficult to assign its proper value to any work of reform, it is not easy to exaggerate the effect of these natural-scientists upon education. The way of study which they inspired seems, to-day, so simple, that one does not realize the change in human thought and in human life itself which was wrought by the overturning of the old methods and objects of teaching. The humanists, great as was their reform, had made no distinct advance in the subjects to be taught in their schools, and the transition of education into the Renaissance had not been a violent one. Attention had been transferred, it is true, from the barbarous and crabbed mediæval to the refined and lucid classical writings, the methods of study had been simplified, the atmosphere of learning had been greatly purified; but, with the humanists, the mind was still the sole means, its culture the sole end, of study. The change which came through Bacon and his scientific contemporaries, however, was a far sharper one. It threw down all the familiar barriers within which learning had been pent, it opened to the student the limitless field of nature and society, it made possible the immediate conception of the modern educational ideal.

But this ideal required two centuries more for its framing. Social and political conditions continued to be, in the post-Baconian days, grievously artificial. The feudal system still fettered education. While the Renaissance had vastly improved the educational opportunities of those few who were permitted to learn at all, the great masses gained little, if anything, by the change. They had to be emancipated, both politically and mentally, before civilization could make any important advance. The men of the Reformation began this work, but it remained for Comenius and the spirit that he aroused to forward it, to methodize it, and to make popular education a living force in the growth of European society. Then began that long struggle for emancipation which is still in progress and which, to-day, threatens a social crisis. While Bacon and the natural-scientists established the direction of modern education, it was Luther and Comenius who determined its ultimate extent.

The homely and common education which Luther and

Comenius made possible remained, like the higher instruction, artificial and one-sided. Scholasticism continued to
so far dominate all education as to limit its field to an
intellectual training, until the materialists, by calling to
their aid the sensual powers, remedied this defect, greatly
simplifying the educational process by bringing to bear upon
it this strong new force. The work of materialism in the
eighteenth century was necessary in order to make that of
the earlier reformers come to fruition in the nineteenth.

The intellect had been freed by the Renaissance, and,
by exercising itself upon the restored learning of the ancients, had been made active and methodical. The natural-
scientists, with Bacon as their leader, had opened vast
new fields in which this active intellect might develop
itself, and might turn itself away from barren learning
towards fruitful experimentation and discovery. To these
fields the founders of public education admitted new multi-
tudes of minds, hitherto kept in passive subjection. To
all these intellects, well-educated and ill-educated, the
sensationalists gave new strength and power by training
and enlarging the sensual powers. But, notwithstanding
this advance, man remained incomplete, his progress
threatened to be barren except of material results, and he
was in danger of destruction by his own success, until a
third and all-important force was enlisted in the work of
education.

This third power, the soul, is an essential factor in keeping due balance between the speculations of intellect and
the grossness of sense. To the development and strengthening of this side of human nature the educational work of
the last century has, consciously and unconsciously, directed its effort. It is during this century, therefore, that
educational questions have risen into such prominence
and the educational ideal has been so wonderfully enlarged.

It is because education has devoted itself to this side of humanity that, during this century, moral questions have been so conspicuous and moral growth has been so marked. It is because, in this short time, education and morality have taken such forward strides, that there is such hope and promise for mankind.

This work, distinctively Christian, was begun, in modern days and on the spiritual side, by the Jansenists and those, Catholic and Protestant, whom their example inflamed; on the material side it was inaugurated by the early sensationalists of whom Montaigne and Locke are types. But their contributions to educational progress were lost sight of in the religious and social tumult of the eighteenth century, until Rousseau, rescuing and reconciling them, gave them an abiding life. This quickened impulse, which Pestalozzi and Froebel strengthened and carried forward, and which is inspiring myriads of parents and teachers to-day, has done more to enlarge the educational ideal than was accomplished in all the Christian centuries which preceded ours. But the slow work of those earlier times was an unavoidable and an essential preparation, and even the splendid advance of to-day is only a first step in that long journey of progress which still lies ahead.

So long as the teaching of children was a matter of the intellect only, so long as the degree of civilization demanded only an educational veneer, just so long did the school remain a separate institution, with its special priesthood, its useless forms, its idle ceremonies, its false limitations. As soon as it was perceived that education is life itself, the agencies of education became illimitable. The process was then seen to be, not one of painful and narrow information, but one of careful guidance among the endless means of training pressing in from every side. Teaching resolved itself into a process of wise and sympathetic selection.

Under this new conception of education, the mother comes forward into hitherto unimagined prominence. She is the natural agent, closest to the child during the all-important period of formation, when the pressure of external conditions must be most carefully regulated, when the channels through which they shall act must be most skilfully planned. Upon her must rest, to an extraordinary degree, the responsibility for the right guidance of the senses and the will of her offspring through the maze of natural phenomena. Only a little less than hers, however, is the responsibility of the father. These two, and these alone, have a direct interest in the child. By its feebleness and ignorance, no less than by the parental instinct, is the child bound to them, and they to it. With them rests the initiative and the final responsibility for the infant's rearing, the child's education, the youth's preparation for the work of life.[1] The school and the schoolmaster are still necessary factors in education, but they are no longer primary ones. They are adjunct only in the holy work that must rest supremely upon the father and the mother.

[1] "It is only by united action, and only through the children, through the care and training of childhood, that the two sexes can reach their lofty aim, the aim of mankind, of our nation, and of every family, — to completely fulfil our common vocation and realize our destiny. . . . The care of childhood is seen to be the one unfailing, perfectly satisfactory condition and means of uniting the two separate sexes to form the one great body of mankind and fully to work out their destiny. This chord of three notes melts together in a higher sense to form an unison, which sounds abroad in a full and clear tone. This larger unity is but the unity of the family over again, where the love of the two parents finds in the child its meaning and its union, attains its purpose and meets its God and Father, reaches its highest development of means and aim, of condition and destiny. Childhood and Manhood melt together to form the unity of Mankind, and this last, as the everlasting child of God, melts in its turn into unity with its Divine Father." — FROEBEL, *Appeal to German Women*, June 26, 1848 (Michaelis-Moore, *Froebel's Let.*, 266).

The schoolmaster's task is not, however, lightened. The new conception of it makes the educational problem simpler, but it makes it at the same time infinitely more serious. Comenius's "mother-school" that "should exist in every house" is becoming possible; upon the fundamental plan of such a mother-school all education must be shaped. It is no longer a simple question of the intellectual value of this study and of that; it is no longer to be decided what manner and quantity of information shall be given. It is a question now of determining those subjects and those methods which shall best supplement and carry forward the training of character, the real education to true manhood and womanhood that is or ought to be given in the home, under the parents' guidance. The solution of the problem is perhaps not greatly furthered; but the problem itself, the questions of what education is, whither it should tend, and upon what broad principles it should be carried forward, are, it seems to me, no longer in doubt.

With the mothers and the fathers, too, aroused to the fact that they are teachers, and that the home is a schoolhouse; with the study which they must increasingly give, under this new light, to that complex organism, the child; with the physiological and psychical sciences resting upon data which shall be thus collected, — the day for a rapid growth in educational methods is not far distant. To know exactly what one's problem is carries one forward with increasing speed towards its solution. Having, after centuries of wandering, brought the child back to his proper atmosphere, his home, having determined who shall be responsible for his teaching, and what shall be the final aim of that teaching, we have, indeed, put the educational question upon a sound and healthy basis. We have at last learned how to follow nature; and we are beginning to understand that the best education, indeed the only right education, is a natural one.

BIBLIOGRAPHY.

FOLLOWING is a partial list of the books read and consulted in preparation for *The Educational Ideal*. The editions noted are those to which the author had access, and, in many cases, are not the best. A number of the English books have been republished in America; and there are, doubtless, other translations from the French and German than those indicated. To make the bibliography of greater value, those books which are believed to be most useful in a general study of the subject of this volume are indicated by a star [*].

GENERAL WORKS.

*Barnard, Henry, [Editor.] *American Journal of Education.* 31 v. 1855–1881. [An invaluable collection.]

Analytical Index of Barnard's Amer. Journ. of Education. [Bureau of Education, 187.] Washington, 1892.

Barnard, Henry, [Editor.] *English pedagogy.* (Compiled from Amer. Journ. of Education.) Philadelphia, 1866.

Barnard, Henry, [Editor.] *German pedagogy.* (Compiled from Amer. Journ. of Education.) Hartford, 1871.

Barnard, Henry, [Editor.] *National Education in Europe.* (Compiled from Amer. Journ. of Education.) New York, 1854.

Bayle, Pierre. *Dictionnaire historique et critique.* 4 v. Rotterdam, 1720.

Browning, Oscar. *An introduction to the history of educational theories.* New York, 1891.

Bryce, James. *The Holy Roman Empire.* New York, 1887.

Buckle, Henry Thomas. *History of civilization in England.* 2 v. New York, 1858.

Compayré, Gabriel. *Histoire de la pédagogie.* (4me ed.) Paris, n.d.

*Compayré, Gabriel. *The history of pedagogy. Translated with an introduction, notes, and an index, by W. H. Payne.* (Heath's pedagogical lib.) Boston, 1894.

*Compayré, Gabriel. *Histoire critique des doctrines de l'éducation en France depuis le seizième siècle.* 2 v. Paris, 1883.

Cournot, M. *Considérations sur la marche des idées et des événements dans les temps modernes.* 2 v. Paris, 1872.

Davidson, Thos. *The education of the Greek people and its influence upon civilization.* (Int. ed. ser.) New York, 1894.

*Draper, John W. *A history of the intellectual development of Europe.* New York, 1863.

*Duruy, Victor. *The History of the Middle Ages.* (Trans. by E. H. and M. D. Whitney.) New York, 1891.

Encyclopædia Britannica. (Ninth ed.) 25 v. Edinburgh, 1875–89.

Fletcher, Alfred E., [Editor.] *Sonnenschein's Cyclopedia of education.* London, 1889.

Gérando, J. M. de. *Histoire comparée des systêmes de philosophie, relativement aux principes des connaissances humaines.* 3 v. Paris, An XII.

Gibbon, Edw. *History of the decline and fall of the Roman Empire.* 6 v. London, 1846.

Gill, John. *Systems of education: a history and criticism of the principles, methods, organization, and moral discipline advocated by eminent educationists.* (Heath's pedagogical lib., from the 14th Eng. ed.) Boston, 1889.

Green, John R. *History of the English people.* 4 v. London, 1878.

Guizot, F. P. G. *Histoire de la civilisation en Europe depuis la chute de l'empire romain jusqu'à la révolution française.* Paris, 1861. ['There is an English translation by Hazlitt.]

*Hallam, Henry. *Introduction to the literature of Europe in the fifteenth, sixteenth and seventeenth centuries.* 4 v. New York and Boston, 1863.

Hallam, Henry. *View of the state of Europe during the Middle Ages.* 3 v. London, 1878.

Lange, Frederick A. *History of materialism and criticism of its present importance.* (Trans. by E. C. Thomas.) 3 v. London, 1877.

*Lecky, W. E. H. *History of the rise and influence of the spirit of rationalism in Europe.* 2 v. London, 1865.

Le Clerc, J. *Bibliothèque universelle.* 26 v. Amsterdam, 1686–93.

Macaulay, Thos. Babington. *The history of England from the accession of James II.* 5 v. Boston, 1860.

Martin, H. *Histoire de France depuis les temps les plus reculés jusqu'à 1789.* 17 v. Paris, 1858.

Michelet, J. *Nos fils.* Paris, 1870.

Painter, F. V. N. *A history of education.* (Int. ed. ser.) New York, 1890.

*Paroz, Jules. *Histoire universelle de la pédagogie.* Paris, 1883.

Payne, Joseph. *Lectures on the history of education, with a visit to German schools.* (v. II. of his *Works.*) London, 1892.

*Quick, Robert H. *Essays on educational reformers.* (Int. ed. ser.) New York, 1894.

*Raumer, Karl von. *Geschichte der Pädagogik, vom Wiederaufblühen klassischen Studien bis auf unsere Zeit.* 4 v. Stuttgart, 1857. [An English translation of a great part of von Raumer is to be found in the Amer. Journ. of Education, vols. 4 to 8.]

Richter, J. P. F. *Levana; or the doctrine of education.* (Trans. from the German.) London, 1876.

Sainte-Beuve, C.-A. *Causeries du lundi.* 15 v. Paris, 1851-62. *Nouveaux lundis.* 12 v. Paris, 1863-70. *Premiers lundis.* 3 v. Paris, 1874-75.

Schmidt, Karl. *Die Geschichte der Pädagogik in weltgeschichtlicher Entwicklung und in organischer Zusammenhangen mit dem Culturleben der Völker.* 4 v. Cöthen, 1860-62.

Shelley, Mrs. M. W. *Lives of the most eminent literary and scientific men in France.* (Lardner's cab. cyclo.) 2 v. London, 1838.

Whewell, William. *History of the inductive sciences, from the earliest to the present time.* 3 v. London, 1837.

RABELAIS.

Ascham, R. *The Scholemaster.* (Edited by Edward Arber.) Boston, 1888.

*Besant, Walter. *Rabelais.* (Foreign class. for Eng. readers.) Philadelphia, 1879.

*Besant, Walter. *Readings in Rabelais.* London, 1883.

Compayré, Gabriel. *Abelard, and the origin and early history of universities.* (The great educators.) New York, 1893.

Deschanel, Paul. *Rabelais;* in *Figures littéraires.* Paris, 1889.

Dimitry, John, [Compiler.] *Three good giants, whose famous deeds are recorded in the ancient chronicles of François Rabelais.* Boston, 1888.

*Faguet, Émile. *Rabelais;* in *Dix-seizième siècle; études littéraires.* Paris, 1894.

Flaubert, Gustave. *Rabelais;* in *Par les champs et par les grèves, accompagné de mélanges et de fragments inédits.* Paris, 1886.

*Fleury, Jean. *Rabelais et ses œuvres.* 2 v. Paris, 1877.

*Gebhart, Émile. *Rabelais, la renaissance et la réforme.* Paris, 1877.

*Guizot, F. P. G. *Des idées de Rabelais et de Montaigne au fait d'éducation;* in *Meditations et études morales.* Paris, 1855.

Hillebrand, Karl. *François Rabelais;* in *Zeiten, Völker und Menschen.* (B. 4, Profile.) Berlin, 1878.

*Jacob, L., bibliophile (pseud. of P. Lacroix), [Editor.] *Œuvres de F. Rabelais.* Paris, 1868.

Laurie, S. S. *The rise and early constitution of universities, with a survey of mediæval education.* (Int. ed. ser.) New York, 1887.

Marc-Monnier. *Rabelais;* in *La réforme, de Luther à Shakespeare.* (*Hist. de la litt. moderne.*) Paris, 1885.

Masson, David. *The life of John Milton: narrated in connexion with the political, ecclesiastical and literary history of his time.* 6 v. Cambridge, 1859.

Michelet, J. *Histoire de France en seizième siècle.* 17 v. Paris, 1857.

Millet, René. *Rabelais.* (Les grands écrivains fran.) Paris, 1892.

Niceron, [le Père.] *Rabelais;* in *Memoirs pour servir à l'histoire des hommes illustres dans la république des-lettres,* T. xxxii. Paris, 1735.

Rabelais, F. *Œuvres.* 2 v. (Bibliothèque Elzevirienne.) Paris, 1858.

Scherer, Edmond. *Rabelais;* in *Études sur la littérature contemporaine,* T. 6. Paris, 1882.

*Stapfer, Paul. *Rabelais. Sa personne, son genie, son œuvre.* Paris, 1889.

Stapfer, Paul. *Rabelais;* in *Les artistes juges et parties. Causeries parisiennes.* Paris, 1872.

Street, A. E. *The education of Gargantua;* in *Critical sketches.* London, 1894.

Vinet, A. *Rabelais;* in *Moralistes des seizième et dix-septième siècles.* Paris, 1859.

FRANCIS BACON.

*Abbott, Edwin A. *Francis Bacon. An account of his life and works.* London, 1885.

Abbott, Edwin A. *Bacon and Essex. A sketch of Bacon's earlier life.* London, 1877.

Bacon, Francis. *Novum organum or true suggestions for the interpretation of Nature by Francis Lord Verulam.* London (Pickering), 1850.

Campbell, John, [Lord.] *Bacon;* in *The lives of the Lord Chancellors and Keepers of the great seal of England, from the earliest times till the reign of King George IV.,* v. II. London, 1845.

Church, R. W., [Dean.] *Bacon.* (Eng. men of letters.) London, 1884.

Craik, George L. *Bacon; his writings and his philosophy.* 3 v. London, 1846.

Dixon, William H. *Personal history of Lord Bacon; from unpublished papers.* London, 1861.

*Fischer, Kuno. *Francis Bacon of Verulam: Realistic philosophy and its age.* (Trans. by John Oxenford.) London, 1857.

*Fowler, Thomas. *Bacon.* (Eng. philosophers.) New York, 1881.

Fouillée, Alfred. *Descartes.* (Les grands écrivains fran.) Paris, 1893.

Huxley, Thomas H. *On Descartes' "Discourse, etc.";* in *Methods and results.* (Vol. I. of collected essays.) London, 1893.

Ingleby, Clement M. *Francis Bacon;* in *Essays.* London, 1888.

Liebig, Justus von. *Francis Bacon von Verulam und die Geschichte der Naturwissenschaften;* and *Ein Philosoph und ein Naturforscher über F. B. v. V.;* and *Noch ein Wort über F. B. v. V.;* in *Reden und Abhandlungen.* Leipzig u. Heidelberg, 1874.

Lowndes, Richard. *René Descartes; his life and meditations. A new trans. of the "Meditationes," with introduction, memoir and commentary.* London, 1878.

*Macaulay, T. B. *Lord Bacon;* in *Critical and miscellaneous essays,* v. II. Boston, 1840.

Maistre, Joseph M. de, [Comte.] *Examen de la philosophie de Bacon, où l'on traite differentes questions de philosophie rationnelle.* 2 v. Lyons, 1852.

Morris, George S. *Francis Bacon;* in *British thought and thinkers: Introductory studies, critical, biographical and philosophical.* Chicago, 1880.

Napier Macvey. *Remarks, illustrative of the scope and influence of the philosophical writings of Lord Bacon;* in *Trans. Royal Soc. of Edinburgh,* v. 8.

Nichol, John. *Francis Bacon, his life and philosophy.* 2 v. London, 1889.

Nisard, J. M. N. D. *Renaissance et réforme.* 2 v. Paris, 1877.

Playfair, John. *Progress of mathematical and physical sciences since the revival of letters in Europe.* Boston, 1820.

*Rémusat, Ch. de. *Bacon, sa vie, son temps, sa philosophie et son influence jusqu'à nos jours.* Paris, 1857.

Rémusat, Charles de. *Histoire de la philosophie en Angleterre depuis Bacon jusqu'à Locke.* 2 v. Paris, 1875.

Saisset, Émile. *Précurseurs et disciples de Descartes.* Paris, 1862.

Spedding, James. *The letters and the life of Francis Bacon, including all his occasional works.* 7 v. London, 1861–1874.

*Spedding, James. *An account of the life and times of Francis Bacon; extracted from the edition of his occasional writings.* 2 v. Boston, 1878.

Spedding, James. *Evenings with a reviewer; or Macaulay and Bacon.* 2 v. London, 1881.

*Spedding, James; Ellis, Robert L.; and Heath, Douglas D., [Editors.] *The works of Francis Bacon.* 7 v. London, 1857–1861.

Stapfer, Paul. *Digression sur Bacon;* in *Les artistes,* etc. (See Rabelais.)

Wrangham, Francis. *Francis Bacon, Viscount St. Alban's;* in *The British Plutarch,* v. II. London, 1816.

*Wright, W. Aldis, [Editor.] *Francis Bacon: The advancement of learning.* Oxford, 1885.

COMENIUS.

[Adelung, Johann C.] *Johann Amos Comenius, ein Schwärmer;* in *Geschichte der menschlichen Narrheit oder, etc.* (Ier Th.) Leipzig, 1785.

Bardeen, C. W. *The text-books of Comenius;* in *Educational Review* (N. Y.), v. III., 3.

*Bardeen, C. W., [Editor.] *The Orbis Pictus of John Amos Comenius.* (Hoole's translation, London, 1728.) Syracuse, 1887.

Beeger, Julius; und Franz Zoubek, [Editors.] *Comenius, J. A.: Grosse Unterrichtslehre. Aus dem Lateinischen übersetzt und mit Einleitungen und Anmerkungen versehen.* (Päd. Bibliothek, IIIr B.) Leipzig, n.d.

Hanus, Paul H. *The permanent influence of Comenius;* in *Educ. Rev.* (N. Y.), v. III., 3.

Holmes, John. *History of the Protestant church of the United Brethren.* 2 v. London, 1825.

*Laurie, S. S. *John Amos Comenius, Bishop of the Moravians. His life and educational works.* Boston, 1885.

Laurie, S. S. *The place of Comenius in the history of education;* in *Educ. Rev.* (N. Y.), v. III., 3.

*Lïon, Theodor, [Editor.] *Johann Amos Comenius. Pädagogische Schriften. Übersetzt, mit Anmerkungen und des Comenius Biographie versehen.* Langensalza, 1875.

Raven, J. H. *An old school-book* [the Orbis Pictus]; in *Macmillan's Magazine*, v. 53, 437.

MONTAIGNE AND LOCKE.

Ancona, Alessandro, [Editor.] *Journal du voyage de Michel de Montaigne en Italie par la Suisse et l'Allemagne en 1580 et 1581.* Città-di-Castello, 1889. [English translation of *Voyage* is given in Hazlitt's *Montaigne.*]

Barthélemy, Ch. *La religion de Montaigne;* in *Erreurs et mensonges historiques*, 5me sér. Paris, 1879.

*Bourne, H. R. Fox. *The life of John Locke.* 2 v. London, 1876.

Brown, John, [Dr.] *Locke and Sydenham;* in *Spare hours*, [Horæ subsecivæ], 3rd ser. Boston, 1883.

Collins, W. Lucas. *Montaigne.* (Foreign class. for Eng. readers.) Edin. and London, 1879.

Courtney, W. L. *John Locke;* in *Studies at leisure.* London, 1892.

*Emerson, Ralph Waldo. *Montaigne; or, the skeptic;* in *Representative men.* Boston, 1885.

*Faguet, Émile. *Montaigne;* in *Dix-seizième siècle.* (See Rabelais.)

Florio, John, [Translator.] *Essayes of Montaigne.* (Edited by J. H. M'Carthy.) 2 v. London, 1889.

Fowler, Thomas. *Locke.* (Eng. men of letters.) London, 1880.

*Fraser, Alex. Campbell. *Locke.* Edinburgh, 1890.

*Fraser, Alex. Campbell, [Editor.] *Locke's Essay concerning human understanding.* 2 v. Oxford, 1894.

Grenville, [Lord.] *Oxford and Locke.* London, 1829.

*Guizot, F. P. G. *Des idées, etc.* (See Rabelais.)

*Hazlitt, W., [Editor.] *The works of M. de Montaigne, comprising his essays, letters, and journey through Germany and Italy; with notes of all the commentators.* London, 1845.

Hettner, Hermann. *Locke;* in *Literaturgeschichte des achtzehnten Jahrhunderts*, Ier Th. Brunswick, 1881.

*King, [Lord.] *The life and letters of John Locke, with extracts from his journals and common-place books.* London, 1858.

Locke, John. *Works.* 10 v. London, 1823.

Locke, John. *An essay concerning human understanding; with thoughts on the conduct of the understanding.* 3 v. Edinburgh, 1801.

Marc-Monnier. *Montaigne;* in *La réforme, de Luther à Shakespeare.* (See Rabelais.)

Montaigne, M. de. *Essais. (Nouvelle éd. avec des notes choisies dans tous les commentateurs,* etc., par M. J.-V. Leclerc.) 2 v. Paris, 1889.

Morris, George S. *John Locke;* in *British Thought and Thinkers.* (See Bacon.)

Owen, John. *Montaigne;* in *The skeptics of the French renaissance.* London, 1893.

Pattison, Mark. *Life of Montaigne;* in *Essays.* (Edit. by H. Nettleship.) 2 v. London, 1889.

Payen, J.-F., [Editor.] *Documents inédits ou peu connus sur Montaigne.* Paris, 1847.

Prévost-Paradol. *Montaigne;* in *Études sur les moralistes français.* Paris, 1865.

*Quick, R. II., [Editor.] *John Locke: Some thoughts concerning education. With introduction and notes.* Cambridge, 1880.

Rémusat, Charles de. *Locke;* in *Histoire de la phil.,* etc. (See Bacon.)

Sainte-Beuve, C.-A. *Montaigne, maire de Bordeaux.* Paris, 1866.

*St. John, Bayle. *Montaigne, the essayist. A biography.* 2 v. London, 1858.

Stephen, Jas. Fitzjames, [Sir.] *Locke;* four papers in *Horæ Sabbaticæ,* 2d ser. London, 1892.

Stephen, Jas. Fitzjames, [Sir.] *Montaigne's essays;* in *Horæ Sabbaticæ,* 1st ser. London, 1892.

Stephen, Leslie. *History of English thought in the eighteenth century.* 2 v. New York, 1876.

Vinet, A. *Montaigne;* in *Moralistes,* etc. (See Rabelais.)

Windsor, Arthur Lloyd. *The mental history of Montaigne;* in *Ethica: or characteristics of men, manners, and books.* London, 1860.

THE JANSENISTS AND FÉNELON.

Balzac, H. de. *Histoire impartiale des Jésuites;* in *Essais et mélanges (Œuv. comp.,* T. XXIII.) Paris, 1879.

Barthélemy, Ch. *La vérité sur le Jansenism;* in *Erreurs et mensonges historiques,* 6ᵐᵉ sér. Paris, 1879.

*Beard, Charles. *Port Royal. A contribution to the history of religion and literature in France.* 2 v. London, 1861.

Bert, Paul. *La morale des Jésuites.* Paris, 1880.

Bowles, Emily. *Madame de Maintenon.* London, 1888.

Brunetière, Ferdinand. *Jansénistes et cartésiens;* and *Les provinciales;* in *Études critiques sur l'histoire de la littérature française,* 4ᵐᵉ sér. Paris, 1891.

Brunetière, Ferdinand. *La querelle de quiétisme;* in *Nouvelles études critiques sur l'histoire de la littérature française,* T 2. Paris, 1886.

*Cartwright, W. C. *The Jesuits: their constitution and teaching. An historical sketch.* London, 1876.

Clémencet, Charles. *Histoire littéraire de Port-Royal.* Paris, 1868.

Crétineau-Joly, J. *Histoire religieuse, politique et littéraire de la Compagnie de Jésus, composée sur les documents inédits et authentiques.* 8 v. Paris, 1859.

Courtney, W. L. *Pascal;* and *Jacqueline Pascal;* in *Studies new and old.* London, 1888.

Cousin, V. *Jacqueline Pascal.* Paris, 1856.

Döllinger, J. I. von. *The most influential woman of French history* [Mme. de Maintenon]; in *Studies in European history.* (Trans. by Margaret Warre.) London, 1890.

Douarche, A. *L'université de Paris et les Jésuites. (16ᵐᵉ et 17ᵐᵉ siècles.)* Paris, 1888.

*Faguet, Émile. *Pascal;* and *Fénelon;* and *Madame de Maintenon;* in *Dix-septième siècle. Études littéraires.* Paris, 1892.

Faugère, Prosper, [Editor.] *Lettres, opuscules et mémoires de Madame Perier et de Jacqueline, sœurs de Pascal, et de Marguerite Perier, sa nièce.* Paris, 1845.

Fénelon, F. de Salignac de la Mothe. *Œuvres complètes.* 10 v. Paris, 1810. [Many of them translated.]

*Huber, Johannes. *Der Jesuiten=Orden nach seiner Verfassung und Doctrin, Wirksamkeit und Geschichte.* Berlin, 1873. [There is a French translation by Marchand.]

*Hughes, Thomas. *Loyola and the educational system of the Jesuits.* (Great educators.) New York, 1892.

Janet, Paul. *Fénelon.* (Les grands écrivains fran.) Paris, 1892.

La Bruyère. *Dialogues sur la quiétism;* in *Œuvres,* T. 2. Paris, 1865.

*Lavallée, Théophile. *Madame de Maintenon et la maison royale de Saint Cyr,* (*1686-1793.*) Paris, 1862.

Libri instituti Societatis Jesu. 11 v. Antwerp, 1635.

Maintenon, Mme. de. *Entretiens sur l'éducation des filles.* Paris, 1854.

Maintenon, Mme. de. *Lettres sur l'éducation des filles.* (Publiées par Th. Lavallée.) Paris, 1854.

Martin, Frances. *Angelique Arnauld, abbess of Port Royal.* London, 1876.

Mavel, J. *Les Monita Secreta des Jésuites;* in *Questions controversées de l'histoire et de la science,* 1ʳᵉ sér. Paris, 1880.

*McCrie, Thomas, [Editor.] *Blaise Pascal; the Provincial Letters. A new translation, with historical introduction and notes.* Edinburgh, 1848.

Migne, [L'abbé.] *Dictionnaire des Jansenistes.* (Appended to Plaquet's *Dictionnaire des hérésies,* T. 2.) Paris, 1853.

Noailles, [Duc de.] *Histoire de Madame de Maintenon et des principaux événements du regne de Louis XIV.* 4 v. Paris, 1857.

Owen, John. *Pascal;* in *The skeptics,* etc. (See Montaigne.)

*Pachtler, G. M., [Editor.] *Ratio studiorum et institutiones scholasticæ Societatis Jesu per Germaniam olim vigentes collectæ concinnatæ dilucidatæ.* 3 v. Berlin, 1887.

Pascal, Blaise. *Œuvres.* 5 v. Paris, 1819.

Prévost-Paradol. *Pascal;* in *Études sur,* etc. (See Montaigne.)

Ranke, Leopold. *The ecclesiastical and political history of the Popes of Rome during the sixteenth and seventeenth centuries.* (Trans. by Sarah Austin.) 3 v. London, 1840.

*Ricard, [Mgr.] *Les premiers Jansénistes et Port-Royal.* Paris, 1883.

*Sainte-Beuve, C.-A. *Port-Royal.* 5 v. Paris, 1860.

Sainte-Beuve, C.-A. *Pensées de Pascal;* in *Portraits contemporains,* T. 5. Paris, 1882.

Scherer, Edmond. *Port-Royal;* and *Ce que c'est qu'un Jésuite;* in *Études sur la littérature contemporain,* T. VII. Paris, 1882.

*[Tollemache, Marguerite.] *French Jansenists.* London, 1893.

Upham, Thomas C. *Life and religious opinions and experiences of Mme. de la Mothe Guyon: together with some account of the personal history and religious opinions of Fénelon, Archbishop of Cambray.* 2 v. New York, 1847.

Wallon, Jean. *Un collège de Jésuites.* Paris, 1880.

ROUSSEAU.

Baudrillart, H. L. J. *Jean-Jacques Rousseau et le socialism moderne;* in *Études de philosophie morale et d'économie politique,* T. 1. Paris, 1858.

Brandes, Georg. *Rousseau;* in *Die Litteratur des neunzehnten Jahrhunderts in ihren Hauptströmungen,* B. 1. Leipzig,. 1882.

Brockerhoff, Ferdinand. *Jean-Jacques Rousseau;* in *Der neue Plutarch,* (herausgegeben von R. Gottschall,) 5ʳ Th. Leipzig, 1877.

Brougham, Henry, [Lord.] *Rousseau;* in *Lives of men of letters and science who flourished in the time of George III.* 2 v. London, 1845.

Brunetière, Ferdinand. *La folie de J.-J. Rousseau;* in *Études critiques sur l'histoire de la littérature française,* 4ᵐᵉ sér. Paris, 1891.

*Caird, Edward. *Rousseau;* in *Essays on literature and philosophy,* v. I. Glasgow, 1892.

[Cajot, Jos.] *Les plagiats de M. J.-J. R. de Genève sur l'éducation, par D. J. C. B.* The Hague and Paris, 1766.

Carlyle, Thomas. *The hero as man of Letters (Johnson, Rousseau, Burns);* in *Heroes and hero-worship.* Chicago, 1891.

Chatelain, [le Dr.] *La folie de J.-J. Rousseau.* Paris, 1890.

Chuquet, Arthur. *J.-J. Rousseau.* (Les grands écrivains fran.) Paris, 1893.

Clarke, Jas. Freeman. *Jean Jacques Rousseau;* in *Memorial and biographical sketches.* Boston, 1878.

Craddock, Thomas. *Rousseau, as described by himself and others; with remarks and explanations.* London, 1877.

*Faguet, Émile. *Rousseau;* in *Dix-huitième siècle. Études littéraires.* Paris, 1890.

Forster, Joseph. *Rousseau;* in *Some French and Spanish men of genius.* London, 1891.

*Girardin, Saint-Marc. *Jean-Jacques Rousseau, sa vie et ses ouvrages.* 2 v. Paris, 1875.

Graham, Henry G. *Rousseau.* (Foreign class. for Eng. readers.) Edin. and London, 1882.

Hettner, Hermann. *Rousseau und die Demokratie;* in *Literaturgeschichte des achtzehnten Jahrhunderts,* Th. II. Brunswick, 1881.

Lowell, Edward J. *The eve of the French Revolution.* Boston, 1892.

*Lowell, James Russell. *Rousseau and the Sentimentalists;* in *Among my books.* 2 v. Boston, 1889.

*Morley, John. *Rousseau.* 2 v. London, 1873.

Musset-Pathay, V. D. *Histoire de la vie et des ouvrages de J.-J. Rousseau.* 2 v. Paris, 1822.

*Payne, W. H., [Editor.] *Rousseau's Émile.* (Int. educ. ser.) New York, 1893.

Rousseau, J.-J. *Œuvres complètes; avec éclaircissements et des notes historiques par P. R. Auguis.* 27 v. Paris, 1825.

Rousseau, J.-J. *Les confessions.* Paris, 1891.

*Rousseau, J.-J. *Émile, ou de l'éducation.* (Garnier frères.) Paris, 1889 (?) [The page references in the text are to these editions of *Les confessions* and *Émile.*]

Steeg, J., [Editor.] *Émile; or concerning education.* Extracts. (Trans. by E. Worthington.) (Heath's pedagogical lib.) Boston, 1894.

Street, A. E. *Rousseau's theory of education;* in *Critical sketches.* (See Rabelais.)

Vinet, A. *J.-J. Rousseau;* in *Histoire de la littérature française au dix-huitième siècle,* T. 2. Paris, 1886.

PESTALOZZI AND FROEBEL.

*Barnard, Henry, [Editor.] *Papers on Froebel's kindergarten, with suggestions on principles and methods of child culture in different countries.* (Revised ed. Compiled from Amer. Journ. of Education.) Hartford, 1890.

*Barnard, Henry, [Editor.] *Pestalozzi and Pestalozzianism. Life, educational principles, and methods, of John Henry Pestalozzi; with biographical sketches of several of his assistants and disciples.* (Reprinted from Am. Journ. of Education.) New York, 1859.

Biber, E. *H. Pestalozzi, and his plan of education.* London, 1831.

*Blow, Susan E. *Symbolic education. A commentary on Froebel's "Mother play."* (Int. ed. ser.) New York, 1894.

*Bowen, H. Courthope. *Froebel, and education by self-activity.* (The great educators.) New York, 1893.

*Channing, Eva, [Editor.] *Pestalozzi's Leonard and Gertrude.* (Trans. and abridged.) (Heath's pedagogical lib.) Boston, 1892.

Froebel, Friedrich. *Gesammelte pädagogische Schriften.* (Edited by Wichard Lange.) 3 v. (I. 1, I. 2, and II.) Berlin, 1862.

Froebel, Friedrich. *Mother-play and nursery songs. Poetry, music and pictures for the noble culture of child-life, with notes to mothers.* (Trans. by Fannie E. Dwight and Josephine Jarvis. Ed. by Eliz. P. Peabody.) Boston, 1893.

Goldammer, Hermann. *Der Kindergarten. Handbuch der Fröbel'schen Erziehungsmethode, Spielgaben und Beschäftigungen.* Berlin, 1874.

*Guimps, Roger de. *Pestalozzi, his life and work.* (Trans. by J. Russell.) London, 1890. [Published, also, in Int. educ. series.]

*Hailmann, W. N., [Editor.] *Friedrich Froebel: The Education of man.* (Trans. from the German and annotated.) (Int. ed. ser.) New York, 1892.

Herbart, Johann Friedrich. *Ueber Pestalozzi's Schrift; wie Gertrud, etc.;* and *Pestalozzi's Idee eines ABC der Anschauung als ein Cyklus, etc.;* in *Sämmt. Werke* (her. von G. Hartenstein), B. XI. Leipzig, 1851.

Herford, William H., [Editor.] *The student's Froebel; adapted from Die Erziehung der Menschheit of F. Froebel.* (Pt. I. Theory of education.) (Heath's pedagogical lib.) Boston, 1894.

Johonnot, James. *Pestalozzi;* and *Froebel and the kindergarten;* in *Principles and practice of teaching.* New York, 1891.

Kriege, Matilda H. *The child, its nature and relations; an elucidation of Froebel's principles of education.* (A free rendering of the German of the Baroness Marenholtz-Bülow.) New York, 1872.

Kruesi, H. *Sketch of the life and character of Pestalozzi.* (Lect. before the Am. Inst. of Instruction, Aug., 1853.) Boston, 1854.

Lyschinska, Mary J.; and Montefiore, Therese G. *The ethical teaching of Froebel as gathered from his works.* London, 1890.

Mann, Mrs. Horace; and Peabody, Eliz. P. *Moral culture of infancy and kindergarten guide.* New York, 1869.

Marenholtz-Bülow, [Baroness.] *Child and child-nature. Contributions to the understanding of Froebel's educational theories.* (Trans. by Alice M. Christie.) London, 1879.

*Marenholtz-Bülow, B. von, [Baroness.] *Reminiscences of Friedrich Froebel.* (Trans. by Mrs. Horace Mann; with a sketch of the life of Froebel by Emily Shirreff.) Boston, 1891.

Meyer, Bertha. *Aids to family government; or, from the cradle to the school, according to Froebel.* (Trans. by M. L. Holbrook.) New York, 1879.

*Michaelis, Emilie; and Moore, H. Keatley, [Editors.] *Friedrich*

Fröbel; Autobiography. (Trans. and annotated.) London, 1886.

*Michaelis, Emilie; and Moore, H. Keatley, [Editors.] *Froebel's letters on the kindergarten.* (Trans.) London, 1891.

Peabody, Elizabeth P. *Lectures in the training schools for kindergartners.* (Heath's pedagogical lib.) Boston, 1893.

Pestalozzi, J. H. *Sämmtliche Schriften.* 15 v. Stuttgart u. Tübingen, 1819–25.

*Pestalozzi, J. H. *Wie Gertrud ihre Kinder lehrt.* (Univers. Bibliothek, 991, 992.) Leipzig, n.d.

Ronge, Johann and Bertha. *A practical guide to the English kindergarten.* London, 1858.

*Rosmini-Serbati, Antonio. *The ruling principle of method applied to education.* (Trans. by Mrs. William Grey.) (Heath's pedagogical lib.) Boston, 1889.

Scudder, Horace E. *Childhood in literature and art.* Boston, 1894.

Shirreff, Emily. *A short sketch of the life of Friedrich Fröbel.* (A new edition, including Fröbel's letters from Dresden and Leipzig to his wife.) London, 1887.

WOMEN IN EDUCATION.

Aimé-Martin, L. *Éducation des mères de famille; ou de la civilisation du genre humain par les femmes.* Paris, 1843.

Baudrillart, Henri. *La famille et l'éducation en France dans leurs rapports avec l'état de la société.* Paris, 1874.

Baudrillart, H. J. L. *Madame de Staël;* in *Études,* etc. (See Rousseau.)

*Blennerhassett, Lady. *Madame de Staël, her friends, and her influence in politics and literature.* 3 v. London, 1889.

Brandes, Georg. *Frau von Staël;* in *Die Litteratur,* etc. (See Rousseau.)

Campan, Mme. *Thoughts on education;* in *Conversations of Mme. Campan, comprising secret anecdotes of the French court, with correspondence,* etc. (Edited by M. Maigne. Translated.) London, n.d.

*Dobson, Austin. *Four Frenchwomen.* London, 1890.

Duffy, Bella. *Madame de Staël.* (Famous women.) Boston, 1887.

Dupanloup, F. A. P., [Évêque d'Orleans.] *La femme studieuse.* Paris, 1869.

*Edgeworth, Maria and R. L. *Practical education.* 2 v. New York, 1801.

Fawcett, Mrs. Henry. *Some eminent women of our times.* London, 1889.

Gasparin, Agenor de, [le comte.] *La famille; ses devoirs, ses joies et ses douleurs.* 2 v. Paris, 1865.

Genlis, S. F. du C. de St. A., [comtesse de.] *Œuvres.* 84 v. Paris, 1825-26.

Genlis, Countess de. *Memoirs, illustrative of the history of the eighteenth and nineteenth centuries.* New York, 1825.

Genlis, Countess de. *Lessons of a governess to her pupils, or journal of the method adopted by Madame de Sillery-Brulart (formerly Countess de Genlis) in the education of the children of M. d' Orleans, First Prince of the Blood-Royal.* (Pubs. by herself. Trans. from the French.) 3 v. London, 1792.

Guizot, Mme. *Conseils de morale.* 2 v. Paris, 1828.

* Guizot, Mme. *Lettres de famille sur l'éducation.* 2 v. Paris, 1852.

Haussonville, G. P. O. de C., [vicomte d'.] *Le salon de Madame Necker d'après des documents tirés des archives de Coppet.* 2 v. Paris, 1882.

Mann, Horace. *A few thoughts on the powers and duties of woman.* Syracuse, 1853.

* Martineau, Harriet. *Household education.* London, 1861.

More, Hannah. *Works.* 8 v. Philadelphia, 1818.

*Necker de Saussure, Mme. *L'éducation progressive.* 2 v. Paris, 1828.

Necker de Saussure, Mme. *Progressive education.* (Trans. from the French: with notes and an appendix; by Mrs. Willard and Mrs. Phelps.) Boston, 1835.

*Oliver, Grace A. *A study of Maria Edgeworth with notices of her father and friends.* Boston, 1882.

*Sainte-Beuve, C.-A. *Portraits des femmes.* Paris, 1884. [There is an English translation.]

Staël, Mme. la Baronne de. *Œuvres complètes. Publiées par son fils; précédées d'une notice sur la caractère et les écrits de Mme. de Staël par Mme. Necker de Saussure.* 17 v. Paris, 1820. [There are English translations of many of Mme. de Staël's writings.]

INDEX.

ENGLISH LANGUAGE.

Hyde's Lessons in English, Book I. For the lower grades. Contains exercises for reproduction, picture lessons, letter writing, *uses* of parts of speech, etc. 40 cts.

Hyde's Lessons in English, Book II. For Grammar schools. Has enough technical grammar for correct use of language. 60 cts.

Hyde's Lessons in English, Book II with Supplement. Has, in addition to the above, 118 pages of technical grammar. 70 cts. Supplement bound alone, 35 cts.

Hyde's Advanced Lessons in English. For advanced classes in grammar schools and high schools. 60 cts.

Hyde's Lessons in English, Book II with Advanced Lessons. The Advanced Lessons and Book II bound together. •80 cts.

Hyde's Derivation of Words. 15 cts.

Mathews's Outline of English Grammar, with Selections for Practice. The application of principles is made through composition of original sentences. 80 cts.

Buckbee's Primary Word Book. Embraces thorough drills in articulation and in the primary difficulties of spelling and sound. 30 cts.

Sever's Progressive Speller. For use in advanced primary, intermediate, and grammar grades. Gives spelling, pronunciation, definition, and use of words. 30 cts.

Badlam's Suggestive Lessons in Language. Being Part I and Appendix of Suggestive Lessons in Language and Reading. 50 cts.

Smith's Studies in Nature, and Language Lessons. A combination of object lessons with language work. 50 cts. Part I bound separately, 25 cts.

Meiklejohn's English Language. Treats salient features with a master's skill and with the utmost clearness and simplicity. $1.30.

Meiklejohn's English Grammar. Also composition, versification, paraphrasing, etc. For high schools and colleges. 90 cts.

Meiklejohn's History of the English Language. 78 pages. Part III of English Language above, 35 cts.

Williams's Composition and Rhetoric by Practice. For high school and college. Combines the smallest amount of theory with an abundance of practice. Revised edition. $1.00.

Strang's Exercises in English. Examples in Syntax, Accidence, and Style for criticism and correction. 50 cts.

Huffcutt's English in the Preparatory School. Presents as practically as possible some of the advanced methods of teaching English grammar and composition in the secondary schools. 25 cts.

Woodward's Study of English. Discusses English teaching from primary school to high collegiate work. 25 cts.

Genung's Study of Rhetoric. Shows the most practical discipline of students for the making of literature. 25 cts.

Goodchild's Book of Stops. Punctuation in Verse. Illustrated. 10 cts.

See also our list of books for the study of English Literature.

D. C. HEATH & CO., PUBLISHERS,
BOSTON.   NEW YORK.   CHICAGO.

EDUCATION.

Compayré's History of Pedagogy. "The best and most comprehensive history of Education in English." — Dr. G. S. HALL. $1.75.

Compayré's Lectures on Teaching. "The best book in existence on the theory and practice of education." — Supt. MACALISTER, Philadelphia. $1.75.

Compayré's Psychology Applied to Education. A clear and concise statement of doctrine and application on the science and art of teaching. 90 cts.

De Garmo's Essentials of Method. A practical exposition of methods with illustrative outlines of common school studies. 65 cts.

De Garmo's Lindner's Psychology. The best Manual ever prepared from the Herbartian standpoint. $1.00.

Gill's Systems of Education. "It treats ably of the Lancaster and Bell movement in education, — a *very important* phase:" — Dr. W. T. HARRIS. $1.25.

Hall's Bibliography of Pedagogical Literature. Covers every department of education. Interleaved, *$2.00. $1.50.

Herford's Student's Froebel. The purpose of this little book is to give young people preparing to teach a brief yet full account of Froebel's Theory of Education. 75 cts.

Malleson's Early Training of Children. "The best book for mothers I ever read." — ELIZABETH P. PEABODY. 75 cts.

Marwedel's Conscious Motherhood. The unfolding of the child's mind in the cradle, nursery and Kindergarten. $2.00.

Newsholme's School Hygiene. Already in use in the leading training colleges in England. 75 cts.

Peabody's Home, Kindergarten, and Primary School. "The best book outside of the Bible that I ever read." — A LEADING TEACHER. $1.00.

Pestalozzi's Leonard and Gertrude. "If we except 'Emile' only, no more important educational book has appeared for a century and a half than 'Leonard and Gertrude.'" — *The Nation.* 90 cts.

Radestock's Habit in Education. "It will prove a rare 'find' to teachers who are seeking to ground themselves in the philosophy of their art." — E. H. RUSSELL, Worcester Normal School. 75 cts.

Richter's Levana ; or, The Doctrine of Education. "A spirited and scholarly book." — Prof. W. H. PAYNE. $1.40.

Rosmini's Method in Education. "The most important pedagogical work ever written." — THOMAS DAVIDSON. $1.50.

Rousseau's Emile. "Perhaps the most influential book ever written on the subject of Education." — R. H. QUICK. 90 cts.

Methods of Teaching Modern Languages. Papers on the value and on methods of teaching German and French, by prominent instructors. 90 cts.

Sanford's Laboratory Course in Physiological Psychology. The course includes experiments upon the Dermal Senses, Static and Kinæsthetic Senses, Taste, Smell, Hearing, Vision, Psychophysic. *In Press.*

Lange's Apperception : A monograph on Psychology and Pedagogy. Translated by the members of the Herbart Club, under the direction of President Charles DeGarmo, of Swarthmore College. $1.00.

Herbart's Science of Education. Translated by Mr. and Mrs. Felken with a preface by Oscar Browning. $1.00.

Tracy's Psychology of Childhood. This is the first *general* treatise covering in a scientific manner the whole field of child psychology. Octavo. Paper. 75 cts.

Sent by mail, postpaid, on receipt of price.

D. C. HEATH & CO., PUBLISHERS,
BOSTON.   NEW YORK.   CHICAGO.

www.ingramcontent.com/pod-product-compliance
Lightning Source LLC
Chambersburg PA
CBHW020347030726
47496CB00007B/2030